OFF RESERVATION

BRAM CONNOLLY

OFF RESERVATION

ALLEN&UNWIN
SYDNEY•MELBOURNE•AUCKLAND•LONDON

First published in 2017

Allen & Unwin
83 Alexander Street
Crows Nest NSW 2065
Australia
Phone: (61 2) 8425 0100
Email: info@allenandunwin.com
Web: www.allenandunwin.com

Cataloguing-in-Publication details are available
from the National Library of Australia
www.trove.nla.gov.au

ISBN 978 1 76029 545 5

Set in 12/18 pt Minion by Midland Typesetters, Australia
Printed and bound in Australia by Griffin Press

10 9 8 7 6 5 4 3 2 1

The paper in this book is FSC® certified. FSC® promotes environmentally responsible, socially beneficial and economically viable management of the world's forests.

Dedicated to my father, Michael Connolly, for his selfless dedication to his children; and Jacky Connolly for her love and support.

There are men among us who have sacrificed. They train while you sleep. They slept while you partied. They have endured physical and environmental hardships just to know they could. They have been tested, over and over again on the basics. When they were perfect at the basics, they learnt advanced skills you couldn't comprehend. Then they were let loose on our enemies. *Foras admonitio*. On behalf of Australia – I thank you.

Bram Connolly DSM 2017

PROLOGUE

SARPOSA PRISON, 10 JANUARY 2013

The walls of Faisal Khan's small cell shook violently. Dust engulfed the perimeter of the prison. There were always explosions just outside the walls. In 2012, Kandahar had been vying for top spot on the suicide bomber hit list, going head to head with Baghdad and 2013 was off to an equally deadly start. In the first few weeks of his captivity, Faisal Khan used to peer out the barred window in the corner of his cell, trying to see the action or the aftermath, but he had grown used to the sound now and he ignored the blasts.

The pressure from the next explosion, however, was immense. It blew Khan halfway across the room. One second he was on his feet; the next he lay unconscious and bleeding from the nose on the dusty floor, his body covered in rubble from the caved-in ceiling.

As if at a signal, other prisoners began to rush towards the ruptured prison walls. The first explosion had blown the gates clear, toppling the guard towers in the process and felling the razor wire. Meanwhile, militants were swarming towards the buildings. One vehicle had even entered the open courtyard, the driver pulling to a stop directly outside Faisal Khan's cell.

A hunched figure, dressed in the flowing brown trousers and shirt favoured by ISIS and carrying an AK-47, jumped down off the back of the vehicle and sprinted through the dust-shrouded opening in the wall. He grabbed a fistful of Khan's long matted hair and proceeded to drag him unceremoniously back through the opening, across jagged bricks and debris.

The militant cleared his throat of the dust and smoke from the explosion and moved his mouth to the microphone on his collar.

'I've got him,' he said.

'Good, move to the first pick-up location,' came the reply.

'I've told you before, it's an extraction point.'

'Whatever, just get him back here.'

The militant picked up the bleeding Khan and dumped him into the tray of the waiting Toyota Hilux. He then leaped in behind him and slammed his hand twice on the roof. The vehicle spun its wheels and disappeared back through the wire as quickly as it had arrived.

• • •

Steph Baumer's iPhone screen came alive with a single thumbs-up emoji. She put her pen down and picked up the phone from among the clutter of folders marked *TOP SECRET* and sent a thumbs-up in reply. Then, she leaned back in her chair and looked up over the top of the computer monitors, printers and radar screens lining the long table. Folding her hands behind her head, she smiled as she gazed out of the huge bay windows to the snow-capped peaks of Italy's Apennine Mountains.

She was a world away from Kandahar, but she was still calling the shots.

1

WESTERN SYDNEY, ZERO DARK HUNDRED

Adjusting the focus on his night vision goggles, Matt could just make out the three-storey industrial building less than sixty metres inside the fence line. Street lamps from an airfield down the road reflected off the low cloud cover and bathed the target building, giving it an eerie glow. On the top floor, someone had left some lights on. Save for that, the rest of the building was in darkness, deathly quiet. Matt's forward scouts held open the chain wire fence for him. For fifteen agonising minutes, they had snipped away at the links, one at a time, covering each other, scanning for threats. Finally, they created a ripped hole barely large enough for a grown man to duck through.

Matt climbed inside the perimeter and then signalled with an infrared torch to the rest of his waiting commando platoon, hidden back in the tree line.

'Thanks, lads,' Matt whispered as he turned around and knelt down. The wet ground immediately soaked through his kneepad and into his flight suit. He raised his rifle to cover the building. Daniel Barnsley, Matt's signaller, moved in on the other side, also raising his rifle to cover the other half of the building's frontage.

The two forward scouts slowly lowered their weapons and started to assist the rest of the assaulters who had just arrived. Some of them had ladders, some had frame charges for windows and doors, and others had dogs. What was required here was teamwork to ensure they all got through the fence and on their way to their entry points without alerting anyone in the building that they were there.

Matt could just make out a low pitch sound off in the distance. He knew it well enough. He had heard it a hundred times before, the sound of helicopters approaching. Still beyond truly audible, it starts off as a change in the ambient noise, almost silent at first, the lowest humming sound. He checked his watch and then looked around at his men making their way to their entry points, all on track. The Sniper Platoon was acting as the other tactical assault platoon. Commanded by Trav Mercardo, it would be here in less than three minutes. Matt's platoon needed to be in position to blow in on the second-floor entry points. They would need to have their ladders and charges in place and dogs in position to synchronise with Trav's platoon, which would fast rope out of the helicopters onto the roof and the top-floor balcony. As if this wasn't complex enough, a platoon of Navy clearance divers would be coming in at speed on V8 Land Cruisers with the intention of making entry through the ground-floor doors. They had practiced this more times than Matt cared to remember, but he still felt a sense of excitement and anticipation.

'All call signs, this is Oscar Charlie, two minutes . . . over.'

'Yankee Alpha, acknowledged,' Matt replied to the radio message from Mike Truscott, the officer in charge of the tactical assault group.

'X-ray Alpha, roger over.'

Matt could hear the helicopter engines screaming as Trav made the call. The pilots would have accelerated the birds to around 140 knots and they would be coming in low and fast on the other side of the treetops. Matt knew that Trav's guys would be sitting with the rear doors open, ready to throw the ropes out and slide down to their target.

'Whisky platoon ready to roll . . .' Matt looked over to the navy platoon's start point and could see the infrared spotlights on top of the Land Cruisers. He twisted the dial on his radio presser switch to change the frequency, allowing him to talk directly to his platoon.

'All call signs, this is Yankee Alpha. Send status . . . over.' He pushed his Peltor hearing protection tighter over his right ear to hear the whispered replies. One by one, each of his teams messaged back that they were at their primary entry points and ready to go.

The officer in charge of the tactical assault group came over the entire radio network to all three platoons. He timed the radio call with perfection, taking into account the speed the aircraft were maintaining and the location of the clearance divers.

'All call signs, this is Oscar Charlie. Ready . . . Ready . . . Ready . . . Ready . . . Ready . . . STAND BY . . . GO GO GO!'

The six teams from Matt's platoon detonated their frame charges. The second-storey windows exploded into the building and a stream of men poured in from the top of the ladders. Dogs ran into the hallways, silhouetted momentarily by flash grenades lighting the building up like a Christmas tree. Four helicopters flared violently overhead and then hovered sixty feet above the roof. Two ropes out of each helicopter delivered lines of assaulters, who no sooner hit their landing points than they sprinted for entry positions, blowing the top-storey balconies and windows to smithereens. At ground level, the Land Cruisers screeched to a halt and the clearance divers, who threw themselves out of the vehicles even before they had completely stopped, sprinted the few feet required to smash open the windows with hooligan tools, jumping through and engaging the meagre resistance offered by the terrorist elements.

Matt moved in behind Team Three with Barnsley right behind him. The lights came on inside. Matt flipped up his NVGs and went to white light on his primary weapon.

'Follow me, Barns.'

'With you,' said Barnsley.

The two of them broke off from Team Three and made their way towards an open stairwell. The lights went out again, plunging them into darkness. Matt tried to flip down his NVGs. A sudden flash from a stun grenade lit up the stairwell entrance.

'Ah, shit . . . I can't see.' Matt let go of the night vision goggles and switched on his torch again. Pivoting to his left, he lifted up his M4 short-barrelled assault rifle and cleared behind the bottom of the stairwell. The torch made him an instant target and rounds whizzed past his face. Barnsley's torch came on next to him. The two conducted a hallway drill, covering each other as they pivoted further in behind the stairwell.

Zip Zip. Two more rounds flew past Matt's ear.

'I'm hit, boss.'

'Fuck, what?' Matt spun around just in time to see Barnsley fall to the floor. At that same moment, he felt the impact on the back of his helmet and neck.

Whack. He crumpled down next to Barnsley. The two men lay at the bottom of the stairwell. Matt looked across to Barnsley.

'I'm sorry, boss. He was in the cupboard on the other side of the stairwell. I didn't see him until it was too late. We didn't stand a chance . . .' Barnsley's voice drifted off.

'It's okay, mate. I should have left my torch off.'

Matt winced in pain as two more rounds slammed into the back of his legs. He closed his eyes tight for a moment then looked again at Barnsley. He could see Barnsley had taken two rounds to the face. In any other circumstance the shots would have been fatal. Instead, paint was smeared all over the left side of Barnsley's Scott protective mask.

One of the attack dogs came barrelling past from the top stair-case and smashed his way into the cupboard, placing a bite on the guy who was playing terrorist. The handler jogged past, giving Matt a cursory glance. No one stopped for a downed assaulter, not until all the hostages had been saved, not in training, not for the real thing. If the tactical assault group was called in there was no other option. Failure wasn't on the cards.

The lights came on inside the kill house, as the guys called it. Matt stood up, helping Barnsley up at the same time. He keyed the microphone on his chest rig.

'Okay, lads, that's a wrap. Move outside and wait for further orders.' Matt and Barnsley strolled down the stairs and out the front door into the warm summer night air. Trav Mercardo came out close behind them.

'That didn't exactly go to plan,' said Trav, slapping Matt's shoulder and wiping the paint off the back of his helmet. Trav was a little shorter than Matt, but with brown wavy hair and chiselled features the two could be mistaken for brothers. Trav eased his way through life. A country boy from outback Queensland, nothing seemed to overly bother him and Matt had always been envious at how easy things came to his younger colleague. Trav was already earmarked as potential commanding officer material. All the other officers knew it.

'It's these bloody goggles.' Matt released his helmet, took off the safety goggles and wiped the fog from inside the lenses. 'I'd rather wear a gas mask, at least they seal properly. These things shit me to tears. No situational awareness and when we use sound and flash grenades the light reflects off the mask.'

'Really good excuse, Matt.'

'Piss off, Trav, you little prick.'

'Good comeback, brother, I wasn't prepared for such a witty reply. Oh wait, yes I was,' Trav laughed. He acknowledged Major Mike Truscott, the officer in command of the tactical assault group, who had walked in from his vantage point.

'That went well. Good work, the both of you. Now that's how we synchronise an assault. Let's just hope we can do the same tomorrow night during the multi-jurisdictional anti-terrorist exercise.'

'Shouldn't be an issue if the water platoon guys can swim into the target vessel on time, boss.'

'Trav, in all my years in special forces I've learnt one thing: don't worry about what the water boys are up to, worry about your own shit. They'll sure as hell take your job if you're not up to it.'

Matt knew that Major Truscott was talking from experience; he had been in the Special Air Service Regiment for some twenty years before coming across to the Commando Regiment. He was a good boss, a little crazy at time with a penchant for speaking his mind in spectacular and abrupt fashion, but get him on a good day and he was more than fair towards his younger officers.

Matt took off his chest rig and placed it on the ground, switching off his radio to conserve the batteries. He stretched out and bent down to wipe the paint off the back of his legs.

'Have you heard the news this evening, Matt?' the CO asked.

'Hardly, I've been walking in the dark for the past five hours.'

'There was a prison break in Kandahar today. Seems your old mate the ever-elusive Faisal Khan is back on the run.'

Matt straightened his rifle on top of his chest rig to stop the barrel falling in the gravel. He slowly looked back up at Mike Truscott.

'Is that right?'

'Yep, I'm afraid so. The commanding officer let me know a few hours ago.'

Matt nodded at the mention of Mark Hoff. The commanding officer had always been good to him. A few years previous, while deployed in Afghanistan, Hoff had been the only one Matt could trust. Back then the murderous Taliban commander, Objective Rapier, had been on a destructive rampage across the country and Matt, commanding Yankee platoon, had been on the back foot the whole time. Sold out by senior CIA operator Steph Baumer, and undermined by his own command structure, Matt's career looked like it was in tatters—that was, until Mark Hoff arrived on the scene and ordered Matt to go after Faisal Khan, Objective Rapier's intelligence officer. Khan's capture lead to the fall of the Taliban commander and his men. Matt dealt out violent justice to them across the province.

'The CO told me that there was a major assault on the prison. It's suspected that it was an ISIS inspired attack. Of course, no one has claimed responsibility yet. Faisal was snatched from his cell and about thirty other prisoners escaped.'

'Makes you wonder why we even bothered going to Afghanistan in the first place, hey, Matt?' said Trav, removing his own helmet and running his hands through his hair. He motioned to his guys, who were now coming out of the kill house, to make their way over to the briefing area.

Matt stared at him, deep in thought.

'What?' said Trav.

'It's got nothing to do with our role in Afghanistan, Trav. This is fucking personal. Faisal was a human intelligence contact for Steph Baumer.' Matt spat on the ground as if her name itself had dirtied his mouth.

'The CIA chick?' Trav knew exactly who Matt meant. He was glad that Matt was actually talking about this. It was the first time he had heard him speak of Steph Baumer since the incident in Kandahar back in 2010. Of course, everyone in the 2nd Commando Regiment knew the story, that Matt had fallen in love with Dutch intelligence officer Allie van Tanken and that Steph had killed her. All the guys had liked Allie. She had been smart and popular across the contingent and everyone had known her to be highly professional. She had also taken a shine to Matt.

'What did this Steph do exactly?' asked Mick Truscott innocently.

'Steph killed a friend of mine, Allie van Tanken. Allie had been trying to warn everyone about a guy she had recognised as a facilitator for suicide bombers, who had arrived to meet Steph. He was also the trigger man for a suicide bomber who was on the inside. He hadn't been checked properly. In all the confusion, Steph shot Allie. I was the first on the scene and she died in my arms a few minutes later. We think Khan had organised a hit on Steph, but we never heard it from him directly.'

'Let's not forget that you shot the suicide bomber,' Trav reminded Matt with a smile.

Matt ignored him. 'Faisal never talked about his dealings with Steph and she simply slipped away into the night, back to the USA, and hasn't been seen or heard of since.'

'Sounds like we should go over there and hunt this Faisal down, get some answers,' said Trav.

Matt picked up his rifle and handed it to Barnsley. He placed his chest rig back on and then took his rifle back. He turned to face Trav.

'I'd love to hunt down Khan again, Trav. But I'd rather have a quiet moment with that bitch Steph, find out if she has any remorse at all.'

'Well, we need not worry about that, gents. Let's focus on the multi-jurisdictional exercise tomorrow night. There will be a lot of people monitoring this and we need to get it right. I just thought you should know, Matt.'

'Thanks, boss, I appreciate it,' said Matt.

'I thought you were going to use "behove" then, boss,' laughed Trav, as the two of them started off towards the briefing area. The rest of the company had now assembled there and were waiting for their commander's feedback on the rehearsal.

'You alright?' asked Barnsley.

'Yeah, mate, of course.' Matt put his hand on his signaller's shoulder. 'It's just disappointing that he's escaped to be honest. And to be fair, I'd jump at the chance of hunting him down again just for shits and giggles, but I have to let this shit go or it will destroy me in the end. I have a job to do and Faisal is the least of my concerns right now.'

Matt walked on in silence and let his mind wander back to Afghanistan a few years earlier. He could almost feel Allie's warm blood soaking across his lap as the life slowly drained from her. He shivered and then blocked out the thought.

2

KABUL

Faisal Khan opened his eyes. He thought he had heard a scream, but now there was only silence. His head throbbed and his vision was cloudy. He appeared to be lying on a bed, but he couldn't make out his surroundings.

When his eyesight did return, he was surprised to see that he was no longer wearing the orange prison uniform and instead was dressed in khaki pants and a soft cotton shirt. He tried to sit up, but his hands had been cuffed to the steel bedframe. Lifting his head, he looked around the room. It was barely large enough to contain the metal bed, a chair and an old prayer rug in the corner. There was an iron door at the other end of the bed, and no windows or ventilation other than between the door and its warped frame.

Faisal had no way of knowing that there were another twenty rooms just like this one running down either side of a long hallway in the longest wing of the compound perimeter. That same hallway opened up into a large rectangular courtyard. There was a deep well in the centre; a fire pit with an A-frame holding an old blackened kettle above the smouldering coals of last night's fire in one corner; and a hole that the locals used for ablutions in the other. A few dogs walked around the courtyard, ignoring the half-dozen hens pecking in the light brown dust looking for small insects. In true Afghan style, each of the walls of the outer perimeter contained small rooms within rooms, and on the roof were hundreds of kilograms of corn, still in their husks, left to dry in the sun. Two green, rusty metal gates were the only way in and out from the dusty street.

The compound was indistinguishable from hundreds of others on the edge of Kabul. It was just an average compound in an average suburb – though the business in which its occupants were engaged was anything but average.

Faisal blinked hard, his focus clear now. His mouth was dry and he licked his chapped lips.

How long have I been here? he wondered. His last memory was of an explosion outside his cell and then a flash of white light. His head throbbed as he tried to make sense of his surroundings. He'd been moved from a prison to a prison, or so it seemed. But who had moved him?

The scream came again, from perhaps three rooms away, no more. The noise made Faisal jolt against his restraints. It wasn't a scream of fear; it was the scream of a man in extreme pain. The scream descended into a gurgling groan, and the sound sent shivers up Faisal's spine. Then came a voice, talking too low at first for Faisal to make out the words, but then the talking rose to a shout and Faisal realised that the man was speaking English.

'You're a fucking traitor and I have told you what we do to traitors!'

The sentence was then repeated by another person in Pashtu.

The door to Faisal's cell swung open and two men burst in. Faisal struggled against his restraints, causing the cuffs to dig into his flesh. He didn't recognise either of the men. One of the men was a monster, dressed in black cargos with a green t-shirt stretched taut over his muscular chest. As he put his hands on his hips, Faisal saw that on his right hand he wore a huge black-and-silver ring. But it was the black scarf wrapped around his head that caught Faisal's attention: no Afghan would wear that. Faisal had only ever seen a man this big once before, when Australian special forces had woken him from his sleep a few years previously by thrusting a barrel in his mouth. The man on the other side of the weapon that night had been a brute. The encounter had ended with Faisal being tortured and imprisoned.

'Hello, Faisal, it's good to see that you're finally awake. I was worried about you.' It was the smaller of the two men who spoke first, his accent confirming Faisal's suspicions that they were British.

'Who are you? What's going on?'

'I'll ask the questions here, brother. I suggest you just lie there and listen.' The smaller of the men closed the door behind them while the monster flipped the chair around so that its back was facing Faisal, and straddled it. He placed his head on his forearms, narrowed his eyes and studied Faisal with interest.

'Do you prefer Pashtu, Arabic or English?' the smaller man asked.

'English is fine,' replied Faisal.

'Good, English it is then. My name is Hassan al-Britani, and this is Abu Brutali. We rescued you, Faisal.'

Despite his fear, Faisal couldn't help but be amused by their names, which had obviously been invented in acknowledgment of their most striking characteristics.

Hassan took a small key from his pocket and went to work on Faisal's cuffs. As he undid them, Abu Brutali watched Faisal like a hawk. Faisal kept an eye on Abu, too, for the big man had removed a double-sided dagger from his boot and was now twirling it slowly in his right hand.

Released from the cuffs, Faisal sat up.

The British man resumed his questioning. 'Faisal, it's true that you trained with the Pakistani ISI, is it not?'

At the mention of Pakistan's intelligence agency Faisal sat up a little straighter and puffed out his chest. 'Yes, that is true.' A small smile crossed his face.

'And for a while you worked as an adviser to the Tarin Kowt regional commanders. I have heard that as a Taliban intelligence officer you had no peer. Ruthless, it is said.'

Faisal nodded. 'Yes – until I was kidnapped by the bearded devils.'

Hassan al-Britani made a dismissive noise. 'Pfft, Australians. What do they know about war?' He peered at Faisal intently. 'Are you still looking to fight the infidel, Faisal? Make them pay for what they have done to you and your friends?'

Faisal screwed up his face. 'I'm not fighting them because they're infidel; I'm fighting them because they invaded my home.'

Hassan ignored the qualification. 'We want you to help us, Faisal. In fact, you will also be helping yourself. You see, we have your son.'

Faisal felt his heart sink. He hadn't seen or heard from his son for many years. His old Taliban commander had made it very clear that he would need to distance himself from the boy, who Faisal had fathered to a local villager before her husband died in an American ambush during the early days of the war. Over the years, Faisal had quietly supported the boy and then when he had come of age he told him the truth and swore him to secrecy. 'Of course you have him.'

'We have a task for you. If you are successful, you get your son back and we will be able to deliver a blow to the foreigners that will make them run from the country like scared children.'

'What task?' Faisal went to stand and Brutali immediately rose from his chair. 'It's alright, brother Abu,' he assured the big man. 'I'm just checking that my legs still work.'

Brutali sat again and tapped the knife against the top of the chair.

Hassan continued, 'We are buying a weapon from the Russians. We have already paid half the asking price and the other half is due on receipt.'

'What weapon?'

Brutali threw the knife with full force into the dirt floor between Faisal's feet. Faisal slowly looked down at it and then smiled up at Brutali.

'You missed,' he said in Pashtu.

'I never miss,' Brutali replied in English.

'Excuse him, Faisal, he doesn't like many people,' said Hassan.

Faisal lowered himself back onto the bed. 'Can you tell me more about this weapon?'

'It's a miniature tactical nuclear weapon,' replied Hassan.

'I see.' Faisal stroked his long beard and thought about that for a moment. He knew something of these devices.

Hassan continued, 'When we detonate it inside the foreigners' base it will kill the lot of them instantly. It can do in one second what ten thousand martyrs would need one hundred years to do.'

Faisal thought back to his time with ISI. He knew Hassan was exaggerating. The weapon was certainly destructive, but it would only realistically clear about a city block. Several years ago, he had seen a dummy version shown to the Taliban's most feared family, the Haqqanis, by a couple of freelance Russian gun runners keen to make a sale without their government's approval. They were smart enough not to travel with the real thing, but too stupid to identify the danger they had put themselves in. Faisal had been in North Waziristan – the Haqqani family's stronghold – under orders from his Pakistani masters at the time. His brief was simple: to foster cooperation between the Pakistan state and the powerful militant group.

The Afghans killed the Russians not long after they had finished their sales pitch. No Pashtunwali – the ancient tribal code that assured protection to a visitor, even an enemy – had been offered or promised. The suitcase had been prised from the dead Russian's grasp and passed from commander to commander as a novelty item, the story attached to it becoming richer in the telling. Faisal himself had taken it apart and reassembled it on a few occasions. It was a copy of a Cold War weapon; the symbolism was not lost on Faisal. He had been surprised at how heavy it was and how easily he could take out the plutonium holders. He had studied the Cold War in depth whilst under training with the ISI and understood what both the USA and the USSR had been trying to achieve strategically with these weapons. Terror.

'Walk with me, Faisal, and I'll tell you a bit about us and what we want you to do.' Hassan moved to the door and Faisal followed. He could feel the presence of Brutali right behind him, close enough to stab him with that knife. They stepped out into the hallway.

'We are from the Islamic State of Iraq and the Levant. Perhaps you have heard of us?'

Faisal nodded. Indeed, he had heard of them, and they were not exactly espousing an ideology that he believed in. His struggle was for his homeland and tribal allegiance; their grievance was with all things that contravened their fatwa council's rulings.

'Yes, I know of your group, Hassan – but I did not realise that you were in my country now.'

'*Our* country, Faisal.'

'Your accent would suggest that you are a recent arrival, Hassan.'

The punch in the kidneys delivered by Brutali knocked the sarcasm from Faisal, a reminder that he was a guest with a tenuous future.

Hassan continued walking, with Faisal holding his injured side. The scream that erupted from the next cell they passed was horrific. Hassan stopped and opened the door, then ushered Faisal into the dimly lit room.

Inside, Faisal could just make out a man hanging from the ceiling by his wrists. He was white, a Westerner. His eyes were closed over and his face bruised and battered. The torturer had a huge scalpel in his right hand and the man's testicles in the other. He acknowledged Hassan with a massive toothless smile.

Hassan leant over to whisper into his guest's ear. 'This is a reporter for the enemy, Faisal, sent here to spread lies. His country has already paid the ransom, and he will go home soon. But not before we give him some memories to take with him.'

He led Faisal from the room and started back down the hallway. Seconds later they heard a loud scream that instantly dissolved into sobbing. Faisal was suspicious. How could a man sustain such an injury and still be conscious? He had seen the Westerners bleed like everyone else; surely they would also pass out with such immense pain. This troubled him.

Seeming undisturbed by the chilling scene, Hassan returned to the subject raised earlier. 'The weapon is going to be delivered in Istanbul. I understand that you know the town well, Faisal.'

'Yes, I know it.' Faisal had visited the Turkish city on three separate occasions to pass on information from the ISI to the Turkish National Intelligence Organisation.

Hassan explained, 'We can't just pop up in Turkey and receive the weapon from our Russian contact without drawing attention to ourselves – nearly all of us have foreign passports and our accents don't allow us to hide our true identities. We can't sneak in without creating more than a little suspicion. For us to get into the country we need to go legitimately, through the airport and through their customs. The borders are watched so closely now and a couple of Brits aren't going to just breeze in'. Hassan turned to Faisal.

'The Russians want to sell it to the Taliban, not ISIS. It seems we are not on Putin's list of bad guys he wants to support.' Hassan laughed at his own joke. 'As I said, travel through Syria is almost impossible now and made all the harder with Western special forces and their warplanes blocking our supply routes, so we couldn't get it in that way even if we wanted to. In short, we need an Afghan who can blend with the Turks and move undetected – which I believe is your specialty, Faisal?'

'I see. Well, yes, it would be nice to get outside and have a look around after being held in prison for so long.'

'Good. Let's go get you some food, then, and a change of clothes. You can sleep in the guest room tonight and then we will put you on the bus to Kandahar and beyond in the morning. And, Faisal, remember: it's your son who will benefit the most from your success.'

Faisal remembered the screams he had heard earlier. If they truly had tortured that Westerner in such a manner, what would they do to his son? 'Yes, I understand, Hassan.'

The men sat on carpets that covered the dirt floor in the main eating area. The large rectangular room had no windows save for the slits where the wooden beams pierced the tops of the walls providing support to the ceiling. These small openings let only a little air in so the room was stuffy with the smell of food and the odour of men who don't shower. Candles sat in recesses in the wall and flickered light shadows danced across the room. Over their meal of goat and beans, Hassan gave Faisal his instructions. He was not to use a phone until he had crossed the border into Iran. There, he was to go to Zabol to rendezvous with an old tailor who was an expert in smuggling contraband across the Middle East and Europe.

After they'd finished eating, Hassan gave Faisal an iPhone and detailed instructions on its use. 'This is how we communicate,' said Hassan, turning on the device.

'Won't turning that on alert the infidel?'

Hassan laughed and so did Abu Brutali, who then rose from the cushion on which he had been sitting to stand upright in one swift movement. The speed and agility of this giant amazed Faisal. The big man walked off towards the prayer room, leaving Faisal and Hassan alone.

'This is a clean SIM card, Faisal. It has been activated only a few times and has never made a call. It's a pinprick of light in a sky of stars; no one knows its significance. See this icon here?'

'Yes.' Faisal knew what it was; he might have been from Afghanistan, but his training in Pakistan had covered social media and its use. 'I don't know what it is though,' he lied.

'This is Facebook, an amazing tool of the modern era for capitalist kids to stay in touch.' Hassan laughed. 'We use it a bit differently, though. We have just the one Facebook account and we all communicate by writing inside the "edit biography" section. This is where. I will send you updates on meeting times and other instructions every day at four pm once you are safely inside Turkey.' He turned off the phone and handed it to Faisal. 'You just have to turn on the phone, open the Facebook account and check the edit bio page.'

'That is clever,' Faisal said.

'We use WhatsApp as well; it's encrypted now and as long as you don't use it while here in Afghanistan it will be secure for you in Turkey. There is only one number in the phone and that's mine. We only have a short window when you can communicate without this phone here giving you up, so check Facebook for the instructions, then use WhatsApp to communicate directly with me. Don't make any calls on it. If I want you, I will call you. The Russian will also have this number and he will be instructed to call you to arrange the pick up.'

'Understood. And the Russian contact – how do I know to trust him?'

'We have already paid him a lot of money, Faisal, and he is greedy: he wants the rest of the money. Take the case from him and send me a photo of the number inside the lid of the case over WhatsApp. Once we confirm that it's the right weapon we will transfer the rest of the money to his account and then forward the receipt to you so that you can show him. He has already been briefed.'

'I understand. May I ask something of you?'

'Yes, what?'

'Could I take a walk around the neighbourhood? I'd like to walk among my people and think for a while. I have been inside a cell for so long.'

Hassan considered the request for a moment, and then he smiled. 'Of course. There is a dry creek out the front; if you follow it, it will take you to the local market. You may go for an hour.'

'Thanks be to God,' said Faisal, standing up.

Hassan stood too. 'But, Faisal,' he added, 'if you run off, I will have everyone in your family killed, not just your son. Do I make myself clear?'

'No need for threats, brother – I am already at your service.'

3

SYDNEY

'Twenty minutes, sir.' The Blackhawk crew chief climbed inside the aircraft and closed the side door to protect the soldiers from the heavy rain. The helicopter lifted off in formation with three others and ascended into the low-hanging cloud above Luscombe airfield. Moving to their first insertion point, or IP marker, the pilots monitored their instruments and vectored in on their target. In this downpour, it was going to be impossible to get a clear visual on the target until they were right on top of it.

Trav Mercardo, the sniper platoon commander, looked around at his team ensuring everything was in place. He focused the left lens of his night-vision goggles so that he could clearly make out the details of his men's faces in the dark. Some of them had yet to pull their NVGs down and were still fastening themselves to the floor of the helicopter with their retaining straps.

Trav raised his voice, shouting above the thumping of the blades and engine noise. 'Lads, switch to NVGs now and get the charges ready. We'll put the detonators in at the six-minute mark.'

Trav looked around at the twelve other men as they readied their equipment. The helicopter shook as it hit some cross winds and the commandos steadied themselves against the airframe. Trav checked his own gear. His black body armour was tightly fastened and the quick-release handle – which he would certainly need if the helicopter ditched in water – protruded through the slimline life jacket that he wore over the top of it all. He checked the small bottle of emergency air attached to the jacket and then the bite valve itself to make sure it was off and ready to go.

One of his men was watching him. 'What's the problem, boss?' the young commando asked. 'Are you nervous?'

'What makes you say that?' Trav checked the night-vision device on his M4. The laser cover was in place. He checked it again, though, just to make sure.

'You're checking and double-checking everything.'

'I just like to be thorough.' Trav looked at the other guys; they were either doing the same or staring out the helicopter windows into the black of night and one of the summer storms that Sydney was famous for, especially in December.

'It's only training, it's not like its real. We're carrying fake charges and paint rounds, for Christ's sake.' The young soldier laughed.

'Train as you fight, bro. Train as you fight.'

Trav steadied himself again as the helicopter hit another strong cross wind. He thought he could see the lights from one of the other Blackhawks out the window and on any other night perhaps he could have, but not in this pea soup. He saw the light again and then realised it was the reflection of one of his team's NVGs in the window.

The four birds descended in formation, hidden from one another, down to where Georges River met Botany Bay.

The senior flight lead of the formation gripped the cyclic control of the Blackhawk and squeezed it hard to keep the airframe steady.

'Winds are rough,' he said to his co-pilot. 'Let's keep it above sixty feet in case there are some downdrafts we can't see.'

'No worries. I have the objective ten minutes out on the port side. Do you still want the approach speed at one-thirty knots?'

'No way.' The senior pilot looked over his right shoulder to make sure that the platoon commander in the back wasn't on the headset. 'It's only a training exercise and there are enough things going against us without adding to the problem with excess speed. This weather is not far from abort criteria as far as I'm concerned.'

'Got it. So, how's this for a new approach profile? Ninety knots approach speed from the south-south-west at two minutes out and then hover at forty feet above the ship's bridge; bird one on landing point two. Confirm, sir?'

'LP two? Yep okay, that's fine. Like I said, it's not a suicide mission. Radio the corrections through to the other birds.'

In the back, Trav checked his watch. By his reckoning, they would be on the target in ten minutes and perfectly synchronised with the other platoons. Then he noticed the aircraft slowly bleeding off speed. He rolled his eyes and groaned.

Here we go, he thought.

• • •

'Slow down, Barns. I need to get an idea where the hell we are; all this bush looks the same in the rain.' Matt Rix tapped his GPS on the front roll bar of the four-seater Polaris and wiped the fog from its screen. He looked down at the sodden map in his hands. Even though he had covered it with contact paper and stashed it in a map cover it was now effectively a balled-up mess of wet paper. 'Christ, this is not going well,' he said.

Barnsley brought the vehicle to a halt and the other seven Yankee Platoon vehicles behind slowed down to a crawl and moved into their defensive formation. The drivers cut the engines and silence settled over the bush, except for the sound of the rain steadily hitting the men's Gore-Tex jackets and weapons.

'I was on track when we went under the highway, then it started pissing down again, which is great for covering our noise but it made navigating near on impossible.' Matt stood up above the roll bar and looked around at their formation.

'Want me to move, boss?'

'Nah, this looks as good a place as any.' Matt flopped back into his seat with a squelch. 'Seriously,' he continued, 'I couldn't see a damn thing. I'm sure this is the dismount point and so the target should be out through there.' Matt pointed to the left to some dull lights about six hundred metres beyond a line of trees.

'Picton.' Barnsley shook his head. 'Jesus, why do people even live out here?'

Matt shrugged. 'I like it,' he said. 'It's far enough from the city not to feel crowded and the bush makes a nice change.'

'You would like it, boss, you're from Bendigo – it's much the same.'

The crackling of Matt's radio interrupted their conversation.

'Boss, shall we cache the raptors here?' It was JJ's voice, asking him the obvious.

'Yep, do it, and get the guys formed up. We'll go out in single file and try to keep to the low ground out to the right.' Matt couldn't even be sure there was low ground to the right with the darkness and rain hindering his vision, but he guessed there was because the treetops were lower on that side.

Yankee Platoon dismounted from their vehicles, double-checked each other's gear and conducted their last-minute radio checks. A few minutes later the teams were assembled ready to move.

The platoon patrolled cautiously, moving towards their final rendezvous point, the place where each team would go off in search of their predetermined entry point. It was also the place where Matt would link up with the sniper team commander, Kiwi, who'd had his team monitoring the stronghold for the past six hours.

Matt's forward scout stopped and the line of operators stopped behind him, rifles pointed, staggered on either side for protection. Through his NVGs Matt could see the outline of a sniper slowly moving towards the front man of his platoon. The sniper closed in and was directed down the line to meet up with Matt.

Kiwi dropped onto one knee beside Matt. He placed his Blazer .338 rifle down on its bipod and leaned in close to Matt's ear. 'Hey, boss, what's happening? Glad to see you made it.'

'Kiwi, how are you?' Matt moved some of the wet camouflage strips from the sniper's face to see him. 'Gee, that ghillie suit looks comfortable.'

'Jesus, bro, it's heavy as hell when it's saturated like this. I thought about ditching it but I can't afford the loss-and-damage bill.'

Matt laughed quietly. 'So tell me – where's the target?'

'It took us a while to find it, to be honest. In the end one of the directing staff had to come and point us in the right direction. All these houses look the same. There are about twenty in that street down there and they're all set in thick scrub. Ours is the one the furthest to the right.' Kiwi pointed to the edge of the clearing and a faint set of lights.

'What's on the target, mate?'

'Nothing; it's been dead as. I think there's a vehicle in the garage matching the description that the police gave us. All your entry points have been identified. I can't see any of the safety guys for the demolitions, though, so I assume they're already inside and out of the rain.'

'Yeah, the brief was to treat it like a real job and just blow our way in. They have an overlay of our primary and secondary points. There are only two charges anyway – the rest of the entry points are through the sliding doors and we're just going to sledge them.'

'Got it, no drama, bro. I put a Cyalume stick up ahead – that's the point where the teams can orientate onto the target. I'll take you right to your point as well, boss.'

Matt adjusted his NVGs and focused them on the small source of white light that shone on the ground a few hundred metres ahead.

'Cheers, Kiwi.' Matt looked down at the fluorescent hands of his watch; it was now 2044 hours. 'Let's get moving then, shall we?'

The wind picked up as the commandos headed off once again; the rain, a little softer now, had started to get inside everyone's waterproof clothing.

Matt watched his lead team make their way through some thicker foliage to approach the house from the left side. The other teams broke off too. This was the most dangerous time for the platoon; compromise now and they would have to crash action into the target. There were ways to mitigate this, certain techniques and procedures, but Matt didn't have this luxury as the other platoon were in helicopters racing towards a ship off the coast of Sydney.

Barnsley stopped at an iron gate that accessed the side of the yard. Matt covered him from the side. Barnsley opened the small gate and walked in with Matt moving in behind him. The pair covered each other as they made their way towards the patio window. Stepping over a discarded bicycle, Matt took the lead from Barnsley and switched his attention to the sliding glass door. Through the curtain he could see two people sitting on a sofa, their backs to him. The TV was on. A third person entered the room. Matt froze, slowly lowering himself to his knee, now maybe six or seven metres away from their entry point.

The person walked towards the sliding door and moved the curtain to one side. Matt quickly flattened himself on the wet ground. Fortunately, the lawn was unkempt and partially con-cealed him. He knew that behind him his other team members would be lying there in the dark, their weapons all trained on the terrorist. The door opened and a dog ran out, barking and yapping.

Matt's heart was beating like a drum. It always sounded louder at times like this, mainly because of the communications earpiece that sealed his left ear. He slowly moved his eyes to his watch: 2058. They had to make entry in two minutes to synchronise with the others. Matt was sure the dog wasn't a guard dog; more likely a labradoodle, judging by the curly coat and the fact that it was now licking Matt's face and trying to play with him. The dog ran off, suddenly interested in a noise from another part of the yard.

The person at the door had retreated inside and away from the curtains. Matt stood up slowly and waited for a second before ghost-walking towards the door, silently lifting one foot up and placing the heel down first then transferring the weight slowly to his toes. He covered the door with his weapon, alert to any threats that might appear. There would be no need for a sledge, of that he was certain; the door was still slightly open. The rest of the team fanned out behind him in assault formation, the same pattern replicated at each entry point.

On the other side of the building, Team Three placed an explosive charge on the back door, while at the front Team One prepared their window frame charge, and as Matt placed his hand on the door the charges went off on either side of the building.

BOOM!

The men rushed in, weapons up, with a stream of sound and flash grenades heralding their arrival. They flowed through the house, moving like so many swarms of wasps in and around the furniture. The bursts of white light from the sound and flash pods made the whole scene look like some crazy nightclub. The scene was being played out in strobe-like segments. One moment a commando was in a doorway, in the next flash he was two metres away, throwing yet another distraction grenade. Any terrorist in location would be completely disorientated and then neutralised in order to save the lives of the hostages. There were no shots fired, and the only noises, save for the distraction grenades, were the terrified screams of those playing the parts of the innocent.

• • •

'Two minutes!' The loadmaster held up a pair of Cyalume sticks to reinforce the shouted verbal command.

The men in the back of the Blackhawk repeated the call in unison.

The loadmaster opened the doors on either side of the aircraft and the wind immediately carried the rain into the back. Trav checked the time: 2105 hours. They had already missed the synchronisation time. He unfastened the strap that had held him in the airframe and stowed it in his flight suit leg pocket. Another check of his weapon retaining hook – in place and secure.

The pilots eased the aircraft twenty metres above the bridge of the ship and settled into a hover. Trav could see that the other aircraft were all at their insertion points and going through the same process. Looking down, he saw the clearance divers, or CDs as they were known, climbing up their steel ladders on the side of the ship. They had timed it well and had waited, fastened by magnets under the ship, until the helicopters had arrived.

The ropes were kicked out of the helicopter and they tumbled to the bridge of the ship below. Trav moved in behind his team on the right-hand side of the aircraft as they lined up behind the big nylon rope. And then they were off: first one, then another, then Trav. He extended his arms into the night air and focused his vision on the rope. His NVGs were set to further out, so a guesstimate was the best he could do. The downwash of the aircraft rotor blades buffeted him as he reached out into the void and the guy behind him was close enough to ensure Trav was given a gentle nudge as he made his way out of the aircraft.

For a moment, there was nothing, and his stomach rose up with the uncertainty. Best case, the fall was about twenty metres to the bridge below; worst case was sixty metres to the water in full kit and, provided he actually survived the impact, a race to get his body armour off and the air bottle into his mouth before he drowned. Finally, Trav felt the rope between his hands. He held it to his chest and created a choke-style hold to slow his descent. His feet found the rope moments later and he steadied himself to time his landing with the roll of the ship. As his feet hit the deck he was off, just as another pair of feet landed and then another, and now the whole team was in a race to get inside the bridge of the ship before the terrorists could respond.

The assault was over within minutes, the six terrorists struggling to hold a three-hundred-and-sixty-metre oil tanker.

Trav stood in the wheelhouse looking over the ship.

'All areas cleared, boss.' The call came from Team One on the middle deck.

'Roger that. Move the crew to the galley and keep them secured. Bravo's on his way now to do the walk-through.'

The door to the bridge opened.

'You guys took your time, Trav,' said Mitchell.

'I don't control the birds; they pulled back speed for some reason. We got here when we got here. Nice flippers, champ.' Trav knew full well this would get a rise out of the head clearance diver.

'They're fins, dickhead.' The CD put his fingers inside his dry suit collar and gave his neck some relief from the choking rubber that sealed it tight.

'Your area secure, Mitch?' Trav liked the CD. He was short and powerful and, as they all were, supremely fit. What Trav really liked, though, was that he had a no-nonsense attitude and strong work ethic, but absolutely no sense of humour – a fact that Trav took great joy in exploiting.

'Of course it's fucking secure. Why else would I be up here?'

'Just checking that you guys didn't just go for a little paddle and then a pleasant stroll around the ship foredeck, that's all.'

'Seriously, you're a dickhead, do you know that, Trav? Just radio it in, for Christ's sake.' The CD threw open the door of the bridge. It bounced back and hit him front on, sending him a few steps back. He smashed it open again and made his way down the ladder. The door crashed closed behind him. Trav laughed to himself.

He spoke into his radio. 'Oscar Charlie, this is Xray Alpha. All areas secure, hostage terrorist count. Prepare to copy. Over.'

'Send. Over.'

• • •

'That can't be right. Guys, send hostage terrorist count again.' Matt looked around the main bedroom of the target house; surely there was some mistake.

The teams repeated their count. There was no change – three hostages and no terrorists.

'What the hell is going on, Barnsley?'

'Not sure, boss.'

'No terrorists, no weapons, what are these guys playing at? A dry hole, perhaps?' Matt was referring to a situation where a target had no enemy or information on it – something he had grown accustomed to in Afghanistan.

'Wrong target, boss?' said Barnsley.

'What? Don't be daft. Right, follow me, and let's go look around. Don't report anything up yet.'

Matt moved off towards the main living area with his signaller in tow. Acknowledging the Team One commander, Matt made his way towards the corner of the room where the hostages were being secured. In the confusion of the assault each one of the hostages had received a palm to the chest and a strong hand to the back of the head, forcing them to the floor. An assaulter doesn't muck around. The roller ball starts and can't be stopped, as they say. The hostages were now cuffed, sitting on the floor and sobbing.

'I tell you what, they're good actors, boss – the screams of the young girl when we made entry caught me out for a moment.'

'Young girl?'

Matt looked at the players on the floor: a middle-aged couple and a young girl, maybe no more than fourteen, dressed in pyjamas. She was rocking back and forth, and clearly in shock. He felt a wave of panic come over him.

'Hey, you.' Matt tapped the man on the shoulder. 'Are you part of this exercise?'

The man only sobbed in response.

'Speak up,' Matt ordered.

The man drew a shaky breath. 'I don't know what you're talking about. Who are you? What have we done? Please don't kill us.'

'*Kill you?* What are you talking about?'

The man shook his head and let out another sob.

'Oh crap, this can't be happening,' Matt groaned. 'Get these cuffs off them and sit them on the lounge.'

The Team One commander immediately complied.

'Someone get the medic in here,' Matt barked. 'Where's he at?'

'Here, boss.' The medic stepped into the room from his position in the hallway.

'Make sure their not injured,' said Matt.

'Boss?' asked Barnsley.

'Not now, Barns,' Matt replied. 'Let me think this through, mate.'

'Boss, it's the CO. He wants to talk to you right now – immediately, he said.' Barnsley passed Matt the handset to the platoon radio.

'Yes, sir?'

'Matt, get your men out of that house and hand over to the police. They're out the front. Take your men back to base. I'll see you in my office as soon as you're back, do you understand?'

'Yes, sir.' Matt gave the handset back to Barnsley and turned his attention back to the distraught family sitting on the couch. The father was shaking and looking at the trembling hands that he was holding up in front of his face. Next to him, his daughter was as pale as a ghost. On the far side of the couch, the mother's arms were wrapped around the crying girl. She looked up at Matt in terror, tears streaming down her own face.

Matt put his hand up to his mouth. 'Jesus Christ, what the fuck have I done?'

4

COMMANDO HEADQUARTERS, SYDNEY

'The weapons are cleaned and back in the armoury, boss,' said JJ as he entered the platoon office, his huge frame filling the doorway.

From behind his desk, Matt looked up at the massive commando sergeant. Jack Jones had been a loyal friend. Even through Matt's worst days in Afghanistan a few years previously, JJ had stood by his young platoon commander. Not just a great warrior, JJ had proven himself as a great administrator for the platoon, and even more pleasing to Matt was the fact that the men still feared and trusted him equally. Matt was happy to have such a great ally.

Matt put down his pen and stood up. 'Thanks, JJ.' He picked up his A4 diary-notebook and walked over to place it back in the filing cabinet. He had been sure to make detailed notes about the situation, times, places and people involved. It was a habit that he had established in Afghanistan during that last deployment. Closing the drawer, he turned back to face JJ.

'What are the lads doing now, mate?'

'Nothing. I've knocked them off and told them to reappear at seven am. We're gonna clean the platoon stores and make a start on the Polaris Raptors tomorrow. Then it's the weekend!' JJ clapped his hands together, did a little shimmy that looked ridiculous given his hulking size and smiled at Matt. He studied his commander for a moment and then lowered his voice. 'What's the matter, boss? You look like your face was on fire and someone tried to put it out with a hammer.'

'Oh, come on, JJ – are you saying I'm ugly?'

'Nah, you're a good-looking rooster alright, but you look like you're upset about something.' JJ grinned.

Matt shook his head. 'Your jokes are ridiculous, you know that, right?'

'Chicks dig 'em,' said JJ.

'Sure they do. Anyway, I'm fine. I'm going over to the officers' mess to get out of these damp clothes and then I'll go up and see the CO, take the arse-kicking that's coming my way.'

'It was an honest mistake, boss,' JJ protested. 'The rain was smashing down on us, the snipers were orientated on the wrong house, there was no safety there to intervene.' JJ counted off the mitigating circumstances on his fingers. 'You'll just have to give the family an apology and that will be that.' He gave Matt two thumbs-up.

'I wish I shared your optimism. Anyway, I'll let you know how it goes. Can you fill out the ammunition acquittal? I'll sign it off tomorrow morning.'

'Of course – it's half done already.'

Matt moved past JJ and walked down the hallway, looking at his watch as he went. It was 0145 hours. Matt knew the commanding officer would be in his office until the company commander called to tell him all the weapons were in and the administration was done for the night. That would be at least another hour because the clearance divers were only just coming through the main gate now.

Matt walked out of the building into the falling rain. It pitter-pattered on the corrugated-iron roof of the all-weather breezeway that linked the commando base and the officers' mess. His GSG 9 Adidas combat boots squelched in the dampness from so many days of rain. He entered the steel security turnstile only accessible with his ID swipe card and then walked down the hill and into the back of the old accommodation building. The red-brick building was constructed in the 1960s and had been the officers' mess for many units over the years. Now it was home to the officers in charge of the 2nd Commando Regiment, the most potent force in Australia's ground assault arsenal. Back in Afghanistan, the commandos were well known to other special forces units as the highly-trained guys who would go out for months on end, rock up to any firefight, violently win and then disappear back off into the dark desert, but it was always the Special Air Service Regiment who got public credit if the media got wind of any successes. It was as if the 2nd commandos were hidden in plain sight.

From the hallway, Matt could hear laughter coming from the adjoining building. He turned the corner and pushed open the saloon doors that led into the dining room. Some officers from another commando company and a few of the various support company officers were still there drinking for Australia, after a formal dining-in function earlier in the evening.

'Hey, there he is – it's quick draw Matt-Graw,' said Dennis Shelby, one of the support company majors. 'Get over here, Rix.

We're doing a validation against the deer's head.' With that he let two bottles of Corona fly in quick succession, both missing their mark by inches and smashing into the wall.

Matt looked at the majestic deer's head hanging over the huge brick fireplace and the pile of broken beer bottles on the floor. So far the deer's head had escaped a soaking but the commando officers were finding their range. The game involved donning a gas mask and standing on a painted X in the middle of the dining room with one's back to the deer. On the command 'Up!', you had to do a close-quarter battle turn and launch the bottle at the deer's nose, then immediately pick up a second bottle from the floor and send it flying. This was known as the double tap.

'Looks like the deer has had enough for one night,' Matt observed.

'C'mon, buddy, have some fun,' said one of the other officers as he thrust a gin and tonic into Matt's hand.

Matt looked down at the drink. *Fuck it, I could use a drink after tonight*, he thought. He slammed it down in one gulp to the cheers of the other commando officers. Another drink was put in his hand and he slammed it down just as fast, raising the glass above his head as a sign of victory.

The noise of the crowd threatened to wake the dead; they shouted their approval at the return of a popular member of their unit.

Standing there in his soaked MultiCams, surrounded by twenty or so drunken commando officers all dressed in red-and-white summer ceremonial dress uniforms adorned with medals, Matt smiled. He had served with some of these men on the most violent operations Australian troops had ever been involved in, and he had completed selection with some of the others years before. They were a brotherhood, the bond between them forged in combat and adversity, and they loved each other like brothers too.

'Hey, Matt, what's this about you totalling some civvies' house tonight?'

The question came from the back of the crowd and it brought Matt crashing back to earth in an instant. He placed his thumbs over his eyelids and pushed in on them as he squeezed his eyes shut.

'Oh shit – the CO,' he muttered, then strode off to his room to get a clean uniform on.

The crowd behind him roared with laughter and then came the call to play carrier landings – nothing good was going to come from that.

Fifteen minutes later Matt was in a clean disruptive pattern camouflage uniform. Walking purposefully under the breeze-way, he headed towards the headquarters. The security lighting softly lit the concrete path in contrast to the darkness between the buildings. The rain was still tapping gently against the iron roof overhead; it was eerily quiet save for the noise from the rain.

What a crappy summer, he thought.

At the end of the covered walkway was a patch of grass over-looked by flagpoles and the commando memorial. During the day, both the Australian and the unit flags flew, but at this time of night the flagpoles were empty. The memorial – a low marble wall inscribed with the names of the fallen – was illuminated by four spotlights. *Lest we forget*, Matt thought. Those names were etched in the surface of the marble for all eternity; he knew he would never forget the names of those who had died under his command.

Matt pushed open the doors to the headquarters and entered the foyer. He paused to gaze at the cabinets that ran along the side wall to the stairs leading to the CO's office. There were photos of some of the fallen, along with memorabilia from Timor, Iraq and Afghanistan and all manner of trophies. The champion platoon trophy was the largest and stood proudly in the centre of a middle shelf. Matt's platoon had won it the year after they arrived back from Afghanistan. Competing against all the platoons in the regiment, over twelve days they had to conduct the same mission – a night parachute jump into the ocean from a C-130 aircraft with their boats bundled onto pallets, a transit under the cover of darkness up the coast to Palm Beach, followed by a twelve-hour sea transit in the inflatable boats back to the wharf near the Commando Base on Georges River. Matt looked at the trophy and read his own name back to himself.

He heard a voice calling from above, 'Is that you, Matt? Come on up here.' It was the CO, Mark Hoff. He must have heard Matt arrive.

'Coming, sir.' Matt hurried upstairs to the CO's office.

As he entered, he noticed that the chair in front of the CO's desk had been moved over to the wall. The only option was to stand. The CO was seated behind his huge oak desk, everything on it orderly and in its place. Even the notes on the whiteboard on the wall above his computer must have been made with the aid of a ruler; all the dates and times and events were arranged in per-fectly straight lines. Hoff himself sat bolt upright in his impeccably pressed uniform, his hair parted to one side like a school rugby captain. He eyed Matt for a moment. Matt caught his own reflec-tion in the window. By contrast his uniform was wrinkled and slightly damp and his hair was uncombed. *I needn't have bothered changing*, he thought wryly.

The clock on the wall showed that it was only minutes from three am, so Matt was surprised when the phone rang.

Hoff answered. 'Yes, hello?'

He paused as someone on the other end of the line spoke. Matt recognised the voice of his own company commander outlining the status of the tactical assault group, ready for their next call-out.

'Thanks, Mike, no worries. Your guys did a great job this evening, all things considered.' Hoff narrowed his eyes as he looked across at Matt. 'Yes, he's here with me now. I'll talk to you about it tomorrow. Come and see me after lunch, mate. It's been a long night.'

The CO hung up the phone and spent a moment looking at the table in front of him. Finally, he said, 'I don't want to get into the details, Matt, but you stuffed up.'

'Yes, sir. I made a mistake and it won't happen again.'

'No. No, it won't, Matt.' The CO stood up from behind his desk. At six foot one Matt wasn't a small man, but he still found himself looking up at the CO, who was a good inch taller. Matt felt the gravity of the situation then.

'You're a brilliant young officer, Matt. From topping your officer courses to your Distinguished Service Medal for leadership in combat, you have excelled in everything the regiment has thrown at you.'

The CO stopped for a moment and turned his attention to the rain still steadily tapping at the window.

'Christ, Matt, you're an inspiration to your men. We did the mountain warfare course together and I saw how they responded to your leadership style. And no one works harder at their fitness or combat skills than you . . .' The CO trailed off, his gaze still fixed on the flagpoles.

Matt spirits sank. 'Sir, it wasn't all my fault,' he countered. 'I mean, the rain . . .' He struggled for a more convincing defence. *What was it JJ had said?* 'The snipers indicated it was the target, sir. It was an honest mistake.'

The CO stood ramrod-straight. 'Stop, Matt, just stop. We are the national capability of last resort. We're not in the business of making mistakes, not like that. You've let yourself, your platoon and your regiment down this evening. Do you have any idea of the fallout that will result from this? The lengths we will have to go to in order to keep that family from going to *60 Minutes* or *A Current Affair*? For God's sake, your men blew up their doorways and handcuffed their fourteen-year-old daughter!'

'I understand, sir. Perhaps I can reach out to them, apologise?'

The CO gently banged his fist on the table. 'Rix, I'm sorry, mate, but I have to relieve you from command.'

'What?' Matt took an involuntary step back. 'Surely you're joking? For this? No way! C'mon, boss. That's bullshit and you know it. Whatever happened to "You can make any mistake in training – just not in war"?'

The CO shook his head. 'Despite being one of the best commando officers to have ever walked through these halls, Matt, this is your problem: you can't take anything on the chin. Your first instinct is always to fight, isn't it?'

'Well, with all due respect, it's got me this far and you didn't seem to mind that when I was leading a platoon in Afghanistan.'

The CO's expression softened. 'I'm sorry, Matt,' he said

again. 'The decision's made. You are to report in six weeks to the International Engagement cell in Canberra. You're being posted there as the ammunition consignment officer and you'll stay there until your promotion at the end of the year. Your promotion will go ahead as scheduled if you let things just blow over, you know, keep a low profile.'

'Sir, please – you can't do this to me. Canberra? International Engagement? I mean – I'm a warrior. This will kill me. Jesus.'

The CO's demeanour softened further and he took a step around the desk to stand in front of Matt.

'This came direct from the top, from SOCAUST, the Special Operations Commander of Australia himself, Matt. I'm afraid there's nothing I can do. Go to Canberra, get yourself set up there. Who knows? You might find the cafe culture a nice change of pace. Let's put all this down to you being stressed and burned out from being continually deployed or on counter terrorism duties. Maybe after a year you'll be competitive for one of the reserve commando companies.'

That felt like a low blow to Matt. He hadn't won a DSM and topped his promotion courses for major only to be relegated to the reserve unit. Matt couldn't believe what was happening. Twenty-four hours ago, he'd been considered one of the highest-performing captains in the Royal Australian Regiment, and now this: the possibility that he *might be* competitive for a reserve company – not even a full-time company. Matt was cut to the bone. He felt something die inside him.

The CO extended his hand and Matt shook it, and just like that his career was over, done.

'Go get some rest, Matt. I'll have the guys pack up your room.

We'll forward your belongings to your new address in Canberra once you're set up there.'

Hoff moved back to his chair and focused on his computer screen; his own reporting duties up the chain of command couldn't wait any longer. He looked up briefly to say, 'Spend the six weeks off relaxing, Matt, and head off to your new job with a clear head.'

Matt turned to leave. He heard the sound of typing begin the moment he stepped through the doorway. No doubt the CO was sending SOCAUST a confirmation that the troublesome Captain Rix was no more.

The rain was heavy as Matt stepped out of the headquarters and into the early morning. The sound of the water hitting the iron roof of the walkway blocked out all other sounds and made it hard for him to think. Matt felt numb. From being in command of the top assault team in the country, he was to become a logistician. For all the command cared, he'd become fat, dumb and lazy in Canberra.

Fuck the army . . .

5

LONDON

Rachel Phillips came out of Green Park station and turned into the grey winter's day. The already bustling morning crowd was flowing along the footpath. She pulled up the collar of her Burberry mac, shielding herself from the cold, and then tightened the Gucci scarf around her neck. A London winter might be unforgiving, but she knew the tricks to survive, as anyone who lived there did. She just survived a little more fashionably than most.

Falling in behind a group of fast-walking businessmen, undoubtedly racing to their nine am coffee meeting, she went over the presentation again in her head.

She broke free from the group – and the welcome shelter they had provided – just past the Ritz and turned right, walking down past the Beretta shop, its windows arrayed with the latest in aristocratic hunting apparel. When her father was still alive she had once bought him a sweater there as a Christmas present. It was a year after she had been accepted into the British Secret Intelligence Service, more commonly known as MI6. She remembered how her father had laughed at her for buying something with brown elbow pads. 'I'm not that old!' he had protested, laughing. He had died only six months later from inoperable lung cancer.

She crossed the top of Jermyn Street and walked past Davidoff, known as a purveyor of premium cigars. A pang of guilt assailed her as she passed; no doubt the cigars she had purchased for him there had contributed to her father's demise.

As always, memories of that time inevitably led her back to Matt Rix. Barely six months after her father's death, she had met Matt in Italy and fallen in love with him. It was a love affair that had never blossomed. She often thought about why she had ended it. She had told him it was because they were too different, that their lives were going in different directions – but, really, it was more to do with the detachment she sensed in him. Matt wouldn't share his feelings with her; he could not even commit to a long-distance relationship. They'd remained friends, which was something, but she still regretted the lost opportunity; she had fallen hard for him and had hoped he might be her destiny.

But her misty memories would have to wait for another time, as she had arrived at 34 St James Street, the entrance to Cording House. From the street, it looked like any other high-end boutique office block in the area. The passive acoustic security monitors that were trained on everyone who entered were undetectable, as were the hidden cameras with facial recognition software that were in constant operation. The small department in which Rachel worked was deliberately hiding in plain sight, a move by MI6 to have its operators dispersed and away from the well-known headquarters in Vauxhall Cross that were monitored by other nation states and any number of threat groups.

Rachel removed her access card from her jacket pocket and held it against the swipe panel disguised as a doorbell that was to the left of the entrance. As she did she poked out her tongue at the hidden camera in the doorframe. There was a buzz and the door unlocked with a click. She pushed it open and stepped gratefully into the warmth generated by the under-floor heating. She strode towards the lift, undoing her mac as she went. Once inside, she pushed the button for the sixth floor, the offices for Transnational Cargo – Shipping and Tracking, an appropriate business alias considering their real occupation. She studied her reflection in the mirrored wall of the lift as it began to rise, running a hand through her long mousy brown hair, which was a bit dishevelled from the wind.

Stepping out of the elevator she found three of her colleagues standing in the foyer, the most prominent of whom was her boss, Milton Lewis, director of Global Pursuit – the MI6 cell responsible for tracking old Soviet bloc nuclear weapons. Sixty-year-old Milton had been a great support to Rachel when her father passed and she now regarded him as something of a father figure. Beside Milton was Tom Wilson, a short but handsome ex Royal Marine Officer. He had been seconded by MI6 as an expert on naval operations and his insights had proven valuable on many occasions. Rounding out the group was Sandra Fox, a strawberry blonde from Essex. She had been recruited in a bar twenty years ago, when the department still used honey traps as a way of eliciting information through pillow talk. However, over the years Sandra had proved her worth as much more than an object of male desire. She had taken part in some of the most dangerous state-on-state missions of the modern era. For her service to Queen and country she had been appointed Milton's second-in-charge in what was surely her ceiling posting. Now in her early forties, she was known as a no-nonsense operations manager and was highly regarded by the senior ranks.

'Ah, Rachel,' said Milton. 'I was just about to call you, save you the trouble of coming up. We're ducking down to Franco's for a spot of breakfast. Do you care to join us?'

'Yes, sir,' Rachel replied. 'I'll come down in a moment; I just need to grab some files. I have that rehearsal this afternoon for the presentation to the Secretary for Defence, I'm on standby to go and brief him and I just want to make sure that everything is ready to go.'

'Very good. Shall I order for you?' Milton pulled on his coat, grabbed his blue umbrella from the stand, and indicated to the others that they should go on ahead of him into the lift.

'No, I won't be too long. I'll meet you down there in ten minutes.'

'Are you sure?' Milton put a hand on Rachel's shoulder. 'I know you were here until past midnight last night – that's the advantage of having our swipe system, Rachel.'

Rachel sighed. 'Well, okay, sir, if you insist – order me a pot of tea, please.' She ignored Milton's subtle enquiry into her wellbeing.

'Do you need me to tag along this afternoon?' Sandra asked, holding the door of the lift open. 'Is it the undersecretary that you're briefing?'

'I should be fine, thanks, ma'am,' Rachel assured her. Sandra shook her head gently and smiled. Rachel knew she hated to be addressed in such a formal manner.

As the lift doors closed, Rachel pushed through the glass doors of their corner suite and went to her spacious office with its view over Jermyn Street. She loved the decor; the walls were painted a distinguished matt grey and the Herman Miller desk and chair were top of the range. She went to her safe and entered her pin number, then opened the door, removed the manila folder containing the presentation she had been working on and placed it in her leather attaché case. Firing up her computer, she waited for it to connect to the secure Intelligence Network Portal and logged in. She opened Microsoft Outlook and scanned her emails.

'Fantastic,' she said under her breath. She hit print, reading the email while she waited for the Epson to spit the copy out. Her agent in Switzerland, embedded within a subsidiary of UBS, suspected that a deal had been done between ISIS and the Russians. Forensic accounting was a powerful tool and ISIS had yet to work out how to money launder like the Russians, or the Mafia, for that matter; in this game the British and the Germans had the upper hand. This was the final piece of evidence required for her to set up her own specific mission; the resources and manpower would be assured. She felt excited to be making headway, even if she was only at the start of the trail of breadcrumbs, so to speak.

Her phone rang as she was grabbing the printout. Glancing at it as she shoved the email printout into the holdall on top of the folder, she was so surprised by the caller ID that she fumbled and nearly dropped the phone in her haste to answer it.

'Matt, hello – hi – how are you?' Her pulse began to race, as it always did when he rang.

'Hey, I'm okay. How are you, Rachel?'

She could hear what sounded like traffic in the background. 'Where are you?' she asked.

'Pulling out of a service station just outside Canberra. Thought I'd grab a coffee; I'm feeling wrecked. I just needed to talk to you, to be honest. I'm not really sure who else to talk to.'

'Is everything okay, Matt? I haven't heard from you in a while. What's going on?' Picking up her attaché case, she walked slowly towards the lift and pushed the button.

'I've been sent to a new job in Canberra, an office job – ammunition consignment, nine-to-five stuff.' He trailed off and she heard his car accelerate. One advantage of being deployed for the better part of the last decade was the tax-free cash. Matt had invested most of his money wisely, she knew, putting it into property in Sydney's buoyant market, but he had also purchased an Audi RS4, a guilty pleasure – basically a super car dressed down as a wagon, the only indication of its insane performance being the small red RS4 badge on its boot.

'You? With a desk job? Well, that's just rubbish,' Rachel declared, wondering what could have happened to cause the Australian army to waste the talents of one of its top commandos.

'Yes, that's one way to describe it,' he said ruefully.

Knowing how disheartened he must be feeling, Rachel was touched that he'd felt the need to talk to her. Perhaps this career setback would prove to be the impetus he needed to step back and discover a softer side of himself. 'How long for, do you know?'

'The posting is until at least the end of this year, and then who knows? I mean, I've spent my entire career busting a gut and this is the thanks I get.' He hesitated, as if he wanted to say more but had checked himself.

The lift arrived and she stepped in, holding the phone with her shoulder as she slipped into her coat.

'Maybe you could take some leave, come stay with me in London for a few weeks?' she suggested. 'We could brave the weather and go down to Dartmoor or even up to Scotland, if you fancy it. I have some days owing to me, so that wouldn't be a problem. Think big fires and even bigger glasses of red.'

'That sounds really good. Let me think about it. I have to get set up in Canberra first, but that shouldn't take too long, I suppose.'

'Matt, I'm sorry, I really have to go. Can we speak again on Friday night, like we used to?' She waited anxiously for his response to her suggestion that they resume the pattern they'd established back in the days when they were still together. His silence did little to reassure her.

'Sorry, I missed that, Rachel – the line dropped out for a second. How about if I ring you on Friday night, at the usual time? Is that okay?'

Rachel felt a rush of delight. As she stepped out into the cold air, it didn't feel quite so cold anymore. 'That would be great, Matt. I'd love to hear from you.'

'Okay, I'll call you then.' Matt sighed again. 'Have a great week.'

'Thanks – you too. And Matt? It's really wonderful to hear your—' She stopped as she heard the phone click. *Oh well, that's progress*, she thought.

Rachel rounded the corner into Jermyn Street and crossed the road towards Franco's. She strode across the street quickly to get out of the rain that had begun to fall steadily. The door was opened from inside by the ever-alert waitress and Rachel stepped onto the red carpet. The 1940s cafe had maintained its old-world ambience, and Rachel found the atmosphere soothing. It was also the perfect place for discreet conversations, and unbeknownst to the Hambro family, who owned the establishment, the cafe had been the location of many a secret decision pertaining to the tracking of weapons of mass destruction.

'Hello again – they're around the corner at Milton's usual table,' said the waitress as she helped Rachel out of her coat and hung it on a hook next to the cash register.

'Thank you, Pippa,' Rachel said. She turned and walked towards her colleagues.

'There she is,' said Milton, getting up from his seat to pull out Rachel's chair before she reached the table. 'We were just discussing the best way to update the database of suspect vessels leaving Croatian ports. Tom thinks that this will be the most likely route for any larger weapons to move out and down towards the Middle East – if that is indeed what we will be seeing coming through the Ukraine.'

'Right, yes, well that makes sense,' Rachel said absently, looking out the window. It had been so good to hear Matt's voice again. What did this sudden desire to talk to her mean? she wondered.

'Yes, my plan is to paint all the suspect ships bright red and the good ones a light blue colour,' said Tom. 'You know, to make it easier to track them on the satellites.'

'That's a great idea,' said Rachel. Had Matt been missing her as much as she missed him? She couldn't wait for Friday to talk to him again.

'Good, it's settled then. We'll leave tomorrow for Croatia. I'll organise the delivery of the paint and if you could get, say, around ten-thousand Polish painters from around the Bristol area we can get cracking immediately.'

'What?' Rachel snapped back to reality and laughed. 'What on earth are you talking about, Tom?'

'I'm just teasing you. What's going on? You were off with the fairies for a minute there.'

'Oh, yes – sorry. I just had a phone call from Matt; I guess it just surprised me. I'm okay now. So, Croatia: what's happening there?' She picked up the glass of water in front of her and took a small sip.

'That's great news, Rachel.' Milton raised his eyebrows at her in query as he poured her tea. 'It *is* good news, isn't it? Matt calling, I mean.'

They all knew about her brief but intense relationship with the special forces officer from Australia. She had been required to declare it as one of the requirements of her job. She had sold Matt her cover story of working for a not-for-profit magazine that highlighted poverty and other issues in Africa. Then, when her department had moved to St James Street, she told Matt she'd taken a job as the marketing manager for a transnational shipping and tracking company. Matt believed her unquestioningly. She hoped to tell him the truth one day, but until then he could continue to assume that she was just some pretty office manager who worked in the centre of London and lived for fashion.

'Yes, it is good.' She shot Milton a wry smile and then looked across at Tom. 'So how do we track these ships, Tom? What are you thinking?'

'Well, it's not going to be easy; most of the ships are already registered on the Automatic Identification System and updated regularly. What we need to do is have a plan to track those vessels that meet certain risk criteria. There's literally thousands of them though.'

Rachel looked up at the ceiling. 'Well, I think it's worth doing an analysis to gain an understanding of the profile that we should be looking at, at least to get us looking in the right ballpark. We can then provide that to the Royal Navy for their use.'

'I agree,' said Milton. 'Let's assemble some of the best and brightest from the navy and the Ministry of Defence some time next week through the Secretary's official channel. We can convene a working group and war-game what it is we're looking for.'

'There is also another layer to this, sir,' said Rachel, sensing an opportunity.

'What's that?'

The group fell quiet as four plates of piping-hot bacon and eggs and multiple baskets of warm bread and jam were distributed with military efficiency across the table.

'I see you ordered for me, sir.' Rachel smiled at Milton and then, when she was sure the waiters were out of earshot, continued, 'My source inside UBS has confirmed that ten transactions occurred from a newly registered agricultural company based out of Turkey to an account that is linked to Milko Orelik, the Russian gun runner I've been tracking.'

Sandra began to cough. 'Sorry – my coffee went down the wrong way.' Her face slightly red, she returned her focus to her food.

'There's not some information you wish to share, Sandra?' Milton asked.

'No, sir, not at this time.' Sandra continued to stare at her plate.

'Very well. So, tell us, Rachel, what are you thinking?'

'Well, sir, the actual brief to the defence secretary is tomorrow morning. It's meant to be about transnational networks and their distribution channels as we have so far determined them. Why don't I hone in on this one piece of the network, see if we can gain approval to raise an MoD mission, MI6 lead and supported by Special Operations?'

Milton looked at the group gathered around the table and then over his shoulder to where the waiters where busy polishing cutlery at the back of the cafe. Finally, he nodded. 'It's certainly worth a shot. Consider it approved. What do you need from us?'

'Well, perhaps Sandra could come along after all; I can pick her brains about Milko on the way there.' Rachel shot her superior a knowing glance, biting on her bottom lip.

'I'd be delighted,' Sandra said, a wry smile on her face. 'I have a feeling that the information I have on him won't be of much use to you, but I'll tag along for giggles.'

'Good, that's the ticket.' Milton picked up his knife and fork. 'Tom and I will get on to the invites for the working group next week. Now let's dig in – all this talk of money and espionage and the like has made me ravenous.'

6

CANBERRA

Steering the Audi into Macquarie Street, Matt saw that the inner-city Canberra suburb looked even more leafy and green than the real estate website had promised. The evening light was slowly fading and the street had a warm and welcoming feel to it. Pulling up behind the grey removal truck he could see that the removalists had already finished unloading.

Matt switched off the engine and got out of the car. Almost immediately he spotted a young man in a badly fitting suit half running, half falling down the stairs leading out of the Barton Apartments. Clearly this was the real estate agent who had promised over the phone to organise everything once he heard that the Department of Defence was paying the lease.

'Hey, man, you must be Matt.' The agent rushed over to the car, arm already extended for the handshake. 'I'm Carl.'

'Of course you are,' said Matt.

He looked across at the modern apartment block and felt pleased with his choice. Behind him he could hear the sounds of kids jumping into a backyard swimming pool in one of the few houses that were interspersed within the new development. Google maps had indicated that the area comprised mostly apartment blocks, a modern hotel precinct and some big houses, all a stone's throw from Parliament House and Lake Burley Griffin. The suburb was dotted with new bars and cafes, all within walking distance. Breathing in the smell of sausages cooking on a barbecue somewhere close by, mixed with the scent of recently cut grass, Matt thought that perhaps he wouldn't mind a year here.

'Right, well, here are the keys. The guys are almost done unpacking the truck and I had them arrange everything just like you asked me to. Are you okay to receive the rest of the stuff on your own? It's just that it's getting late and I should really be heading home.'

'What other stuff?' Matt knew where this was going.

'Well, I mean, this can't be all of it. There's only, like, ten boxes, a plastic army trunk and an old leather chair.'

'That sounds about right.'

Carl gently punched Matt's right shoulder. 'What are you – a serial killer?' he joked.

'I could be if you touch me again, Carl,' said Matt, giving him a fierce look then a small smile as he returned the little tap to the shoulder but four times as hard.

Carl stepped back to steady himself. 'Right, yes, of course.' He laughed nervously. 'Okay, well, the garage is just down there; this is the remote for the roller door and the card for the security access upstairs.' He presented the remote and card to Matt. 'The post box is by the front door . . . What else? Oh, yes – the electricity and water are both on and I've sorted out the payment scheme. So, that's about it, I guess. If you could drop by the office tomorrow, we can have you sign the rest of the documents.'

'Cool.' Matt nodded and leaned back against the car.

'Gee, that's a sweet ride.' Carl gazed at the car and whistled admiringly.

'Thanks, buddy.' Matt opened the car door and got in.

'Well, I'll be off then,' Carl said. 'Oh, there's a great little cafe at the bottom of the building on the other side. It opens really early and doesn't close till late.'

Matt turned the key in the ignition. 'Thanks, Carl. I'll be seeing you, pal.' He eased the RS4 away from the kerb, and watched in the rear-vision mirror as Carl fumbled for his phone and dropped it in the grass. Matt laughed to himself and manoeuvred around the removal truck and then down the driveway that led into the underground garage.

• • •

A few minutes later Matt was standing in his new apartment. He looked around at the softly lit, open-plan living area and the adjoining marble kitchen. His old leather chair sat in the middle of the room. Moving down the hall and into the bedroom, Matt admired the removal men's handy work. Everything unpacked, and folded on shelves, his camouflage military uniforms all hanging in a row on the left of the wardrobe and the polyester formal uniform on the right, boots at the bottom and training gear on the top shelf. He studied the Sherwood green 'smashed moth' para wings on the sleeve of the polyester uniform.

I guess I better get used to wearing ceremonials, he thought.

He walked back to the lounge room and slumped into the chair, resisting the urge to go in search of a bottle shop. It was an urge he had been finding harder to resist over the last few days, but he knew nothing good was going to be found at the bottom of a bottle. His phone beeped to signal the arrival of a message and he picked it up and glanced at the screen. The message was from JJ.

How goes it, boss?

Matt ignored the message, choosing instead to stare out the window. The apartment was on the top floor and looked out over the lake. The last rays of sun bathed the tops of the gum trees in the most incredible orange light and hundreds of galahs circled and squawked above before settling for the night. As the sun slipped away, so did Matt, into the type of sleep that helps the mind to make sense of situations that people sometimes have to endure just to get to the better stuff.

• • •

One week on, Matt ran across the bridge over Lake Burley Griffin and extended his stride. Even at six in the morning the track around the lake was thronged with people trying to reach their own fitness goals. He focused on the same woman he had seen the past few mornings and matched her pace, ten metres behind and closing in. Matt watched as her ponytail bobbed up and down and focused for a moment on her pale orange running tights.

He was beginning to like Canberra. The CrossFit gym around the corner had been a revelation. No one cared who he was or where he was from; he just turned up, trained hard and left, and he was planning to do that every day of his remaining five weeks of leave before starting his new job at army headquarters. He had deliberately avoided calling Rachel, even though he had promised he would. Going to London would only complicate things further, he'd decided. He was probably never going to be able to give her what she wanted. It hurt to recognise that, but he had to be realistic. He'd thought that maybe he could, but if he was really going to commit to being honest with her, that would mean telling her about Allie van Tanken, the Dutch intelligence analyst he'd met during his 2010 deployment to Afghanistan. Not that there was much to tell; they had only just been getting to know each other when she had died so tragically in his arms. He still wondered about the circumstances leading up to Allie's death at the hands of Steph Baumer, who had then been so promptly whisked away by the US government. The whole affair had been shrouded in a veil of secrecy.

To take his mind off Allie, he focused instead on the woman in front of him. She had just increased her pace. *Oh no – not today you don't*, he thought. She had done the same thing the last few days right around the monument and Matt knew she would maintain the new speed for the last five kilometres. She was quick, probably a triathlete, although in Canberra she could also be an Olympic athlete. It was the home of the Australian Institute of Sport, after all. Her tank top showed off the type of muscle definition that you can only get from lifting, and lifting often.

The alarm on his watch started to beep and he already knew what it was going to tell him. His heart rate was reaching the max zone, a hundred and eighty-four beats per minute and climbing. He maintained the pace.

Shit, she's turning it on today.

His lungs screamed at him to slow down, the faintest taste of blood starting to creep into his mouth, an indication that he was now burning lactate for fuel. Glancing quickly at his watch he saw the pace: three minutes and thirty-five seconds per kilometre. There was no way known she was going to hold this; he certainly wasn't.

The first kilometre came to a close and Matt's legs were burning. The pace hadn't let up and, if anything, Ponytail had pulled ahead by another couple of metres.

The second kilometre clicked over at the same pace and by the end of the third Matt was off in the desert of his own mind, finding the happy place he had been trained to go when pain washed over him. His body was screaming, his watch beeping, his legs burning and vomit threatening. Then his body just quit. He buckled and slowed his pace to just above a walk.

Ah, damn it!

Ponytail looked over her shoulder and smiled at him and then, to add insult to injury, she took the steps of the last bridge two at a time.

Matt chose to walk the last kilometre back to the cafe in his apartment building where he'd had breakfast after his run each day that week.

'G'day, Matt. Have a seat, cobber, and I'll bring you the usual: long black and warm cow juice on the side.' The Australian colloquialisms sounded odd coming from the lips of Bruce, the diminutive Asian waiter. Matt had really warmed to him though. Hearing that strong Australian accent made him laugh. The name made him laugh too: with his jet-black hair worn spiked up, Bruce looked like an extra from a Bruce Lee movie.

'Thanks, champ.' Matt took a seat in a plastic orange chair and emptied the contents of his pocket onto the table; iPhone, apartment access card and the money that he had brought to pay for breakfast. The bi-fold doors of the cafe were wide open, merging the early morning with the dining room.

Bruce yelled some instructions in Vietnamese to the staff back in the kitchen, most probably family members, and he then disappeared behind the long glass counter. The kitchen was a hive of activity as they prepared for the day ahead. In two hours' time, Matt knew, the place would be full of civil servants demanding eggs and coffee, and then at lunchtime half of Canberra would pop in for laksa and pad Thai.

Matt's iPhone vibrated and he looked down at the illuminated screen.

You disappoint me, Rix. I didn't take YOU for one who would set patterns.

What the fuck? Matt thought. He looked quickly around the cafe. He saw a couple who had also been jogging earlier in the morning; they were now lost in each other's eyes and holding hands across an outside table. A middle-aged man in a well-tailored suit sat in the corner. He was buried deep in the *Sydney Morning Herald* while sipping his cappuccino. And there was an attractive young woman sitting two tables away with her back to him, dressed in smart casual clothing and focused intently on her laptop. Not your usual public servant – probably a journo or perhaps a blogger.

Usually the cafe was empty at this hour of the morning, but today it was busy. Other than that it didn't seem like anything out of the ordinary was going on. No one registered as an immediate threat to Matt. His eyes darted back towards the kitchen and he spied the knife block. That would be his first port of call should an armed threat emerge.

Matt's phone vibrated again. This time he took notice of the number – it had an international area code.

Want to catch Faisal Khan again? Reach under the table and take the envelope.

Matt scanned the area again, this time looking out to the street. He saw a couple of executive drivers in conversation across the street. Nothing going on there either.

He slipped his hand beneath the table and felt the envelope stuck to its underside. He removed it in one swift motion.

'There ya go, chief: one long black, warm udder juice on the side. Now, what ya gonna wrap your laughin' gear around this morning?' Bruce licked his index finger and flipped open to the next page of his little yellow notebook.

Matt looked up at him, still trying to make sense of what was going on. 'Huh? Ah, nothing, thanks.'

'Alrighty.' Bruce rushed off to clear the table recently vacated by the attractive young journalist.

Matt stared at the envelope. He ruled out explosives, as the envelope wasn't that thick and wasn't even sealed. He opened it carefully and saw that it contained airline tickets and a business card. He looked up just in time to see a black Statesman pull up out the front and the journalist jump in before it sped off.

Matt stood, almost knocking the table over. He caught the coffee cup before it fell to the floor.

'Shit!' Matt looked around. 'Bruce? Hey, Bruce!' Matt resettled the cup on its saucer and stood up ready to go.

'What's up, man?' Bruce walked out from behind the counter, wiping his hands on a tea towel.

'Was anyone in this seat this morning? Before me, I mean.'

Matt already knew the answer before Bruce replied. 'Yeah, the lady that was sitting over at that other table. She sat here first for a little bit and then moved to where she could plug in her laptop. Why?'

'I don't suppose you know her, do you?' Matt asked.

'Never seen her in my life.'

'No, of course you haven't.'

Matt looked again at the envelope and took out the first ticket. It was from Canberra to Melbourne, departing that very afternoon. The next was from Melbourne to Dubai and the third and last ticket was from Dubai to Bologna. The flights were all business class.

'Is something wrong?' Bruce asked.

'I'm not sure. At least, I don't think so.' Matt frowned at the tickets, his mind racing as he tried to make sense of it all.

'She was in a bit of a rush, huh?' Bruce wiped Matt's table down with the tea towel and then stood back up, looking out to the street.

'What?'

'The American girl – she left here quickly, is what I meant.'

'She was American?'

'Yeah, I think so, she ordered an Americano and I'm pretty sure she had an American accent.'

Matt took out the business card. It was for a cafe called the Lupo Bianco in a town called Abetone, Italy. He turned it over; there was a message written on the back.

Meet me at 7 am on 17 January if you want answers. Steph Baumer.

Classic CIA espionage 101, Matt berated himself. He had been stalked all week and hadn't even seen it. He had allowed himself to set a pattern. They had worked him out and set up a contact. The journalist sat side-on to him, her computer camera capturing his image in real time so that Steph could positively ID him before she sent him the text messages. Then, when he was distracted by the envelope, she had slipped away to a waiting extraction vehicle. No doubt there was backup somewhere close by too, just in case he had worked it out before the she could safely exit. Matt recalled the loving couple who had been sitting just outside at right angles to the woman. They were gone now too.

Far out – I just got worked over by the bloody CIA, Matt realised. He was kicking himself. He looked again at the airline tickets and then he looked straight up at the older man who had been reading the paper. They locked eyes and the gentleman got up, nodded his head at Matt and slowly left the cafe. He seemed a lot more suspicious to Matt now than he had before. Was he part of the set-up, or someone else entirely? Someone from his own government, perhaps?

Matt placed twenty dollars under his cup.

'Gotta go, Bruce. Keep the change, pal.' With that Matt hurried upstairs to pack. The adrenaline had awakened something within him, something that had been dormant.

It's time to get some bloody answers from Steph Baumer, he thought. This would be the last time the CIA got the better of him, he swore to himself. Faisal Khan was on the loose, and if he was honest with himself chasing Khan would provide him with some much-needed excitement. And now he had the opportunity to get some answers about Allie. Then, maybe, he would be in a better space to make something of the relationship with Rachel. After all, there was no reason he couldn't go to London after he was finished in Italy.

7

DELARAM-ZARANJ HIGHWAY, AFGHANISTAN

The suspension creaked and groaned as the old bus bounced slowly along the broken bitumen. The Delaram–Zaranj Highway was the best in Afghanistan, but would be considered dismal by Western standards. The road provided the fastest route from Kandahar to Zabol, but it also meant more scrutiny by security forces. There were US military patrols on every corner, and roadblocks and vehicle checkpoints in every culvert and on every bridge; war planes circled high overhead and Apache helicopters responded to the ground forces' calls for support. The road was chaos.

The late-afternoon sun beating down on the roof of the bus intensified the foul odour inside, a smell that told of men with questionable bathing habits. Faisal didn't notice the pungent smell, however; he just sat in silence on the half-shredded vinyl seat of the Toyota Coaster stroking his beard and watching as the scenery slowly went past the greasy window. He hadn't washed for a few days himself, except for his hands and feet before prayer time.

The bus pulled over in a clear area on the side of the potholed road. It was obvious that this spot was well known to the driver, given the rubbish and empty water bottles that lay around the small desert shrubs. There had been a firefight here recently too, as evidenced by a small pile of machine gun link and empty brass casings. The other travellers, prayer mats in hand, left the vehicle to conduct their rituals. Faisal waited until the last of the passengers got off. He had been listening to the conversations of his fellow passengers and he knew who was going where. Three of the young men towards the back of the bus were heading to Iran. Although they were Sunni Muslims, one of the lecturers at their university had assured them that they would be well received in Iran. He had promised them safe passage in exchange for US dollars, and the students had jumped at the chance to escape the violence in Kabul, which was becoming ever more prevalent on the streets of the capital.

When he was certain that he was unobserved, Faisal went down to the back of the bus where the students' bags were stowed. He checked the weight of each bag in turn and then, selecting the heaviest of the three, unzipped it. Looking over his shoulder quickly to ensure he was still alone, he removed a block of opium about the size of a standard house brick from under his shirt and tucked it in among the clothes. Faisal then reached into his vest pocket and pulled out one of the two mobile phones he had bought at the market the evening before. With this phone, he had rung every number that he could remember and told them all he was free. Then he had turned off the phone and removed the SIM card.

Now Faisal turned it back on and shoved it inside a shoe, stuffing a rolled-up sock in after it. Then he alighted from the bus and joined the group at prayer, first washing himself and discarding his own water bottle along with the other rubbish, then facing Mecca to recite the first chapter of the Quran. He continued the ritual and then rolled up his prayer mat. He always felt a sense of relief after prayer. He wanted to keep his mission in the front of his mind and he felt the best way to do that was to keep Allah aware of his feelings and to draw strength from his own faith.

Faisal walked back down the side of the bus with the other men. The driver, standing at the front, caught Faisal's eye.

'Are you coming all the way to the border?' the portly driver enquired of him.

'Yes.' Faisal watched as the other passengers boarded. 'I'm going into Zabol.'

'What are you running from? Afghanistan herself? The Taliban? The Americans?' The driver put his cigarette out on the front wheel and flicked the still-smouldering stub into the dirt at his feet. Faisal couldn't help but be disgusted at the decaying mouth of the driver, his teeth rotting in place.

'I'm not running, just visiting a brother in Iran; he helps look after a mosque. Afghans can still travel, can't they? Or would the world rather we just stay in the one place?' Faisal had known the driver would approach him at some point; they were all on the take. A day ago Faisal had paid him with Iranian rial, suspecting that he would be watching his passengers throughout the trip. The US dollars that his new ISIS 'friends' had given him would have led the driver to suspect that he was on the run or a spy, so he had strapped the cash to the inside of his leg. Those in the south of Afghanistan, that had business between the two neighbouring countries, often used the Iranian rial, and so it would draw less attention.

Still, the driver eyed him with suspicion. 'How old are you? Early thirties? I don't see many older Afghans make this trip all the way anymore – not after word got out at how the Iranian border guards treat us.' And it was true that this exit for the Afghans had ceased to be viable unless safe passage – meaning advance notice to the guards at the border post along with a decent bribe – had been arranged. Most Afghans had neither the money nor the contacts to make what used to be a straightforward journey.

'Well, I work for a family that has connections in the Iranian government. I shouldn't think I will find too much trouble in Iran, God willing. I keep myself to myself and I will answer any questions that are asked of me.'

'I see. Well, we'd best get going if we are to make the border post before it shuts. I hope the Iranians receive you as warmly as you seem to think they will.' The driver snorted and wiped his fat nose with the back of his hand. 'Things have changed you know.' He lit another cigarette, breathing it in deeply.

'I'll take my chances.' Faisal hitched up his pants and climbed the Coaster's stairs, resuming his seat in the stench. He stretched out and placed his feet on the Adidas sports bag containing his travel documents and a change of clothes. His bag also contained a letter from the Fayaz family. The head of the family was Ayatollah Mohammed Ishaq Fayaz, the most powerful voice in the Shia minority in Afghanistan promising unity and inclusion across both sects. The letter, only a few lines in total, told of Faisal's intention to pay a cultural visit to the Imam Reza shrine in Mashhad.

Faisal amused himself for the rest of the journey by listening to the students discuss what they thought Iran was going to be like. They had no idea of the experience that Faisal had just organised for them.

8

ABETONE, ITALY

The door to Steph Baumer's office flew open.

'Ma'am, we have a problem – or, rather, you do,' declared Fiona Prince as she strode into the softly lit office on the top floor of the mountain hideaway. People referred to Fiona behind her back as Princess Fiona, a reference to the troll princess in *Shrek*. She was in her late thirties and, mainly due to her personality – or lack thereof – was unlikely to advance further than her position as an intelligence analyst for the CIA. Steph tolerated her abrasive nature because she was handy to have around and excelled at menial tasks, but Steph also kept her firmly in her place.

'I told you not to disturb me. This better be important, Fiona.' Steph was poring over a file she had recently received from MI6 and was reviewing notes on Milko Orelik and his recent movements through Europe. She looked up over her desk and out the huge window to the panoramic view of the snowy Italian mountains. She watched Fiona approach in the reflection.

'It's the project you're working on in Afghanistan. It's Faisal Khan, ma'am.'

Steph turned her chair slowly and eyed Fiona, who looked particularly frumpy in her tartan skirt and long-sleeved blouse. *Combat pants and t-shirt, ready for anything*, was Steph's mantra.

'What about Faisal Khan?' Steph tapped her finger on the desk impatiently. 'Well, come on – get to it.'

'They know he's on the move. I just saw some traffic come over the RIPCADMAT requesting a Reaper. They're looking at hitting a bus he's on with a missile – like, now!'

'You've got to be joking! Who? Who is looking to do that?' Steph stood up and placed her hands on her hips. 'This will fuck everything!'

Fiona took a deep breath and stepped back from Steph. 'It's the Special Operations Joint Task Force in Kabul. The request came from Brigadier Mark Smyth. He's looking to approve the strike on Khan – they're only waiting for a positive ID. If he uses his phone again they're going to locate him and launch.'

'Right, well, of course they are.' Steph brushed a strand of hair from her eyes and ran it back into her tight ponytail. 'What on earth is a RIPCADMAT anyway?' she asked, as she turned back to the desk and gathered all her files into a single pile.

'It's the new software system for joint fire assets that was installed in the Joint Operations Room. It's the Recon, Intelligence, Planning, Combined Arms Directory for Missions and Training. It was installed last month and I can now monitor assets all over the world. I briefed you on it last month. It's awesome.'

'I'm the bloody Italian station chief, Fiona – do you think I give a crap about that shit?!'

'Assistant to the chief . . .' Fiona trailed off, looking at the floor.

'Sorry, what was that?'

'Nothing, ma'am.'

'No, didn't think so. Anyway, how do they even know where he is?'

'He made a series of phone calls two days ago and again today. It appears that he was excited to let everyone know he was out of gaol. Did you know he had a teenage son?'

'No, I didn't know that.' Steph focused on some dirt under one of her fingernails and picked at it with her other hand.

'Well, none of us did. His son's name is Mohammed Al Faisal, and Faisal Khan rang his number. The conversation was interesting. It turns out his son is being held against his will. Khan was given permission to talk to him, told him that everything was going to be okay and he mentioned that God had given him and his son a mission. The call was transcribed in the report attached to Smyth's request. Plus, the National Security Agency intercepted a call between Faisal Khan and our friend the facilitator in Egypt and then a call to one of the known narcotic targets on the Drug Enforcement Agency's hit list. The NSA matched his voice from past records and they realised he was one of the escaped prisoners from the Sarposa prison break in Kandahar, as well as a registered medium-value target. They alerted ISAF SOF and they passed the information to the Special Operations Joint Task Force HQ. Now they're trying to locate him.'

Steph slammed her hand on the desk. 'Goddamn it. I told those retards to give him a smart phone with instructions not to turn it on until he was in Turkey. We have to make sure they don't get a shot at him.'

'Ma'am, we're eight thousand kilometres away. How can we stop them?'

'Shit, I don't know, but we better think of something, and fast.'

Steph turned her gaze to the view again. Finally, she asked, 'This RIPCAD thingy – does it have footage too?'

'Of course; it's an interactive platform. We can access it, see everything, we could even request a strike through it if we wanted to and our request met the criteria.'

Steph opened the bottom drawer of her desk and grabbed an old Nokia. She switched it on to make sure it was charged.

'Right, let's go.' Steph moved out the door, eyes fixed on the phone as she dialled a number.

'Mohammed Al Bahari, is that you? . . . Hello, yes, it's been a long time, my friend. So, I need you to do me a favour, right now . . . Yes, it's extremely important – I'll pay you triple the normal fee.'

There was silence at the other end of the line except for the sound of a car's engine and then that too fell silent.

'I'm listening,' came the reply.

'Can you locate Jawid Fartouk for me? I need to talk to him urgently.'

'Ten times.'

'What?' said Steph.

'I want ten times the normal amount, then I'll do it.'

'Don't be stupid, Mohammed, I don't have access to that sort of money.'

'Fine, I'll take three times the normal amount.'

Steph heard him yawn lazily and felt a flare of anger. He had pissed her off now, and she decided to change the game they were playing.

He spoke again. 'If you had agreed to ten I would have been worried anyway. Give me half an hour – I'm not that far from there now.'

'Thank you, Mohammed.' She heard the car start again as he hung up the phone. Steph stuffed the handset back in her pocket and shouldered open the door to the operations room. On one side of the room there were four small cubicles, each with a computer for the staff to write their reports. In the centre of the room was a long desk covered with reports and files. On the far wall were three giant maps – two of Italy and one of Croatia – as well as a smaller map of Afghanistan. One of Steph's staff, at Fiona's instigation, was already hooking up a projector to the main computer so they could all watch the Reaper footage.

'So what's the plan, ma'am?' asked Fiona.

'Gather around, everyone – we have about thirty minutes to stop this from becoming a really crappy day!' Steph turned to Fiona. 'You just get me that Reaper feed and I'll do the rest.'

'Yes, ma'am.'

• • •

'Sir, the MQ-9 Reaper has plenty of time left on station but it has only one hellfire left after it supported a para regiment patrol today in Helmand Province.'

Jim Rafter, the Joint Task Force operations officer, replaced the handset on the secret telephone located on the far side of the brigadier's private office. He turned to face his commander, who was standing behind his stately desk. Although located in Kabul, the office of the Special Operations Joint Task Force commander was spacious and opulent, as you would expect for someone of such high rank. It was Brigadier Mark Smyth's preferred place from which to run these types of operations. He found the operations room too loud, not allowing him time to sit quietly and process important information. Standing there behind his desk, at six feet tall and dressed in immaculate MultiCams, he looked every bit the thirty-year military veteran. His salt and pepper grey hair softened his looks slightly, but this was offset by his bright blue eyes, and the sharp gaze that often made people uncomfortable.

'Thanks, Jim.' Smyth turned to his intelligence officer. 'Karen, do you have the positive ID yet? Is this definitely our guy?'

'Not yet, sir, he's only just turned the phone back on. Once he makes a call, and if he speaks clearly enough, we should be able to get positive ID in a matter of seconds.'

'And you think it's this bus that we are watching on the screen now?'

'Most probably, sir. The Reaper that's on station has searched the length of the highway. There were twenty buses in total but this one is about the correct distance away from the point where we first intercepted his transmission. They started tracking it just after its last stop. Simple matter of time past a point based on average speed and requisite rest breaks.'

Smyth smiled at her. 'Great work, Karen.'

'Thank you, sir. Do you mind if I help myself to a coffee? It's been a long couple of hours.'

'Yes, yes, of course, you know where it is.' Brigadier Smyth folded his arms as he turned back to watch the screen.

Karen moved to the Nespresso machine located in the small alcove off to the side of the room. 'Do you want one, boss?'

'No, thanks.' Smyth kept his focus on the screen. A few cars overtook the bus as it exited another urban area and started to make its way further out of Kandahar proper. 'Tell me, Jim, collateral damage – what's the story?'

'Well, it's a twenty-two-seat bus, sir, so there could be two or twenty-two or even fifty aboard; you know how they jam into these vehicles. We could stay on station for a few hours to get ID and follow him until we have him by himself, or we could just smash him and whoever he is with and put it down to bad luck for them.'

'I'm going to pretend you didn't suggest that, Jim.'

'Yes, sir.' Jim looked down at his feet and then up to the screen.

'But when the time comes,' Smyth added with a wry smile, 'there's nothing off the table.'

Karen's voice chimed in from the alcove, 'Sir, the Reaper pilot can update us on how many are on the bus; they watched it during its last stop and would have recorded the footage.' She walked in with two cups of coffee and handed one to Jim. He took it and she smiled at him, raising her eyebrows as she did. 'I'll establish communications with them now, boss. Won't be long.'

She moved across to the stack of radios by the secret phone and scanned the laminated card on the wall for the correct frequency. She pushed the digital keypad on the Harris radio and the sound of the Reaper controller in Kandahar came through the handset.

'I didn't think of that,' Jim said to the Brigadier under his breath. 'Sorry, sir.'

The brigadier waved away the apology, his eyes still on the bus, playing over in his mind how to deal with the problem.

Karen spoke up. 'They're pretty sure that's the bus, sir. They still don't have positive ID but the Reaper picked up the phone signal itself. Also, there are seven people on board including the driver.'

'Right! Okay, tell me again, Karen: how important is this guy, in the grand scheme of things?'

'He's a medium-value target, boss.' Karen listened to some information from the pilot and then continued. 'The Reaper is asking for your authorisation codes – they're ready to launch.'

'But how does he rank, where is he in the fight, what effect will this have, if any?' Smyth started to pace the length of the room.

'Sir, if you're going to do this you have to do it soon, they're approaching another village area.' Jim had moved closer to the screen and was now cross-referencing the video feed with a map in his hand.

'He's important enough to eradicate, boss,' said Karen.

'Eradicate? What about the other six, Karen? Is their *eradication* going to save the lives of others?' Smyth stopped walking and watched as the bus pulled over again.

'I can't answer that, boss. How would I know?'

'I need some more information, Karen,' Smyth told her.

'Perfect chance now, boss,' Jim said. 'No other cars, static target and off the road to boot. Launch it, I'd say.'

The brigadier ignored him.

'Karen, give me something.'

'Sir, he's on the Joint Prioritized Effects List, and we are authorised to capture or kill people on the list – that's why we have it.'

'Do it, boss! I think the bus is going to move again!' Jim was now standing a foot from the screen and almost bursting with excitement.

'Jesus, Jim, calm down. Karen, there are other people on that bus; I need to know where he is on the list.'

'They might be all part of his group, boss,' said Jim.

Smyth shot him a glare.

'He's on the bottom end of the list, sir,' Karen said.

'How many names are on the list, Karen?' asked Smyth, knowing the answer only too well.

'Around two thousand two hundred, sir – but it should be remembered that he was much higher at one point, before he was in prison. He has links to the Pakistani intelligence service, al-Qaeda, the Taliban and others. Sir, he's a nasty piece of work.'

'I see.' Smyth looked at the screen and sighed. 'Very well.'

Karen was interrupted by her mobile ringing in her pocket. 'I'd better take this, sir – it should be the intelligence cell calling with an update.'

Jim said urgently, 'Sir, the Reaper has it locked now – they're ready to release on your command.'

Smyth straightened up and walked over to the radio stack.

'Alright, I'm ready. Let's do this. Pass me the handset, Karen.'

Karen ended the call she was on and looked up at her commander, the colour gone from her face. 'Sir, you're not going to fucking believe this!' she said.

'What is it, Karen?' Smyth hadn't heard her swear before.

'You're never going to guess who just popped up on our radar ...'

• • •

'Mohammed Al Bahari, thanks for calling me back.' Steph pointed at Fiona, who in turn pointed to one of the other intelligence staff.

The woman quickly began to type on her desktop and an automated message came instantly back from the NSA.

'Hi, Steph, I have Jawid, he's here with me now. I'll hand him over to you.'

Steph could hear them talking; she knew that Mohammed would have promised Jawid one-third of the money. Taliban at this level were not easily deceived; at least, not until one of their own offered them a large amount of cash. Steph had made Mohammed rich over the years, and now it was his turn to pay back the debt, and pay he would.

'Yes?' said Jawid quietly.

Steph handed the phone to Qasim Darya, her Afghan translator.

'This is Qasim, I work for a friend of Mohammed Al Bahari. Are you Jawid Fartouk?'

'Yes, it is me. What can I do for you?'

'I need some information about a family in Arghandab,' Qasim said. 'Perhaps you know them?'

Steph nodded to Karen, who patched the phone call back to the NSA.

'I'm the rightful governor, I know everyone in Arghandab,' Jawid said with authority. 'If they are from my area, I surely know them.' His pride at being the shadow governor for the Taliban was obvious.

Steph rolled her fingers over at Qasim, indicating for him to keep Jawid talking.

'It's a family who have links to the Pakistani construction company that are maintaining the road.'

'Yes, I know this family well. What do you want of them? I can tell you now that they own half of—'

Jawid would utter no more words in this life. The hellfire punched through the roof of the car. The eight-kilogram high-explosive warhead detonated behind the driver's seat, vaporising Mohammed Al Bahari and Jawid Fartouk instantly. The blast was so intense that if they truly had souls, they too would have been obliterated and not much use in an afterlife.

The sound that came back to Qasim made him drop the phone and the NSA message that appeared on the intelligence analyst's computer confirmed the strike had taken place on Brigadier Mark Smyth's orders.

'I'd say that was effective.' Steph smiled at Fiona, who looked back at her in disbelief. 'Well, what did you think would happen?' Steph looked around at her shocked staff. 'Okay, carry on everyone – fun's over.'

She picked up the phone from the floor where Qasim had dropped it and made her way out the door. She closed it quietly, smiling to herself, and went down the hall back to her office.

'Jesus, did that actually just happen?' asked one of the intelligence staff under his breath.

Fiona looked around the room at the intelligence staff. They all looked back at her with their mouths open in shock.

'She just totally wasted one of our top informers in Afghanistan,' said another analyst.

'Right, so let's have a few minutes' break, gather ourselves a bit.' Fiona was shaking. She looked at the door that her boss had just left through and slowly shook her head. She couldn't believe how quickly Steph had burned a valuable contact in order to save a mission. If the station chief should ever return from sick leave –

probably taken as a result of trying to rein Steph in this past year – she would be sure to inform him of what had just happened.

. . .

Back in Kabul, Karen reported, 'Target neutralised, sir. Battle damage assessment indicates complete destruction.'

'Thanks, Karen, and top twenty on the JPEL – not a bad day's work,' said Brigadier Mark Smyth.

'Yes, sir, great result all round.'

'Should we get back to the bus now, sir?' asked Jim.

'The Reaper is empty now, Jim – that was its last hellfire. Plus, they lost contact with the bus for five minutes; there's no telling if the objective is even on it anymore until we go through a whole ID match again.'

'And in any case, all the other assets are on task,' said Karen.

'Yes, that's enough for one day, I think. Thanks, guys, can you give me a few minutes alone now?' Smyth lowered himself into his seat and turned off the large monitor with the remote control. He put his hand on the cupboard next to his chair, ready to open it as soon as they left. A quick shot of Irish whiskey would be just the recharge he needed.

'Yes, sir.' Karen nodded to Jim and they left the brigadier's office.

In the hallway Karen stopped and turned to face Jim.

'God, that was intense. Can you believe that guy just popped up on the radar like that?'

Jim shook his head. 'I know, right? We're going after one low-level guy and all of a sudden – boom, there's Objective Citroen, right there for the taking.'

'Massive boost for the boss.' Karen smiled. 'Let's go get dinner. I'm starving.'

Smyth sat quietly in his office looking at the blank TV screen. Moments before he had watched two lives wiped out on his command. Opening his notebook, he started to pen his thoughts on what had just occurred; no doubt it would come in handy one day.

9

AFGHAN-IRANIAN BORDER

Faisal could see a group of Iranian border guards gathered by the boom gate as the Coaster approached. Not long from now, he would be in the city of Zabol. Faisal thought back to the instructions he had received from Hassan al-Britani.

'In the centre of the city is a small tailor's shop known as Stitch in Time Threads. This is where you are to meet Bahbak Khorasanhi, whose job it is to smuggle you into Turkey,' the ISIS militant had said as he gave Faisal a single sheet of paper with the address of the tailor's shop. 'Destroy this once you have memorised it, Faisal. And I'm sure I don't need to remind you not to carry a phone.'

Faisal had ignored this; he had bought ten different SIM cards to go with his new phones. As long as he switched between SIM cards with his remaining phone he should have no trouble evading detection.

As the vehicle came to a stop the guards gestured for the men to get off. The largest of the guards talked to the driver, who seemed to nod in Faisal's direction.

Faisal exited behind some of the others. He stayed silent as he went down the steps and produced his documents for the guards to inspect. The other three men behind him joked and laughed as they in turn stepped off.

'Line up here, have your papers ready and put your bags at your feet.' The commander of the Iranian guards was all business. He took Faisal's passport and checked it, then looked back at Faisal suspiciously. 'Not much travel over the last couple of years,' he said.

'No, there were things in Kandahar that held my attention,' said Faisal. He could see the driver watching the exchange from the front of the bus.

'Where are you heading to?'

'Imam Reza shrine.' Faisal produced the envelope containing the forged letter and passed it to the guard, who opened it and perused the contents.

'Hmm, I see.' The guard raised his eyebrows and showed his commander, who was hovering next to him. The commander pushed the letter into Faisal's chest and indicated for him to move to one side.

'You three can stop joking around and produce your papers too!'

The students stopped laughing and stood quietly as the guards took their documents. The first guard went over their papers while a second went through the bags at their feet. 'Sir, look at this.' The second guard stood up, holding the block of resin in his hands.

'What?' one of the students protested. 'No! That's not mine. You must have put it there.'

'What did you just say?!' The commander belted him across the face. 'You come to the border with this poison and then you try to deny it!'

The commander called for more guards and they streamed out of the concrete guard house to surround the men. The commander kicked the legs out from beneath the student and the other guards followed suit with his friends. The students lay in the dust while the guards went to work on them, kicking and punching them into submission.

Faisal watched quietly as the young men were dragged away, along with their bags and Faisal's drop phone. He smiled to himself.

'What are you looking at?' The commander eyed Faisal suspiciously.

'At justice being served, I'd say,' Faisal replied smoothly.

'You'd best be on your way too,' said the commander gruffly, clearly satisfied by Faisal's response. 'I've got some work to do.' The commander turned his back and marched off towards the guard house.

Faisal headed through the barrier towards the waiting taxis and walked up to the one at the head of the line.

'Zabol, please.'

10

ABETONE, ITALY

Stepping out of the Hotel Bellavista and into the cold, Matt pulled up the collar of his Arc'teryx jacket. A quick glance at his watch showed that it was seven am, although it could have just as well been two am given that the sun was yet to rise. An Italian winter could play tricks on the mind.

Matt's boots crunched along the frozen cobblestones as he walked slowly up the hill. About twenty metres ahead he could see a Transit van parked in front of one of the small shops that lined the ancient Italian street. Soft light from the dashboard was reflected on the faces of the two men inside. Both their heads were down, but as Matt approached he could see that their eyes were looking in his direction. *That's a rookie mistake,* he thought. Not checking if the car lights could be completely blacked out while the heater was still on was the sign of an amateur as far as he was concerned.

Matt patted the small Walther PPK in his pocket. Finding a decent gun in Italy without attracting the attention of the Mafia had proven to be a lot easier than he'd thought it would be. However, this firearm felt like a novelty item compared to the Heckler & Koch USP – Matt's weapon of choice. *How the hell did James Bond survive using this thing?* Matt wondered.

Approaching the car from the driver's side, he turned the pistol in his left pocket to cover the two men while at the same time he slowly moved his right arm up, as if scratching his nose, so that it was clear of the proposed line of fire. He continued walking with the barrel trained on the driver's side window. The weapon probably wasn't going to be enough to kill anyone at this range, but it would provide enough of a shock to allow him to put some distance between himself and them should they be looking for trouble. The two in the van gave him only a cursory glance as he passed, and then lost interest in the stranger walking towards them, going back to the paperwork required for their deliveries. Matt breathed a gentle sigh of relief.

'Hanging on too tight,' he whispered to himself.

Matt continued on up the hill, past the Hotel Miramonti, once the summer residence of the famous composer Giacomo Puccini and a favourite spot of poets Byron and Shelley. He knew from the quick search for hotels he had conducted on the internet that behind the traditional wooden shutters and stone facade the rooms were chic and modern – probably not a bad description of Abetone in general.

At the top of the hill were two stone pyramids signifying either side of the border between the provinces of Pistoia and Modena. Here the road turned in a dog's leg, giving Matt a view out across the dark mountains and deep valleys below. The vista of snow-capped peaks was just becoming visible as dawn was breaking. Matt had to admit the jagged, frozen monsters in the distance were breathtaking.

Looking across the frozen car park, he could see the lights were on in the Lupo Bianco cafe on the other side of the road and there were signs of life inside. He walked in a wide arc away from the cafe and across the car park so that he could get a better look through the windows and the entrance. This would give him more time to gain situational awareness as he made his approach to the doorway.

There appeared to be six people inside: two staff as well as the two customers standing at the bar and two sitting by themselves at separate tables. The people standing were almost certain to be Italians enjoying their morning espresso, so Matt focused his attention on the tables. One of those seated looked at this distance to be an old man, so Matt discounted him. The other was a woman with her back to the entrance. This seemed strange to Matt. Why would someone sit in such a vulnerable position?

He crossed the road and made for the door. While walking, he removed the PPK from his jacket and secured it inside the belt of his trousers. It nestled snugly in the small of his back, the cold steel against his skin making him shiver. As he stepped inside he was enveloped by warmth; there was a fire flickering in the fireplace and Roberta Flack's 'Killing Me Softly with His Song' was playing softly. The whole setting was so calm and serene it made Matt nervous.

He announced his arrival in the customary way, with a '*Buongiorno*' addressed to the room in general.

No one other than the waitress showed any interest in him as he took off his jacket and hung it on the back of a wooden chair.

'Welcome, what can I get you?' the waitress asked him in Italian as she approached the table. Matt guessed her to be in her early forties, but it was hard to tell because most of the women smoked heavily in Italy and he had always thought that this made them age faster. Still, she was pretty and slim, with tight permed hair.

'*Vorrei un cappuccino, grazie,*' Matt replied.

As the waitress moved off Matt kept his peripheral vision focused on the woman sitting across the room with her back to him. She hadn't moved an inch nor appeared to have registered his entrance. She just sat there staring into a mug of something.

The cappuccino arrived.

'Are you skiing today?' the waitress asked casually.

'Maybe later. I might make my way up to the *rifugio* at the top of the mountain for lunch. I hear that there is an amazing log fire and that the wine itself is worth the trip.'

'Yes, it's true.' The waitress smiled at Matt. She stood there in silence for a moment, as if weighing him up. 'Where are you from?' she asked.

'I'm up from Rome,' Matt replied in fluent Italian. He took a sip of the cappuccino.

'No, no, I don't think you are. At least, you're not Italian, are you? I mean your accent is good, but it's not from here.'

'What makes you say that?' Matt asked quietly. He glanced around quickly to check on the positions of the other customers. Nothing had changed.

'Your jacket,' she said, pointing to the blue down-filled hoodie that Matt had placed on the chair. It's Canadian, right? Arc'teryx?

Well, no Italian gentleman would ever wear that. Those Scarpa boots, yes, of course, but the jacket, no. And who drinks cappuccinos?' She laughed softly and walked back to the counter.

Figures, Matt thought. When he was a boy it had been mandatory to learn either German or Italian at his school in Bendigo. He had excelled in Italian and had befriended an Italian boy at the school who had helped him learn to speak like a native. He had spent two winters and three more summers in Italy with his family over the years, too, not to mention the holidays he'd taken there while on leave from the army. It was on one of these holidays that he had met the beautiful Rachel. He'd felt sure he could pass himself off as Italian, only to be let down by his practical dress sense.

Thinking about this, he looked down at the Suunto GPS watch on his wrist and let out an involuntary groan at another example of his own ineptness at blending in.

'Hello, Matt.'

He hadn't noticed her entering the cafe. She must have been in the ladies' room, he realised: the corridor leading to the restrooms was the only area he wasn't able to cover from where he was sitting. She must have been waiting there for Matt to arrive.

'Steph, how are you?'

Matt watched her as she approached the table. She hadn't changed from when he had last seen her two years ago. She still looked fit and wore her brown hair tied back in a single ponytail. While she was not unattractive, she certainly wasn't Matt's type.

'I'm fine. As well as can be expected being here, I guess.' Steph nodded towards the waitress who already knew what to get for her. Matt could see that the penny had dropped for the waitress too;

it was obvious she knew Steph and now associated Matt's appearance in this high alpine town with the American CIA agent.

'Why here then, Steph?' Matt gestured towards the window and the wider expanses of the Tuscan mountain range. 'Why did you need me to come halfway around the world to meet you?' Matt came straight out with it; he didn't want to play games and knew only too well the capacity that CIA agents had for twisting a conversation.

Taking a seat opposite Matt, Steph said, 'See that mountain up there?' She gestured out the window to the ridgeline that ran away from town and up into the clouds. The morning dawn now bathed the valley in warm light and the mountaintop was just visible through the fog. 'That's Monte Cimone, the highest mountain in the Apennines. It has a restricted US base at its peak.'

Matt could just make out a few buildings and what looked like a small antenna farm on top of the ridgeline.

'The locals think that the mountain is hollow and contains nuclear missiles.' Steph laughed to herself and shook her head.

'What does any of this have to do with Faisal Khan?' Matt's patience was already wearing thin. The last time he had seen Steph was before the enquiry into the botched suicide bombing in Kandahar, and that was only from a distance as she was whisked away. Steph's abrupt disappearance had left Matt with many unanswered questions, especially about the death of his close friend, the Dutch intelligence officer Allie van Tanken. He had been determined to find the CIA agent, to have his questions answered, but she had become a ghost. Matt had been threatened with disciplinary action should he continue requesting that the Department of State investigate her involvement in Allie's death, so, reluctantly, he had let the matter drop. But now here they were, face to face – and *she* had summoned *him*.

'This is where I'm based now. They called it a promotion, but I think of it more as a sideways move to get me out of everyone's way and as far from Washington as possible. I'm the station chief here – well, technically the deputy chief, but I'm the one who's running the show. The site no longer contains ballistic missiles; I mean, it's not the Cold War, right?' She smiled. 'It's now a CIA listening post. As the highest point in central Italy, it's perfect for looking into Europe.'

'Yeah, whatever. Who gives a fuck? Let's talk about Allie, shall we?' Matt took another sip of his coffee and looked out the window at a couple of skiers dressed in bright clothes who had just arrived in the car park. The cafe was starting to fill up now with ski patrol staff, emergency service workers and locals all looking for their morning espresso hit.

'I killed her, Matt. What do you want me to say?'

Matt looked back at her face; he thought he saw the briefest sign of regret flash across it, but it was gone before he could be sure.

'So that's it then, Steph? That's all you have to say about it? No apology, no sorrow?'

'It just is what it is, Matt. Move on. I have. Anyone would think you were in love with her.'

Matt could feel the rage mounting in his chest; in the space of a week he had lost everything he had worked for and he wasn't in the mood to be patronised. He moved his hand around to the small of his back and leaned across the table towards Steph, narrowing his eyes.

'You had a team stalk me and then you lured me here. I suggest you tell me what the fuck is going on, Steph, before I do humanity a favour and put a bullet in that twisted little brain of yours. Trust me, I don't feel like I have too much to lose right now and I'm not sure that you'll be missed.'

Steph took a sip of her coffee, her eyes never leaving Matt's. She put the cup down ever so gently and then pushed it and the saucer out of her way.

'Don't be alarmed, Matt, but I'm taking out my Glock and I am going to put it right here on the table in front of me.' She indicated where she intended to put it with a movement of her eyes and then she slowly withdrew her weapon from the front of her cargo pants. She slid it under her beanie on the table. She took a deep breath. 'Anyway, are you sure that PPK even works, Matt? Have you test-fired it?'

Matt did a double take at the question.

'Oh, you seem surprised. You're asking yourself, *How could Steph know what weapon I have?* Take a moment to think about it, genius; I control all the lowlife thugs within a hundred-mile radius.'

Matt leaned back in his chair, defeated. He remembered the guys hanging around the Bologna train station and their eagerness to sell him stuff. They weren't surprised at all when, jokingly at first, he asked for a gun, and they had become a lot keener when he showed them US dollars. *Checkmate*, he thought ruefully.

'This is all just a big game to you, isn't it?' He slumped further back in his chair.

'Of course it is, Matt; it's espionage, the purest of all games, and you're only a beginner. Sure, you have an excellent reputation as a blunt tool of destruction, but this takes a bit of finesse.'

'Well, I'm not sure I want to play your game.' He leaned forward. 'You're obviously not going to discuss Allie's death in any real detail. I was a fool to think you'd give a shit. I know there's more to it than meets the eye though and I can't help but think it was convenient for you to kill her in the crossfire.'

'Give it a break, Matt. As I said before, it was an accident – do you really think I could just kill a person in cold blood because it would be to my advantage?' Steph smiled sweetly at Matt. 'She and I were after the same guys in Afghanistan and it just got confusing in the end. She was playing the game as much as anyone. Her death was . . . well, it was regrettable.'

'Jesus, what are you playing at? Why don't you just get to the point?'

'Fine, I will. Do you want to be a sheep, Matt? Walking around blindly in a brainwashed haze, responding to stimulus without questioning the society that we've created for you? Or do you want to be let in on the secret? You can be a sheepdog, Matt, protecting the lambs; a protector who keeps the wolves at bay. You see, we created this game and the wolves play on our terms. We remove them when we want and we prop them up for a feed when we feel like it.'

Matt rolled his eyes and shook his head.

'Nice analogy, Steph, but I've never been a lamb; I know how your government works. I, like most people, just tolerate the way that people like you play your stupid games at our expense. And I don't want to be one of the sheepdogs, either, enforcing some sort of false protection over the masses. If that's what you think you're actually doing, you're fucking delusional.'

Steph smiled and put her hand up to her face to brush an

eyelash from her cheek. She looked at it on her finger and then flicked it away.

Matt studied her face for any emotion. There was none.

She raised her eyebrows at him. 'And is your life's work really so much more noble than mine? We're not different, Matt, you and I.' With her left hand, she picked up her cup and raised it to her lips, her right hand staying close to the Glock.

'Well, that's where you're wrong. How about I give you my analogy, Steph? I'm a fucking lion. I was once in charge of a whole pride of lions just like me and we would hunt wolves – no silly games, just total devastation whenever we were released on them. And you know what, Steph, it has just occurred to me that when I'm done with the wolves, I'd be just as comfortable chasing the mangy sheepdogs that can't be trusted.'

Steph slowly removed the Glock from under her beanie. For a moment, she trained it on Matt; her finger went inside the trigger guard. Then her expression relaxed and she eased the weapon back into the front of her pants. She looked around at the transient espresso crowd.

'We hear a lot up here, Matt, mostly chatter about Russia and the Ukraine. Last month, though, some ISIS chatter made everyone sit up and take notice. They were talking about trying to buy a new weapon from some Russian gun runners: a nuclear weapon. It's a miniature nuclear weapon and I want to get it off the streets. I had it confirmed by London and also by the Italian spy agencies.'

'So what has that got to do with me?'

'I have Faisal Khan. He thinks he's working for ISIS now and is going to do the trade with the Russians. It had to be done through a third party because none of our agents has the background to make it seem convincing. Russian intelligence would blow holes in any of our cover stories. It has to be a guy who thinks he's doing it for a greater cause.'

Matt's mouth was agape. 'What? Faisal Khan? You're certifiably insane! How on earth have you got Khan?'

'Easy – I broke him out of prison using my Afghan CIA force. I recruited a bunch of British Muslim boys who had been radicalised online and marginalised by society. They were looking to join ISIS and we intercepted them; it was easy to make them my own once we offered them cash and a sense of purpose. Just like us, they were only looking to belong to something bigger. Khan thinks they're ISIS and he's willing to work with them. Actually, I turned most of them myself, and the ones who aren't British are from the Haqqani network. I've assembled a great little team and they've been knocking off commanders all over the capital.'

At her mention of the Haqqani network Matt's anger started to rise again. 'Jesus, you are a piece of work. But I still don't get what this has to do with me.'

'I need someone to shadow Khan. He's going to take possession of the weapon and then deliver it to my people. I want to make sure that he doesn't give us the slip and take off with it once he has it. He's a crafty character, and I want some insurance. It looked to me like you didn't have much going on at the moment, and so I thought you might like to do something for democracy and freedom and all that rubbish. After all, you're a fucking lion . . .' She smiled sweetly and took a sip of coffee.

'You're out of your frigging mind! Help you? I don't trust you an inch, Steph. Why can't you use one of your own? Or, better still, a special forces guy from DELTA or a SEAL?'

'State denial, Matt. I can't have an American do this. The Russians will be watching everything around the drop area. Australians love to travel and many of you travel alone; you wouldn't look out of place there at all, especially given your country's relationship and history with Turkey.' Steph looked at Matt's Suunto watch pointedly. 'Well, you won't look out of place if you play it smart, that is.'

Matt looked at his watch and then folded that arm under his other across his chest. 'What makes you think I would want to do this anyway?'

Steph leaned across the table. 'It's a nuclear weapon, Matt,' she hissed. 'ISIS have said if they get it they are going to let it off in the centre of the Green Zone in Kabul. We don't want that now, do we?'

Matt thought about it for a moment. He had been following the rise of ISIS closely and had already developed a deep hatred of its murderous ideology. He looked out the window at the snow-covered peaks now bathed in morning sunshine. The truth was, he felt alive. Maybe it was the alpine air, or maybe it was the sense of purpose that he had been missing since being relieved of his commando duties. He felt the excitement and the thrill of the chase, a mission greater than just getting up in the morning and living.

The two sat in silence for a while. Matt sensed that Steph was watching him, looking for a reaction.

Finally, he spoke. 'I'm going to need cash.'

'Of course, you'll have more than you need.'

'A weapon, surveillance equipment – the most up-to-date you have.'

'Understood. I have people who can make sure it's waiting for you in the hotel room that we organise; that's not even an issue.'

'And documents.'

'Yes. I know.'

'Intelligence support, tracking, satellites.'

'All at your disposal, Matt.'

'I'm going to want to get some blokes to help me; some support, backup.'

'Bring whoever you want. Do what you have to do to stay in touch with Khan; it's deniable on my part, just so we're clear.' Matt watched as Steph unzipped the front of her green polar fleece and reached inside. She produced an envelope and slid it across the table. 'Everything you need is in there, Matt. WhatsApp me a list of whatever you need, anything. The room is already booked in the name of the passport inside; the equipment will be there.'

Matt opened the envelope and fished out an Australian passport. The name inside was Regan Dransfield. The picture was of Matt and the passport wasn't a fake. 'Who came up with that name?'

Steph smiled at him. 'Thought you'd like it. So, you're all set.'

Steph rose from her seat. Matt stood too and in an instant he'd moved around the table to grab her right upper arm, his left hand flashing to the handgrip of her Glock. She was trapped. She had also underestimated his athleticism. He squeezed her hard enough for her to know how powerful he was. Steph took in a quick breath as if she was considering fighting back, but then thought better of it.

'If you double-cross me, Steph . . .'

'Get your hands off me, Matt,' she rasped.

'All I'm saying is, if this is a trick I don't need too much of a reason to come after you – and I *will* come after you, and I will fucking *end* you.'

Steph relaxed in his grasp and smiled at him, more to reassure the other patrons who had become interested in their conversation than out of any show of warmth. 'Matt, Matt, Matt . . . a lust for revenge just doesn't suit you. You're one of the good guys, remember? The sooner you accept your place in all of this, the sooner you'll get good at this game.'

Matt let her go and took a step back. He caught the waitress's eye and gestured for another coffee before sitting back down. 'Where is it that I'm off to then?' he said as he picked up the envelope and turned it over in his hands.

'Istanbul. Enjoy the trip.' And with that Steph turned and left.

Matt watched her walk across the car park and disappear down a set of stairs on the far side. Then he returned his attention to the envelope, tipping the contents onto the table in front of him. The first thing he picked up was a secure GSM phone. He looked at the instructions taped to the back. Then he inspected the papers and cards, placing them back in the envelope one by one as he went: one return ticket to Istanbul from Bologna, flying Pegasus Airlines; hotel accommodation booked under the name of Regan Dransfield; booking receipts, hire car details and an American Express card and PIN.

Matt thought for a moment longer and then took out his phone and dialled a number he knew well. The phone rang three times before it was picked up. In the background Matt could hear the familiar sounds of the Room Floor Combat Range at Luscombe airfield, as guys manoeuvred through and double-tapped their targets, sound and flash grenades going off; it was the roar of lions hunting in packs.

'Hey, boss, where the hell are you calling from?' asked JJ. 'Hang on.' He raised his voice to yell, 'Guys! Make your weapons safe and place them down against a wall, then go and have a five-minute break and think of all the shit I would have said you did wrong!'

'How are the boys, JJ?' Matt asked when the sergeant was back on the line.

'They're okay. We have a new boss, Kris Smith; he's taking some work, but I'll train him up. He's actually pretty good. How you doing?'

'I'm good, JJ. Kris, huh? Yeah, he was an operations officer a few years back; it's about time he had a platoon. He'll make a good commander. I have a question for you though.' Matt tapped the table with his fingers as he looked out at the snow now falling gently in the car park.

'Send it, skipper.'

'Do you have some leave? How would you like to come to Istanbul for a week, all expenses paid?'

'Sounds good. What's the occasion? Did you finally see the light and decide to elope with that British chick, what's-her-name?'

'Rachel . . . No, it's nothing like that.' Matt watched as a group of ski instructors came in for their morning espresso. He turned away from them and looked over the now-glowing mountains, the reflection of the sun shimmering through the pines and across the valley.

'It's Faisal Khan, JJ. He's in Turkey.'

'Well, I'll be a monkey's uncle. That prick is busier than a one-armed bricklayer in Baghdad.'

Matt snorted his agreement at the joke. 'So, when can you get away?'

'At the end of the week, maybe a day or two later – not sure, but it can be pretty soon. How's that sound?'

Matt heard JJ cover the handset and start yelling at the platoon again, telling them to run around the range; clearly someone had just antagonised him.

'JJ, you there?'

'Yeah, sorry, just sorting out a weak link.'

'I'm going to need your passport number and date of birth. I'll organise the rest and send you the details tonight. Keep this close hold, though; I don't need the command knowing anything about this – I'm in enough shit already.'

'What? This isn't a special ops mission? You're joking.'

'No, mate, it's someone else's mission.'

'Well, then I'm in, balls and all!'

'That's another image I didn't need, big guy. Cool, I'll wait for your information and get back to you soonest.'

'Good stuff. I'm going to get back to beasting these guys and then I'll fire it off to you. Catch ya over there.'

Matt hung up the phone. *Well, that's some serious firepower secured*, he thought. He opened the email app on his phone and typed in a quick message containing much the same content as he had discussed with JJ. If Todd Carson, the US Special Forces captain Matt had become friendly with a few years ago, could also get away, then he wouldn't just have firepower; he would have assembled an arsenal.

Matt's thoughts turned back to Rachel as he gazed across the mountains. Why had he always kept her at arm's length? When they'd broken up he had found himself falling for the beautiful Allie van Tanken. Rachel was so far away, living a different kind of life altogether, while Allie had been right there in Afghanistan, in Matt's world. It was no wonder he'd been drawn to her – but he'd never had the chance to tell her. If he was to learn anything from Allie's death, it was that he shouldn't run away from love. Matt picked up his phone and tapped in another message, this time to Rachel.

Sorry to be out of touch. Will see you in a couple of weeks.

It was time to open up to her, he thought. Time to stop running away from love.

Matt took one more look out the window as he placed a handful of coins on the table.

He pulled his jacket back on and left the cafe. Stepping out into the cold he spotted a ski hire shop three doors down. He checked his watch; he had hours to kill before needing to leave for his flight.

Might as well get some skiing in then.

11

ISTANBUL

Matt elbowed the guy behind him in the middle of the solar plexus. The breath rushed out of the Indian businessman who moments before had been pushing against Matt's back in the aisle of the cramped aircraft. Personal space wasn't given much respect by those from the subcontinent, even cashed-up creeps like this one. Matt put it down to India's huge population, but he didn't excuse the bloke for his lack of manners.

'Are you right there, turbo?

The skinny businessman just looked at Matt vacantly.

Matt grabbed his leather bag from the overhead locker and turned to face the front of the aircraft. The doors had been opened up ahead and those at the front of the line started making their way out of the plane.

'Hope to see you again, sir.' The flight attendant smiled.

As Matt walked past her through the small galley, he noted that she had been very attentive during the flight; perhaps a little too attentive . . . or was he just feeling paranoid after the operation Steph had orchestrated to get him to Italy in the first place?

The flight from Bologna to Ataturk airport had taken three hours, which was more than enough time for Matt to pore over the city guides and maps and memorise the layout of the streets around his accommodation. Clearing customs, he walked out into the modern airport terminal and picked up his roller bag. A line of orange Fiat taxis waited for customers on the road out the front. Matt made a beeline for the taxi at the front of the queue. The driver opened the boot, grabbed the roller bag from Matt's hands and threw it in. Even at four in the morning local time, the place was a chaotic jumble of taxis, police cars and trucks beeping and wailing for supremacy. The driver lit a cigarette as he got behind the wheel; he turned to Matt and said something in Turkish, smiling a decayed brown smile – the result of four decades of Turkish coffee and sweets, no doubt.

'Do you speak English?'

'Well, maybe a little,' said the driver, his cigarette hanging precariously from his bottom lip. He tilted his hand from side to side, indicating that it was probably less than a little English.

'Can you take me to the President Hotel in Sultanahmet?'

'President Hotel, of course.' The driver pulled out into the early-morning traffic.

Matt rested against the headrest and took in a deep breath, mostly of second-hand smoke. He let sleep slowly wash over him as they drove.

Thirty minutes later Matt was standing out the front of his hotel in Istanbul's old town. The street was covered in a gentle dusting of snow. Matt shivered and raised his collar.

Grabbing his bag, Matt made his way up the short flight of steps and looked around the hotel lobby. The place smelled of fresh linen and sandalwood. In the corner of the golden room a fountain gently frothed and bubbled away, seeming to keep time with the classical guitar music being piped through the foyer. Giant blue and turquoise mosaics adorned the walls, and large smoked mirrors made the room appear much larger than it was. In the corner was the entrance to an old English pub, complete with a red British phone box.

Matt approached the reception desk, sizing up the staff member who was there waiting for him.

'Ah, man, am I beat.' Matt laughed. 'Seriously, not doing the red eye again.' He dropped his roller bag and leather holdall on the ground and let out a sigh. Hunching over to disguise his natural size, he said, 'Hey, can I leave my bags here? I'm checking in later this morning and can't be stuffed draggin' 'em round Turkey anymore.'

The middle-aged man at the reception desk slowly lifted his eyes from whatever he was reading and regarded Matt thoughtfully. He rubbed his chin with his giant hand, and looked Matt up and down. 'You can check in now, if you like, sir,' he offered. He started his computer. 'And I can hold your bags here until the room is ready later this morning. May I have your name?'

'It's Rix, Matt Rix.'

'Very good, sir. Can I have your passport and credit card, please?' He extended his hand.

Matt handed over his passport, checking it was indeed his and not Regan Dransfield's, and then thumbed through the cards in his wallet. He found the CIA American Express card that Steph had given him and moved it to one side and then located his personal card and handed that over.

'Gee, it's early. What time did you start?' Matt feigned a yawn and stretched his arms over his head.

'I started at six last night, sir. Only an hour to go now and then I am finished for the day.' The man finally gave Matt a wry smile. After a pause, he added, 'I double as the night watchman, too.'

Matt sensed a message in that comment. He looked at the man more closely. He was powerfully built, and with his shaved head he didn't look like the standard Turk. Maybe he was Armenian? A power lifter or wrestler, perhaps.

'We don't seem to have any reservation for you, sir.' He looked at Matt for another long moment and stroked his chin.

'What? Well, there must be a mistake – my travel agent assured me it was all confirmed.' Matt leaned over the counter as if to check the screen himself.

'Please don't do that,' said the man behind the desk, placing his giant paw on Matt's shoulder and slowly pushing him back. 'It isn't a problem; we are not fully booked this day.'

'Oh, well that's a relief. I'm going to have something to say to that travel agent though.' Matt pulled out his phone as if intending to send a message.

'There you are, sir, it is all fixed up for you. If you come back at ten, the room will be ready. There's a lovely little bakery behind our building.' He drew a quick circle on a small tourist map with a red biro. 'And some of the cafes on the road in front of us are very good for watching the morning float by. Most of them are open. You may leave your suitcase with me.'

'Great, thanks; I'll keep this one though.' Matt folded the map and stuffed it in his jeans pocket, then slung the leather bag over his shoulder.

'Just be careful of your valuables, sir,' the man called after him. 'There are many people in Turkey who would take advantage of a weary traveller, especially at this time in the morning.'

Matt made his way outside and decided to go for a quick walk around the area. He checked the laneway that ran alongside the hotel; there was a back entrance, he noted, with a double door that looked like it had an alarm. The narrow street behind the hotel was packed tight with low-rise buildings. He walked down it, then turned into a street that snaked its way up the hill. The place was already a hive of activity. Large groups of skinny, tanned men with varying degrees of facial hair hauled boxes off small trucks. The street was lined with shoe shop after shoe shop. In between the shoe shops were belt shops and accoutrements for men, all the latest and oldest brands in stock. Each shop had a group of at least five men running in and out, gathering stock and setting themselves up for the trading day. Matt sensed a nervous energy hanging in the air.

A lanky kid hauling a trolley piled high with boxes banged into Matt's side. He shouted some abuse in Arabic, confirming Matt's suspicion that he was Syrian.

Matt glared at him; he knew better than to say something in English and be exposed as a foreigner, especially in the back streets of old Istanbul. With his olive complexion, Matt could fit in, much the same as he could in Italy, but if he spoke then the game would be up.

The kid shouted something to his older mates and they paused in their work. Looked like they'd clocked him anyway. Matt did a quick scan of his surroundings. There were no fewer than twelve guys in his immediate proximity and at least one hundred up and down the street. Of the twelve, two were much older, so he discounted them. There were four in their teens, so they were less of an issue. That left Matt with six middle-aged males to contend with. There was a clear space just up ahead, on the other side of a pile of boxes. Matt kept walking casually to get into this space, securing his leather bag over his shoulder as he went. Further up the hill he spied a side street; Matt guessed it ran back to the main road.

'What's your name then, boy?' The question, in heavily accented English, came from a burly Syrian. He wore jeans and a black t-shirt and his face, etched with deep lines, looked like it had been made from brown putty. He had to jog to cut Matt off.

Matt stopped walking and the other men put down their boxes and moved in to surround him. He noticed that two of the men held box cutters in their hands.

'So this is how it's going to be, huh?' Matt cracked his neck from side to side and clenched his hands into fists. They might not realise it, but he represented a very real threat to these guys.

'Let me tell you, we don't like strangers here, not at this time of morning. Especially not Americans, it's just how we roll.' After delivering this string of clichés, the burly Syrian spat on the ground.

Matt didn't bother to respond; there just didn't seem like much need for talking at this point. Hollywood movies were full of examples of one man beating a dozen, flying kicks and back fists reigning supreme. The truth was that when outnumbered it paid to be extremely violent. Don't go to ground at any cost and get the hell out of there once the initial damage has been done, that was the rule. Matt was now in beast mode, the state of mind that can only be achieved by years of training with the specific intent of using your body to fight for survival.

Feet shoulder-width apart, left foot slightly forward, Matt pointed his finger at the nose of the self-professed tough guy.

'I'm not looking for a fight,' Matt said, poking at the Syrian's face with each word, as if to reinforce his point.

The Syrian laughed as Matt spoke and looked around at his friends, raising his bushy eyebrows.

He stopped laughing quick smart, though. Matt poked him one more time and then closed his hand into a fist and slammed it into the Syrian's nose. Matt then pivoted at the hips and threw a murderous left hook at the Syrian, who was still holding his face.

The sound was horrific, stopping everyone in their tracks; there was no coming back from an impact like that, not in the short term.

Matt then spun around and threw a punch at another nearby target, the full weight of his shoulder behind the strike. The young man collapsed, his head hitting the ground.

The rest of the men stood dazed, dumbfounded by the speed of the assault.

Matt thought about throwing caution to the wind and dropping them all right where they stood – and why the hell not? They were a bunch of opportunists who thought they could prey on a stranger. But he didn't want to cause more of a scene than he had to. He punched one more guy in the throat, just to give himself an exit, and then he broke into a sprint, charging up the hill.

By the time it occurred to the Syrians to give chase, he was gone, darting down the side street and off up to the main road, melting into the crowds of workers pouring off the trams into the old town.

Matt made his way back to the hotel and settled himself in the cafe across the street; from his table he had a perfect view through the doors to the reception desk. He watched the shift change and waited another hour. Three Turkish teas, a cappuccino and a pastry later, Matt returned to the hotel to check in, this time as Regan Dransfield. He received the swipe card for his room, then headed to the elevator.

Later in the day, when the shift had changed again, he would go and get the key for the room he'd checked into under his own name. Instinctively, he knew it would be best not to stay in the room Steph had arranged for him. She had set up the alias, and would be monitoring his movements, no doubt, but he wasn't yet convinced that his safety would be her priority. Staying in another room, under another name – even if it was his own – would afford him some protection, and it might just buy him some time when he needed it.

Matt sat on the edge of the bed and flicked through the channels on the remote control, bringing the BBC up on the screen. He lowered the volume.

Pulling the secure GSM out of his leather bag he typed in the four-digit pin to unlock it and then hit the speed dial button, followed by the same number to go secure. A garbled voice indicated that they were trying to establish a connection.

'You are now secure – go ahead, please.'

'Hi, Matt, are you settled in?' Steph asked.

'Yes. When's Khan getting in?'

'I'm not sure. I know he made it safely over the Turkish border, but his movements now are up to him. He's going to be staying down the road from you, in the Hotel New House. He's coming by train and he was briefed on the hotel and the locations for the pick-up and drop-off. It's all straightforward, really.'

'Hang on,' said Matt

He grabbed the notepad off the desk and scribbled down the hotel name.

'Where's the equipment I asked for, Steph? When can I get it?'

'It's locked in the safe, right there in your room. The code is 3443. Everything you wanted is there.'

'How? You have someone in the hotel?' Matt asked as he wrote down the code. He heard her laugh on the other end of the phone.

'Like I've told you before, Matt, I've been playing this game for a long time.' She paused. 'Find Faisal Khan, Matt. Track his every movement and make sure that he remains safe until he hands that weapon on to my guys.'

'I understand, Steph. I don't understand why your guys are travelling here to pick it up though. Surely it would be better for Khan to take it back through the way he came in?'

'It's not going to the Middle East. My guys have arranged to get it to a boat in the Bosphorus and bring it back here to Italy, where it will be delivered into the hands of the CIA. You just need to make sure that Khan is monitored from the point he receives it from the Russians until he delivers it safely to my guys, understood?'

'Right. And how will I know they're your guys?'

'Faisal will set up an exchange with them. I'll let you know when it's to take place.'

'So, I'm to shadow Faisal, make sure he stays safe and wait for him to deliver the weapon to your guys? Easy.'

'Exactly.' She hung up.

Matt turned off the mobile and tossed it on top of his leather bag. He stretched out on the bed and looked up at the ceiling.

Something was splattered across the plasterwork. He wondered what it was; bodily fluids of some sort, he suspected. He rolled onto his stomach and thought about the task at hand and then looked at the hotel safe. Time to get to work.

12

LONDON

'Tell me, Sandra, what do you know of this Milko Orelik?' In the back seat of the black Mercedes, Rachel placed her laptop bag at her feet and fastened the seatbelt over her plain black skirt. She looked across and watched as her superior rifled through her own handbag for something.

Sandra produced a little black band and with one hand she deftly pulled her sandy grey hair back into a tight ponytail then used the band she held in the other to secure it. She then checked her makeup in the mirror of a small compact. Stylish and sophisticated, Sandra had learned how to be admired by women and desired by men. However, Rachel hadn't seen her go to so much trouble over her appearance when they'd met with other ministers in the past; her superior's behaviour now struck her as a bit odd.

Folding her hands in her lap Sandra raised her chin in the air and cleared her throat, turning slightly to face Rachel. 'Well, he certainly likes to fuck,' she said.

Rachel caught her breath, but she knew better than to reveal her shock, though this was clearly the effect Sandra was after. 'I see, but what about his connections? Everything I've seen suggests that he wasn't a particularly big player in the grand scheme of things. Connected, yes, but not someone who would consider pushing a WMD across Europe.'

'He was considered small fry back in the day.' Rachel saw a small smile flit across the older woman's face as she recollected some private memory of years gone past. Finally, she spoke again. 'Milko's problem is that he likes to live like the rich Russian mafia; I assume he got into trouble with some real players and now he has no alternative but to do their bidding. I might be wrong, but ten years ago he was all about money and hookers. He was easy prey and we extracted a lot of information about the lower levels of the Russian establishment from him, that's for sure.' Sandra turned to stare out the window and Rachel sat in silence, wondering what horrors Sandra had endured in the service of her country. What would her previous life have been like?

They didn't speak again for the rest of the drive to Whitehall.

• • •

'The minister will see you now.' The Minister's secretary led Sandra and Rachel out of the anteroom and down the white hallway. Rachel read the brass plate on the wall opposite the oak double doors: *Secretary of State for Defence, The Rt Hon Michael Faulton MP*. The three women walked into the corner office, the secretary clearing her throat to herald their arrival.

Faulton turned from the window. A tall and powerful older man, his presence dominated the room and his authority was further emphasised by his sharp black suit and crisp white shirt. His blue and red Household Division tie hinted at a man who had been handy in his day.

'Ah, MI6.' He approached the pair with his hand extended and then saw Sandra and stopped in his tracks. 'Good lord – Sandra. Well, well, this is a pleasant surprise.' The minister's face went bright red; his white hair seemed to turn even whiter. 'Please, have a seat.' He gestured towards the huge leather sofas in the far corner of the room.

'Thank you, that's very kind of you,' Sandra said. 'May I introduce you to Rachel Phillips, sir? She's the operations officer for the MI6 Department known as Global Pursuit.'

The minister nodded at Rachel and again gestured to the sofa. He sat down opposite them.

Rachel looked quickly around the room. It was massive, and sparsely furnished, other than the gigantic desk opposite the window, the leather sofas and a coffee table. The desk near the window had an old computer monitor and a notebook on top, but other than that the surface was bare.

'Catherine, get us tea, please – and a weak coffee, one sugar, for Sandra.' He smiled at Sandra. 'See? I haven't forgotten.'

The secretary left, closing the oak doors behind her, and they heard her footsteps retreating down the hallway.

Faulton turned his attention to Rachel. 'Now, why don't you tell me what this is all about.'

'Yes, sir,' Rachel said. She took her laptop from her bag and the screen came alive. She handed the minister and Sandra each a printed copy of the PowerPoint presentation she had been working on and updated the minister on the backstory as well as outlining the progress that Global Pursuit had made in recent months in tracking down various weapons of mass destruction. When she had finished, she withdrew a manila folder from her bag. Inside the folder was a document; on the first page was a photo of a man and on the second an image of a suitcase bomb.

'This brings us to Milko Orelik, sir. We have varied intelligence to support our theory that he is seeking to deliver a nuclear weapon to an extremist group. He has been very vocal over recent weeks trying to get the item moved. In fact, he has received some rather large payments over the last few days into his personal bank account from an agricultural business in Turkey, indicating that a deal has been made – and leading us to suspect that the handover will occur in Turkey.' Rachel produced the banking transcripts and laid them in front of the minister.

They paused the discussion as Catherine returned with a tray of tea and coffee and served it.

After she'd left, Faulton sipped on his tea and ran his eyes over the transcripts. 'I see. Well, we must stop him.'

'Yes, sir. Our understanding is that the weapon he's selling is a Soviet-era suitcase bomb, which makes the task more difficult as he can move reasonably easily with it.'

'That's nasty stuff,' Faulton said, genuinely shocked. 'Where on earth did he get it?'

'Yes, sir – and nasty is an understatement,' added Sandra. 'It would be devastating if it fell into the wrong hands, such as ISIS or Al-Qaeda. It's our theory that he's working for someone else, probably not state-sponsored but someone with access.'

'What steps have you taken so far? To prevent him from delivering it, I mean.' Faulton dropped the folder back onto the coffee table.

'Well, sir, I have notified the French and Croatian governments, as well as the Italian government, and of course I have notified my Turkish counterparts since the transactions were initiated there. They checked out the agricultural business but it's already been wound up.'

'Of course it has. So, what makes you so sure that he will go to Turkey?' Faulton sat back on the sofa and loosened his tie slightly.

'Well, someone has been there already to set up the fake business; they've had to launder money there and not small amounts either. It's possible that they're trying to throw us off the scent, but I don't think they even realise we are watching. So, it seems likely they're either in Turkey or they're going in and out.'

'So the person paying for the weapon is either in Turkey or will be going back to Turkey to take delivery, which means that's where our man Milko is headed?'

'Yes, sir, that's my belief,' said Rachel.

'Well, I'm not sure about all of this. It seems we would be very exposed if we went hunting for Milko Orelik.'

'Sir, Rachel has done some concrete work on this.' Sandra leaned forward and made eye contact with the minister. 'You know, sir, if we could get your approval to proceed, we could make this department – you – look very good. It's a fantastic opportunity.' She smiled at him and nodded, then sat back.

The minister continued to gaze at her for a few seconds then turned to Rachel. 'So, what do you need from me?'

'A tactical team to go to Turkey with me, including technical enablers, and a budget, sir.' Rachel winced as she mentioned the money, knowing full well that Whitehall was not as flush with cash as back in MI6's heyday when the Cold War had been in full swing and spying was the front line of defence.

Faulton looked from Rachel back to Sandra. 'Of course, anything you want. Will two weeks be sufficient?'

Rachel watched as Sandra held the minister's longing gaze. 'Yes, sir, I think that should be more than sufficient,' she replied.

Faulton stood up. 'We are stretched thin at the moment, but I will contact the special forces commander. I'm sure the Special Boat Squadron would like to do something other than partici-pate in this year's Golden Beagle exercise on the Isle of Skye. Get a decision brief to me by the end of the week, Rachel, including your budget requirements – and advise on your required rules of engagement, too. I'll pass it through to the Foreign Secretary and brief COBRA on Monday. I don't anticipate there being any problems.'

'Of course, sir – thank you,' said Rachel. 'Your support is very valuable to us.'

'No. I think what Global Pursuit is doing is valuable. Good job – now go get that thing off the streets.'

'Thank you, sir; yes, sir,' Rachel said.

Faulton stood to walk them to the door. 'Oh, and I assume you have contacted the CIA to keep them in the loop?' he asked.

'Yes, sir. I passed all the information on to the station chief in Italy when I first came across Milko, some weeks ago now.'

'Good, that's good. It always pays to keep the Americans on-side. Catherine will see you out, ladies.' He added softly, 'Sandra, you have my number if you ever need anything.'

'Yes, sir, thank you.' Sandra shot Rachel a wry smile as they left the room.

. . .

Back in the car Rachel was still on cloud nine. 'Well, that went well.'

'Yes, that's a great outcome, but what's the plan? What are you thinking?'

'Do you think we can track him through his phone? That's the obvious starting point.' As she spoke, Rachel checked her own phone for messages.

Sandra considered this. 'That should work; he's not very bright. Getting that authority should be easy enough. Put in a request for Signals Intelligence when we get back to the office and I'll sign it off for approval. Your request for Cyber tracking was confirmed yesterday, we probably should have submitted them both together, but you know how hard it is to get authorisation for phone monitoring. But with the minister's approval it should all be pretty easy now. Anyway, if the cyber monitoring has been approved then we should start seeing some information coming in today. It might be a good idea to get a detailed brief to the IT guys. Get them to monitor more than just his emails. Let's access his camera – really build up a picture of his movements and intentions. Anyway, let's see how this all plays out.'

Rachel nodded, impressed with her superior's thoughts on the matter. Scrolling through the messages that had come through while they were in with the minister, she spied one from Milton. She read it quickly. 'Seems Milko is indeed on the move, Sandra.'

'Really?'

'We've already had a hit on Milko's computer; he booked flights to Turkey for six people. He travels in five days, and we have a location for the exchange too.' Rachel couldn't believe it even as she said it.

'Looks like you and the SBS are going to Turkey then.'

'Yes, indeed it does,' said Rachel, still staring at the email.

13

ZABOL, IRAN

Stepping out of the taxi, Faisal surveyed the built-up urban area. He was in a small street near the city centre. Most of the buildings lining the street had two storeys, and most were decrepit, the paint peeling, and fixtures like drainpipes and window shutters either missing or rusted away. The tailor's shop that he had been instructed to visit was directly across the road. On one side was a small bakery and on the other were an electrical shop and a laundry, both of which had already closed for the day.

Faisal could sense that he was being watched. The place had just come alive again after the evening prayers and the city had a strange electric energy to it, as if an evil resided there. Faisal shivered as he paid the taxi driver and dragged his bag from the back seat. The taxi pulled away and Faisal was left standing in the streetlight looking at the tailor's shop.

Taking a deep breath, he crossed the road and pushed on

the door. A bell above the entrance tinkled to signal his arrival. The shop was long and narrow and dimly lit. To Faisal's left, the wall was lined with rolls of fabric in every possible shade of blue and brown. On the right of the narrow space were three long tables, and behind them stood three young tailors, measuring, cutting and stitching trousers and jackets. They smoked as they worked, and the smoke hung heavy in the air, adding to the gloom. At the back of the shop was a low table behind which sat an old man – Bahbak Khorasanhi, Faisal assumed. The elderly tailor was almost bald, save for a few tufts of grey hair on the sides of his head. Portly and wrinkled, he was hardly a picture of health, but his eyes were bright and sharp as they observed the Afghan. Through the bluish haze, Faisal saw Bahbak raise a hand to summon him.

As Faisal stepped forward, one of the young men moved away from his table to close the door behind him.

Faisal took another step, and another of the younger men launched himself at Faisal, scissors in hand, and threw Faisal against the rolls of fabric, holding his scissors to Faisal's throat.

'Easy there, boy,' said Faisal. 'I've had a long day and I just want to speak to the old man.'

'Who are you? I haven't seen you before.' The young tailor kept a strong hand on Faisal's chest and didn't move the scissors from Faisal's throat. Faisal should have been more cautious; he cursed himself for not changing out of his traditional shalwar kameez, the loose-fitting body shirt and drawers were comfortable but he stood out. He should have worn something more modern, like what the Iranians were wearing.

'Leave him be, Arman,' said the old man. 'Let him through.'

Arman looked Faisal up and down then spat at his feet. 'I'll let you go now, Talib, but listen carefully: yours won't be the first Afghan throat I've ripped out with these blades.' He stepped back, letting Faisal go.

Faisal could see that the young Iranian tailor was powerfully built, but a good six inches shorter than Faisal; he wouldn't let the young man get the upper hand again.

Faisal adjusted his waistcoat over his brown robes and proceeded to the back of the shop.

'Please excuse my son,' said Bahbak. 'My boys are very protective of me. You are Faisal Khan, I assume?'

'Yes.' Faisal put down his bag then stood up straight, as if presenting himself to the old man.

'Sit. Can I get you chai? Or something to eat? Maybe something to smoke, perhaps?' The old man coughed as if to emphasise the health benefits.

'Some food, yes, that would be good,' said Faisal, who couldn't remember when he'd had his last meal.

The old man yelled something in Farsi and the two other sons disappeared down a set of stairs near the front of the shop, presumably to a kitchen somewhere.

'Those two, Basim and Jafar' – he waved in the direction of the stairs – 'are not so bad, but Arman has a hot head. One day it will get him killed, I'm sure.'

Faisal smiled at the old man and nodded his head in understanding, while also deciding that he could help the old man's son to the afterlife if the opportunity arose.

'Now, I've been paid to get you into Turkey, so that is what I am going to do.'

'Good, and how are we going to do that?'

'I have my ways – but first, let's eat.'

One of the old man's sons put down two bowls of steaming lamb stew and a dish of black-eyed peas. The smells of turmeric and cumin had Faisal salivating. The second son put some flatbread on the table along with a pot of chai and two small glasses.

The old man ripped his bread apart and used a piece to scoop up the deep red stew. Faisal followed suit and soon the two men had devoured the meal. Faisal sat back feeling content; he felt much better with a good meal inside him.

'You will be needing some rest, Faisal. Up those stairs is a small room and a bed. There are some clothes on the bed, too; you should bathe and change out of this.' The old man waved a hand up and down to indicate Faisal's vest and robes. 'We will wake you early in the morning and you will leave before daybreak. My sons will take you. It won't be a pleasant trip, my friend, but you will get to Turkey and no one will know you are there.' Bahbak reached under the table for a white plastic bag, which he handed to Faisal.

'What's this?'

'We had these made for you. Hassan al-Britani was very specific about it.'

Opening the bag, Faisal found two battered passports, brilliantly forged with stamps from surrounding countries. One was in Faisal's name and another in an alias.

'Thank you, brother.' Faisal stood and stuffed the passports into his bag.

The old man gestured to someone standing behind him, and when Faisal turned he saw Basim, the youngest of the old man's sons, standing there with a M1911 Browning, fitted with a silencer. It was pointed directly at Faisal's face.

Faisal took a hasty step backwards and almost fell over the table.

Arman who was standing further back in the room, laughed aloud. 'Typical Talib coward.'

'What's this?' said Faisal.

'It's a gun, Talib,' said Arman mockingly.

The younger man then turned the weapon around and handed it butt first to Faisal. 'It's for you,' said Basim.

'I see.' Faisal felt the weight of the weapon and decided that it probably wasn't loaded. If it had been, he might have just shot the lot of them right there and then for their trouble. He placed the gun into his bag.

'I'll give you ammunition in the morning, Talib,' said Arman, walking back down the room towards Faisal.

'Right, well, if there are no more surprises planned for this evening, I might take my leave of your kind hospitality.' Faisal picked up his bag with his left hand and took a step towards the stairs.

'Don't be smart.' Arman moved closer to Faisal, only this time Faisal was ready; in fact, he had deliberately moved off on his wrong foot in order to be in position when it counted. In a lightning-quick move, Faisal dropped the bag and punched the young Iranian in the throat. Arman landed heavily on the floor with Faisal following him down and placing a knee on his back.

The other sons circled, but the old man barked something in Farsi and they stayed back, watching.

Faisal grabbed a fistful of the Iranian's hair and yanked his head back. With his mouth close to Arman's ear, he whispered, 'If you cross me again, boy, I will kill you, make no mistake about it; I've killed better men than a mere tailor's son.' Faisal shoved the Iranian so hard that his head cracked a tile on the floor.

Faisal stood up and turned to face the old man.

'Thank you for your hospitality, Bahbak, the meal was especially enjoyable. Please excuse my bad temper; it has been a long week.'

As he climbed the stairs Faisal could hear Bahbak cursing his eldest son, and Arman apologising profusely.

Faisal pushed open the door at the top of the stairs and entered the small room. He stripped off his Afghan robes and washed in the small bath. When he was done, he took the scissors and razor that had been left by the sink and first trimmed his long beard, then shaved it close to his face. For the first time in twenty years he could make out his jawline. He looked at the shape of his face in the mirror. In years past he had worn his long black hair slicked back and applied surma, a black mineral powder, under his eyes, believing it would increase the power of his vision. This had given Faisal an evil appearance and helped to reinforce his status in the tribal areas. He took a fistful of hair and chopped at it with the scissors, and then he kept chopping until his hair was shorter at the sides, though still long and curled at the back, in the tradition of the Pakistanis from the border regions.

Faisal held up the clothes that had been placed on the bed. A pair of brown trousers, a white cotton button-up shirt, a grey woollen jumper and black oilskin jacket. These things looked like the clothes of the West to Faisal. He put them on and looked at himself again in the mirror above the sink. The reflection looking back at him made him shudder; he could be one of them.

Faisal checked that the wooden door was locked then lay on top of the single mattress and let sleep wash over him.

He had no idea how long he'd been asleep when there was a gentle knock at the door. He jumped with a start. He could see through the small window in the corner that it was still dark outside, with not even a hint of morning.

He opened the door slightly and saw Arman.

'Come on, it's morning prayer time. We can leave once the day breaks.' He looked Faisal up and down. 'At least you don't look like a Talib now,' he observed. He pushed the door open further and passed Faisal a small bag containing flatbread. 'And here's some ammunition for the gun.'

Faisal took the bread and the box of ammunition and tossed it onto his sports bag.

'I'm going to need some other things, too, Arman.'

'What? What do you need?'

'Can you get me some explosives? Military grade would be best – something light and portable, like C4. Also, two garage door remotes, some thin wire and a roll of black tape.'

The younger man shrugged. 'No problem; I can give you this and more besides. Under the old man's desk is a trapdoor – go down and fill your bag with whatever you need. He has instructed me to provide you with anything you require until you are in Turkey. I don't know who sent you or what your mission is, but my father seems to think it is of the highest importance.' With a nod, he left the room.

Faisal checked the ammunition; it was subsonic. The Iranians knew what they were doing. He quickly loaded the magazine of the Browning then placed the rest of the ammunition in the side pocket of his sports bag.

An hour later Faisal had a second bag, this one packed with enough explosives and electronics to start a war in Turkey. He smiled to himself.

'Here's the truck now, Faisal.' Arman pointed at the vehicle as it pulled up outside the shop. Basim was at the wheel and his older brother Jafar was next to him.

'Jump up here with me.' Arman climbed into the back of the truck and started to move some boxes. He lifted a small metal plate on the floor to reveal an opening that was barely a metre wide. The cavity beneath it was about two and a half metres by one metre; barely enough room for Faisal to lie in with his bags at his feet.

'You need to get in here when we get to the checkpoint, or if we beep the horn twice. Just lift this plate and lower yourself in; it latches closed on the inside behind you. It's not comfortable, but you will be well hidden.'

'I see. And for the rest of the trip, I just sit in the back here?'

'Yes, it's an eighteen-hour drive. It's rough going in places but you will just have to make do.' Arman jumped back down onto the street. 'Time to leave.'

• • •

The trip was indeed rough. All day the old Bedford truck bounced and heaved its way along gravel roads and over mountain passes. The landscape changed from fields and woods to escarpments dotted with ancient pines and as they rose higher the temperature dropped. They stopped twice, taking the opportunity to relieve themselves by the side of the road and to drink cold tea and eat stale flatbread.

They had been travelling for a few hours in the dark when the truck came to a shuddering stop. Faisal was thrown from where he was sleeping on the boxes and slammed into the metal grid below the window separating the cabin and the tray. The horn sounded twice in quick succession.

'*Allahu Akbar*,' Faisal muttered under his breath.

He darted for the hatch and clambered in, barely managing to pull it down behind him before the back tarp was ripped open.

Someone jumped up into the truck. Faisal could hear them walking around above him. He held his breath and tried to slow down his breathing. There was shouting outside and he thought he heard someone getting kicked and then someone crying out in pain. Faisal tried to make out what was being said. Lying there in the dark he weighed up his options. Reaching down between his feet he located the sports bag and slowly dragged it up by his side. He unzipped the bag, a tooth at a time and then, working quietly in the close confines of the secret hold, located the Browning. He checked the silencer was on tight and that the magazine was secure. He had cocked it before they started on their journey, so he knew it was ready to fire. The person above him yelled out something and laughed and then Faisal heard him jump from the truck.

Faisal held his breath as he released the latch and slowly climbed out of the hold. Peering out beneath the bottom of the tarp, he confirmed that the coast was clear and dropped onto the ground then rolled under the truck. On the side of the road Faisal could just make out the three Iranian brothers sitting in the dirt, their hands on top their heads. The area was dimly lit by the headlights of the truck and the lights from a car on the track. Faisal could see the giant log that had been laid across the road; the driver wouldn't have had but a second to react as they rounded the bend. Faisal crawled from the back wheels to halfway under the truck to get a better look. Someone was standing above the Iranian tailors with an AK-47.

Faisal waited and watched while the bandits moved around; they were discussing what to do with their captives and the loot. He counted three bandits in total – one guarding the brothers and two at the front of the truck. They were all armed.

Faisal took a breath and steadied his hands; lying under the truck he took aim at the bandit behind the Iranian brothers. He applied a firm grip with his master hand and focused on the foresight of the weapon until the rear sight slowly came into focus. He let two rounds loose from the silenced Browning. Both thudded into the back of the bandit's head and he fell on top of Jafar, who let out an involuntary yelp.

The noise alerted the other two bandits, who came running around from the front of the truck. They spotted their colleague dead and the Iranian brothers now standing above his body. One of the bandits levelled off his AK and let rip with a ten-round burst, but the brothers had already dived out of the way and the rounds cracked past them and off into the side of the hill in the distance.

Faisal eased himself out slowly from under the front of the truck, and then he moved fast, firing two rounds at each of their backs. They crumpled to the ground and he ran to stand above the bandits. They were writhing in the dirt, moaning in agony.

Faisal put one bullet into the back of each of their heads. Then he looked over at Arman and levelled the Browning at his face.

Arman screamed and placed his hands over his eyes. Dropping to his knees in the dirt, he pissed himself where he sat; the violence of the past thirty seconds exceeding anything he had seen before.

'Want to call me a Talib coward again, Arman?'

Arman was shaking as he took his hands away from his face.

Faisal lowered the Browning. 'Let's get this mess cleaned up, shall we?'

The brothers looked at each other then, after thanking Faisal, they dragged the bandits off the side of the road and hid their weapons in the undergrowth; they would recover these on the way back, they agreed.

Then they set off again. The three brothers sat in silence up the front and Faisal sat in the back. He looked up through the gap in the tarpaulin into the clear night sky. He thought about Allah and the importance of his mission and what it all must mean.

• • •

When they approached the Turkish border crossing the next morning, Faisal was concealed in the cavity beneath the floor of the truck. The Iranians bribed the Turkish guards the same way they always had: with money and cigarettes.

A few hours later Faisal was stretched out on a bench seat of an express train hurtling towards Istanbul.

14

RAF BRIZE NORTON AIRFIELD

Rachel pulled the black Range Rover Sport into the car park opposite the aircraft hangar. She switched off the engine and took in a deep breath. The steady beat of the windscreen wipers was much more audible now that there was no engine noise. She looked down at her phone. It had been a few days since Matt had messaged to say that he would be coming to visit. She had replied suggesting that he call her so they could make firm arrangements, but he never had. She wondered if she should call him; if it was two am here, what time would it be in Australia? No, this wasn't the time – she needed to focus. Sighing, she put the phone away.

The hangar in front of her was one of many that lined the runway at the RAF Brize Norton airfield. It looked like all the others: grey and nondescript. This particular hangar was different, though; it housed the necessary equipment, computers and communications support to enable the men based there to deploy anywhere in the world at a moment's notice. And they had. On more than one occasion the hangar had been the staging area for men preparing to face their country's adversaries. It had been the 'temporary' home of the Special Boat Service's Rapid Response Team for more than a decade.

Rachel finally switched off the ignition, the wipers freezing in the middle of the windscreen. She stepped out of the car and into the cold night air. Lifting her suitcase out the back of the car, she struggled under its weight and let it crash to the ground at her feet.

'Oh rubbish,' she whispered.

She picked it up and pulled it along behind her, the wheels crunching awkwardly over the gravel. She shivered as she walked past the hangar's giant roller doors. Light seeped from underneath, the only indication that there was life in there. These doors were very rarely raised and the hangers and their contents had remained inconspicuous for years. She continued around the side of the building to a smaller side door and whistled softly to herself when she saw the fit-looking Royal Marines captain she had previously only seen in a file photo; he looked even better in the flesh.

Glyn Thomas was double-checking the aircraft pallet loaded with green military trunks and black Pelican cases, the type used to protect sensitive equipment. He was dressed in dark blue jeans and a grey woollen V-neck jumper which was stretched tight against his muscled torso. He resembled the archetypal university rower – probably because he had been one in his younger years, representing first his grammar school and then Exeter University. Rachel knew from his file that he excelled in both the sporting and academic arenas, and he had breezed through the Marines and SBS selections.

As if sensing Rachel's eyes on him, Glyn turned towards her and greeted her with a nod.

'Hello, you must be Rachel Phillips. How was the drive?' He beamed at her and held out his hand. She took it, feeling weak at the knees at the strength of his grip.

'It was alright, I guess. Not much traffic at this ungodly hour.' She gave a light laugh and then, realising they were still holding hands, abruptly released her grip. He stood back and put his hands on his hips, surveying her from head to toe, smiling the whole time. Realising she needed to say something – anything – to fill the silence, she gestured to her suitcase. 'Where do you want this?'

'Just over there, next to that pallet.' Glyn waved his hand towards the third pallet in the row. She rolled the bag over and struggled to lift it onto the green dive bags. She finally managed to heave it up and left it sitting there precariously. She walked back over to Glyn.

She waited as he finished looking through a manifest and then he looked up at her. Their eyes met again and for a second time they stood there in awkward silence. Eventually Rachel recalled why she was there and slipped her hand into the pocket of her Puffa jacket. 'My presentation is on this thumb drive. Would you mind bringing it up on a projector somewhere?' She handed it over.

'Yes, of course, the men are in the briefing room now. Shall we?' He indicated for her to follow him.

She moved in close behind him and could smell the faintest hint of his aftershave. *Stop it*, she scolded herself as she felt a blush creeping up her neck.

Glyn strode purposefully to a door on the other side of the hangar. As they entered the room the nine men inside stopped talking and slowly rose out of their orange plastic seats. Rachel was surprised to see that they had to wedge themselves under wooden desks made for primary school students. Apparently, the Ministry of Defence supply chain had decided that these highly trained instruments of foreign policy should receive all their briefings squashed under tables meant for children.

Glyn scanned the room. 'Bluey, are you happy with the equipment load out?'

'Yep, it's all ready to go. Weapons are bubble-wrapped, ammunition is boxed in the diplomatic trunk. Radio gear and batteries have all been checked. Once the personal bag pallet is finished we can roll out the door just as soon as you give the word.'

'Good. I checked the manifest and load list and also the AD straps. When we've finished here just get the lads to make sure they're all secured and tucked away.' Glyn inserted Rachel's thumb drive into the computer's USB port and picked up a laser pointer that was sitting on the lectern. He gestured towards the interactive whiteboard on the wall.

'Lads, you've all seen the deployment orders.' He circled the mission and the administrative details with the laser. Then he turned to his left and indicated Rachel. 'And this is our mission commander, Rachel Phillips from MI6. She's going to update us on the task.'

Rachel took a step forward and nodded to the men; they smiled back at her. She sensed that some of them were smirking, as if amused by the fact that their mission commander was a young woman. She stood taller and assumed a serious demeanour; she had to persuade them of the gravity of their mission.

'Gentlemen, it's great to meet you. I shouldn't need to remind you that our task is in the national interest.' She paused and clicked the mouse to bring up the first slide of the presentation before continuing. 'Actually, it's in the interest of humanity. We can't afford to allow a weapon like this to reach the hands of terrorists. I want to thank you in advance for your professionalism. I know you will do yourselves, your service and the nation proud.' She turned to the captain. 'Glyn, can you do the introductions, please?'

'Certainly.' Glyn started to his right with his second-in-command.

'This is Warrant Officer Bluey Reid, my 2IC and an expert in maritime operations. He's the Team Bravo commander.'

'Evening,' said Bluey. He looked Rachel squarely in the eye and extended a big paw for a handshake. His bright red hair was cropped tight on his giant head which had the effect of making his huge shoulders even broader.

'Hello, Bluey,' said Rachel. 'So what's your real name then?'

'Blue, ma'am.'

'Oh, I see, of course.' Rachel nodded.

Bluey smiled at his boss, who gave him a frown in return and then moved to the next member of the team.

'This is Corporal Stuart Ganley, a new addition to the team. He's the Alpha Team sniper and a general nuisance, but he makes me laugh so we keep him around.'

'Turn it up, sir.' Stuart looked at Rachel with wide eyes. 'Good evening, ma'am.' He gave a little bow. 'Well, I must say, I have always wondered what spies look like and going by first impressions ... '

'Stop talking, Stu,' Glyn ordered. 'Moving on then, Rachel, this is Sergeant Simon Reid, the Alpha Team signaller. He's from Southall originally and has been in the SBS for fifteen years. He knows Turkey well and will be an asset for us over there. Two tours of Iraq and five of Afghanistan. And this here is Corporal Johnny Brookes – he's my team driver.' Both men smiled at Rachel and said hello. Glyn put his hand on Johnny's shoulder. 'Johnny's background is electronics and electronic counter measures. That's the Alpha Team complete then.' Glyn nodded to Bluey, who had already assembled the other small group.

The first man stepped forward.

'Hello, ma'am. I'm Corporal John Higgins, the 2IC of Team Bravo. I'm from Cornwall originally. I've been in the SBS for four years, with three tours of Afghanistan.'

'Ma'am, I'm Corporal Oisín Donough. I'm the Bravo Team sniper. As you can probably tell, I'm Irish. I was in the Royal Marines for eight years and have now been in SBS for the past two. I've had a few tours of the Ghan too.'

Rachel nodded her approval and the next man stepped forward.

'Corporal Nathaniel Xue, I'm the Bravo Team signaller. I'm originally from Mexico.' At that the whole team broke out laughing. He looked around as if shocked at their response, which only made the men laugh all the more. 'Just jokes – I'm from Hong Kong but have lived here in the UK since I was a teenager. I deployed to Iraq with the Marines and have been to Afghanistan as well.'

'Right. Very good,' said Rachel. She turned her attention to the next guy. A six-foot-two Pacific Islander, his presence dominated the room.

'Ma'am, I'm Corporal Semi Taufolo,' he boomed. 'I'm the Bravo Team driver. My heritage is Tongan, but I'm a dual British and Australian national. I'm just happy to be here and part of the mission, thanks.'

Rachel smiled. 'Excellent, thank you – it's good to have you all on board.'

'Wait, there's one more, ma'am,' said Bluey. 'Darryl, introduce yourself.'

Darryl stepped out from where he had been standing behind Semi. 'Ma'am, I'm Marine Darryl Tate. I'm the demolitions operator for Team Bravo. That's about it, I guess.'

Rachel wondered how old he was but knew better than to ask; he looked so young compared to the others, but clearly he was beret-qualified and therefore his competence was assured.

'Okay, gentlemen – have a seat then and I'll bring you up to speed on developments,' she said. Rachel moved in behind the laptop. 'This is Milko Orelik.' She used the laser to circle his face.

'He looks like your typical Russian punter,' Bluey observed. 'Medium height, stocky with blond hair, blue eyes.'

'And Cold War dress sense,' added Stuart. 'Seriously, that geezer looks like someone Bodie and Doyle should be chasing through Padstow.'

'How do you even know *The Professionals*, Stu?' Oisín demanded. 'You're like twenty-five or something.'

'Okay, lads, let's keep it relevant, shall we?' Glyn said quietly. 'Please continue, Rachel.'

'Thanks, Glyn.' Rachel clicked to the next slide, which showed a photo of Milko and another man, whose face had been blacked out. 'This is where we had the first indication that Milko was trying to sell the nuclear device. This is a meeting between him and one of our double agents in Russia, who was asked if he had contacts in ISIS. In his report, our agent made it clear that Milko had moved on from the export of booze and the occasional AK-47. What we now know is that Milko has made contact with someone working either on behalf of or with ISIS. We've seen the money trail forming and we've built up enough of an intelligence picture to know that the transfer is going to take place later this week. We even have a rough location and now we're just trying to work out exactly when and where that transfer is going to take place.'

'Why don't you just ask the double agent?' said Johnny Brookes. He turned to Nathaniel and said in a stage whisper, 'Seems a no-brainer, right?'

'That wouldn't be terribly successful, I'm afraid.'

'Why's that, Rachel?' asked Glyn.

'Because his head is no longer attached to his body. He was found in Paris a week ago cut into fifths and floating down river. Suffice to say Milko and his associates are the key suspects.'

'Oh. Right.' Johnny looked at Glyn and then back down at his notebook, pretending to write something inside it. The rest of the SBS team smirked at each other and focused their attention back on Rachel.

'A few points about the weapon then.' She clicked on the mouse and a new slide flashed up on the screen. On one side was a photo of a medium-sized grey Samsonite, the plastic type. Down the side of the slide was the tabulated technical data of the Soviet-era tactical nuclear device. On the other side of the screen was a picture showing the inside of the weapon. It comprised two coal-coloured cylinders, a nest of wires and a fuse box, nestled between all sorts of electronics and radio receivers. The men looked at the device in awe and Rachel detected a subtle shift in the atmosphere. They were focused now.

'What are we dealing with here, Rachel? In terms of effect, I mean.' Glyn was studying the slide with concern.

'Best case, it's about a kiloton of destruction. Enough to destroy a city block or render a country's airport or harbour inoperable.'

'For how long?' asked Bluey.

'For the people in the immediate area, forever,' Rachel replied. 'And for the infrastructure, well, depending on the nation, possibly decades.'

'What if the bloody thing goes off while we're trying to recover it? Jesus, we'll all be wasted.' Semi shook his head. 'We're going to have to go into this hard.'

'Not necessarily, Semi. To arm the device requires a code sent from Russia. It's safe to assume that the code was negotiated in the price of the deal, but the device can't be activated instantly. You have to give the USSR some credit; they too had some protections in place for this type of scenario.'

Glyn moved closer to the screen to look at the internal parts. 'So, doesn't that mean that someone in Russia – in the government, maybe – would have to broadcast that code in order for the device to work? Perhaps an option is to block all transmissions in the area as we do the recovery.'

'That's not a bad idea. In fact, it's an excellent idea. However, I think that it's more likely that Milko has replicated a government COMCEN with the ability to broadcast the codes for this device and maybe others that he has too. Our theory is that there will be a final transaction for the codes required to arm the device. Think about it: he gets paid big for the initial device, but his real payday is when the codes are requested.'

'Right. That makes sense.' Glyn nodded.

'Also, it's not too difficult to render the device safe; it's just a matter of removing the receiver. That's this small device attached to the bottom inside of the case.'

Rachel moved next to Glyn in front of the whiteboard screen and indicated its location. She felt him move an inch closer to her. His elbow brushed the side of her breast and she felt her skin tingle. She blushed and swallowed hard. Taking a step back, she continued.

'You see, it disconnects here and slides right out, leaving an antenna and coaxial attachment. The weapon is effectively rendered useless.'

She nodded at Glyn to indicate that she had finished her presentation.

Glyn stepped forward to address his men. 'Gents, let's wrap this up. The C17 will be here in an hour; I want the pallets loaded as soon as its engines are off so we can get out of here before daybreak. Simon, get on the computer and knock out some ground reference guides for the target area, get them distributed to each bloke.'

'Yep, no worries, sir.'

'Johnny, you need to think about electronic counter measures. Work out what frequency or bandwidth or whatever that device is on and see if you can figure out how to block it, just in case. If you need any other equipment, let Bluey know and we'll see what we can rustle up.'

'Understood.' Simon got up and went over to the screen to take a closer look at the device.

'Rachel, make yourself comfortable. We'll get this stuff loaded and I'll give you a yell when we're ready to leave. Next stop: Samandira army air base.'

. . .

Two hours later Rachel was sitting in one of the twenty passenger seats that had been configured inside the massive cargo plane. She adjusted the small pieces of hearing protection inside her ears, the noise of the aircraft seemingly passing through her whole body. Rachel couldn't believe the size of the aircraft. She had been on C-130s before, but she found the space of the C-17 incredible. Apart from the three rows of seats, the rest of the space behind them was taken up by eighteen large cargo pallets and supplies for the Turkish government. Among the pallets was Glyn's team's equipment.

She looked around at the men, most of them now asleep. They all looked so fit and strong, in the prime of their young lives. If she were to recover this weapon it would be up to them to contain the incident and maybe – most likely – use lethal force. She looked across at Glyn. He was reading a book; an old copy of *Fatherland*. As if sensing her appraisal, he raised his eyes from the page and gave her a wink. She couldn't help but smile back and then felt annoyed at herself. She was in charge of this mission, for Christ's sake; this was no time to be flirting with handsome captains.

She closed her eyes to get some rest. Who knew when she'd have a chance to sleep again in the next seventy-two hours?

As she allowed her thoughts to drift, Matt's face came into her mind. She remembered a special dinner they'd had together once; a dinner that had ended up in the bath and then . . . All of a sudden, Matt's face was replaced by Glyn's. Startled, she opened her eyes slightly and saw that the captain was still looking at her.

Uh-oh, she thought. *This might get messy.*

15

ISTANBUL

As luck would have it, Regan Dransfield and Matt Rix were staying on the same floor. Matt had unpacked his own room and organised himself then made his way back to the room booked under the name of Regan Dransfield. Entering the room, he went directly to the safe and typed in the number that Steph had given him. Opening the door, he removed the contents from the safe and placed the various packages on the bed. Turning his attention first to a plastic bag, he pulled out two small black boxes and a cable. Matt studied the larger of the boxes, which bore the label Thales. He had requested the best gear and here it was: a secure Tetra multiband radio with all the ancillary equipment. The second box was wrapped in plastic, obviously brand new, and contained a retransmission device. Matt next upended a cloth bag and tipped a jumbled mess of electronics onto the bed, along with a weapon. Picking up the pistol he whistled to himself.

'The CIA is legit!' Matt said under his breath. He studied the Heckler & Koch P30SK. At only a little more than six inches, the weapon would be perfect for a concealed carry. He grabbed the paddle holster, which had tumbled from the bag with it, and jammed it in his cargo pants, then added the pistol. Matt took off his jacket and pulled his t-shirt down over the holster and looked in the mirror, turning to inspect himself from different angles. Nothing visible.

With his left hand, he clutched his t-shirt in a ball and then pulled it up in one swift action, his right hand flashed down towards the P30 and he ripped it out of the holster; his left hand flashed up and he intercepted the draw as the weapon came up to the centre of his chest. He punched it forward and held it with an 80/20 grip: eighty percent master hand and twenty percent non-master hand. He kept both eyes open and looked through the sights into the mirror. Pleased with himself, he returned the weapon back to the holster as fast as he'd drawn it and put his jacket back on.

Returning to the stash on the bed, he picked up a small plastic bag containing two micro listening devices and receiver that resembled a Nokia phone, as well as a disc containing software to be loaded onto his computer that would link all the communications and surveillance devices. At the bottom of the bag was a five-millimetre plug and a small circuit board. He stuffed it into his jacket pocket. A tracking device and a target indicator beacon rounded out the equipment. Steph had provided him with everything he'd asked for. Satisfied, Matt returned the things he didn't need back to the safe.

Matt checked the corridor and then, when he was sure it was clear, made his way back down the hall to his own room. He turned his back to shield what he was doing from the security camera located above the elevators, and pulled the plug and circuit board from his pocket. Feeling under the hotel door lock, he located the small opening for the plug and inserted it into the hole. He switched on the power to the circuit board and the green light on the door lock flashed. He pushed open the door. Then, switching off the circuit board, he closed the door again and tried to open it with his room key. This time the light flashed red, as the lock failed to recognise his key. He would have to go and get the card recoded at the reception desk. But at least he knew now that he could access any room. Using the circuit board, he let himself into his room and set up his computer on the small desk next to the balcony door. He ran the coaxial cable from the small box next to his computer. The multiband receiver would allow him to use the monitoring devices within about a kilometre and a half of his room. The retransmission booster that he would later place on a high rooftop terrace would ensure that was the case.

Time to go and find my old friend Faisal Khan, he thought.

• • •

Walking along Divan Yolu Road, Matt mingled with the late afternoon crowd. The breeze had picked up slightly since the morning and spots of rain now heralded the storm front that was approaching. Matt's stomach grumbled, and he remembered that he hadn't eaten since breakfast. After he found where Faisal would be staying, some street food might be the best economy of effort. He kept an eye open for the dissecting street that he would need, and then spotted it in the distance: Evkaf Street. Fifty metres down the hill on the right-hand side was the Hotel New House. The building had been painted a soft pastel yellow, except the ground level, which was painted black. He surveyed the building; four storeys high, iron bars on the windows of the first storey. The entrance was set back from the street and the reception was down a set of stairs. Down the side of the hotel was a covered walkway leading into a garden. Matt suspected the walkway continued on around the back as well, but he would have to confirm that later. On either side of the archway were two lanterns. The fact that both were still on, even at this time of day, suggested that they were never turned off and that the garden area would also be well lit.

Matt walked up to the hotel. He held his phone up to his ear and hit the record button, filming the hotel while having a false conversation – in Italian, to further disguise himself – about buying a new dog. He entered the reception, still talking on his phone. He smiled at the small lady behind the counter, mouthing hello as he walked past. He walked straight to the elevators at the back of the reception area. Testing the elevator, he found that no card was required to operate it; he was able to access each of the four floors. He then conducted a detailed recon of each floor, recording it all on his smart phone. There was an exit door at the end of each corridor, he noted, and these exits were not alarmed. Satisfied that he had all he needed, Matt returned to the ground floor and exited the hotel through the back garden, then continued up the hill towards the main road.

The modern tramline ran the length of Divan Yolu Road. Matt walked up to the token machine and purchased a red token for his trip then walked through the turnstile and waited for the next tram. Once on board the trip was straightforward. After fifteen minutes, Istanbul's main train station came into view. Exiting with the crowd, Matt made his way to the large central hall and sat on one of the many steel benches. Settling in with a copy of the *Lonely Planet* guide to Istanbul he had purchased back in Bologna, he watched the comings and goings of the crowd over the top of his book. There was no telling how long he would need to wait. Perhaps he wouldn't even pick up Faisal Khan here and would need to go to the hotel and get access to the guest list. He ran through multiple scenarios in his mind while scanning the hall for the Afghan. Presumably he would be wearing the shalwar kameez common to Afghanistan . . . or would he? Even though Turkey was predominantly Muslim, not many locals wore traditional dress, unless they were attending prayers – and even then, the style of dress was more progressive and Western. If Faisal Khan wanted to blend in, he might well be dressed in something other than his usual brown robes and vest.

A few hours passed and Matt was starting to feel restless. *Perhaps he had missed him.* Then someone approaching among a wave of passengers from a recently arrived train caught his eye. Matt almost didn't recognise him at first. Taller than the average Turk, his hair was jet black and parted to one side, longish and curled at the back – similar to the way Pakistanis wore their hair in the border regions. The long traditional beard of the Taliban fighter was gone and instead Khan was sporting a three-day growth. But it was the clothes that gave him away. Khan stood out from the crowd, dressed in light brown pants and a black oilskin jacket; the outfit just didn't look right.

Matt followed Khan as the crowd exiting the station swept him along. The Afghan militant made his way out of the station and towards the tram stop, but rather than board a tram he instead walked alongside the tracks. He proceeded slowly up the road that snaked its way back towards the Blue Mosque. Carrying an Adidas sports bag on one shoulder, pulling a roller bag behind him with his right hand and clutching two plastic bags in his left, he made slow progress.

He stopped in front of several of the shops lining the street, gazing in the windows, occasionally entering one, making small talk with the shopkeepers. Matt realised Khan was employing classic counter surveillance techniques. He would stride briskly for a hundred metres or so before abruptly slowing down to a plodding pace. Stopping at a brightly lit shop to purchase a chicken shawarma, he suddenly looked over his shoulder and back down the hill. Matt, who had by this time moved ahead of Khan, rather than tailing him, watched with interest. Khan wouldn't be looking for him, he knew. Rather, the Afghan was checking to see if the Turkish intelligence apparatus had picked him up. Matt decided to get on the next tram and continue up the hill to the hotel; there was a little Starbucks almost opposite the tram stop that would provide a perfect vantage point. Now that he knew what Khan looked like in his Western clothing, Matt would have no problem picking him out again.

Forty minutes later Faisal Khan came striding past the Starbucks. He turned and walked down the stairs into the reception of the Hotel New House. Matt gave him a few minutes then proceeded around the side to the fire stairs. He opened the ground-level door slightly and peered through. He spotted Khan waiting for the elevator. Matt made his way up the stairs to the second floor and waited, watching through the small window in the fire stairs door.

He counted down twenty seconds then, when there was no sign of Khan, ran up the next flight of stairs two at a time. He was just in time to see Khan exit the elevator and proceed down the hallway towards his room. He entered the room and closed the door behind him. Matt waited for five minutes, then left the safety of the stairwell and walked quickly down the corridor to check the room number. The Afghan was in room 313. Matt had just returned to the door to the fire stairs when he heard a sound behind him. He slipped into the stairwell then, holding the door open a crack, looked back down the corridor.

Faisal Khan was leaving his room, dressed now in white and a black vest.

Bingo, thought Matt. This was a lucky break. Khan was off to evening prayers.

He hurried down the stairs and out the garden exit, then rounded the corner of the hotel in time to see Khan leave through the main door and walk up the street. The call to prayer echoing from minaret to minaret across the city gave Matt a fair idea of where the Afghan was headed. Matt looked down at his watch and smiled to himself.

He made his way back up the fire stairs to room 313. Taking the plug from his pocket, he pushed it into the electronic lock and pressed the small switch on the circuit board. The green light flashed on the door and Matt pushed it open and went inside.

The room was smaller than Matt had anticipated. There was an old leather chair in one corner next to a wooden wardrobe, a small desk and metal chair against the wall, and a double bed. The bathroom was immediately to the left of the door. Matt crossed the room to peer through the green curtains – which clashed horribly with the orange carpet and tan walls – he saw that a sliding door gave access to a small balcony.

Matt turned his attention to Khan's belongings. He looked into one of the plastic bags sitting on the table and found it full of flat-bread. Opening the wardrobe, he saw Khan's jacket on a hanger. Matt took the small passive listening device he'd brought with him and fixed it to the inside of the jacket's lapel, then moved on to inspect Khan's sports bag. He carefully unzipped the bag and rummaged through the contents, which included what looked like a couple of garage remotes and a small battery pack and antenna.

I see you're up to your old tricks, mate, thought Matt.

Matt removed the GPS tracking device from his pocket and took the plastic covering off the adhesive backing. He placed it firmly inside the bottom of the bag.

'That should do it,' Matt muttered. 'Now, what else do you have in here, you sneaky prick?' He looked over to the other side of the bed, and noticed the roller bag. Unclipping the locks, he opened the case.

'Jesus Christ, Faisal, really?' Matt said under his breath on seeing the contents. He closed the lid, locked it again and stood up.

Just then, the door lock clicked and the handle moved.

Matt jumped half a foot in the air. Moving across to the sliding door in two quick strides, he ripped it open and leaped outside onto the balcony, closing it just as the room door opened. He looked for an exit. There was a fire escape, but an old rusty padlock had secured the access grate. 'Shit, that'd be right,' he whispered.

Through the gap in the curtains he saw two people enter. The first through the door appeared to be a woman from house-keeping. Short and plump with greying hair held back by a black scarf, she looked like someone's sweet grandmother – except she held a Browning 9mm in her left hand.

Behind her was a tall, skinny Turk dressed in dark chinos and a blue polo shirt – the universal dress for secret police trying not to look like secret police. He breezed into the room with an air of authority and looked around.

Satisfied the room was empty, the woman put the pistol away in the small cloth shoulder bag she wore. Meanwhile, the tall Turk had moved over to Khan's sports bag. Pulling a biro out of his pocket, he moved some of the contents of the bag around. It was a rudimentary search and he didn't really look that interested. He then gave the wardrobe a cursory once-over and shrugged as if he was done. He had completely overlooked the roller bag, Matt noticed.

The woman, noticing that the sliding door to the balcony was slightly ajar, began to move towards it.

Oh shit, thought Matt. He looked around frantically for another way to escape. At three storeys, the chances of getting down in one piece were slim. The balcony below was a possibility, but it would require some time to lower himself down – time Matt didn't have. Matt cursed inwardly; just like that, the whole mission was going to be jeopardised.

Then the Turkish man's phone rang and Matt heard him answer it. He said something to the woman and she closed the door she'd begun to slide open.

Releasing a small sigh of relief, Matt looked through the crack in the curtains to see the pair leaving the room. Judging by the speed of their withdrawal, he presumed they had been alerted to Faisal Khan's imminent return.

Matt went back into the room and quickly attached the last listening device to the bottom of the bed. Satisfied all was in order, he left through the front door and jogged down the hallway back to the fire exit stairwell. Leaving the hotel, he zigzagged his way through the streets and back to his own hotel room, where he set up the computer and receiver and searched for a signal from the listening devices.

White noise came across the small handheld receiver and then some coughing. Khan was back in the room. No doubt he would have had to get his key recoded after Matt had broken in. The Turkish secret police clearly had a master key card to access the rooms. Hopefully Faisal hadn't thought twice about his access card not working. Matt settled back on the bed with the receiver in his hand. He leaned over and grabbed the remote for the TV and put CNN on in the background, volume down low. If someone was listening in to his room, they would have to contend with the background noise. Then he looked at the room service menu. He hadn't eaten anything since the morning and his stomach was churning with hunger. Khan coughed again, and this time he spat as well. Matt screwed up his face and put the receiver down on the bench. He dialled for room service and ordered a steak and then went in search of beer in the minibar fridge. It was well stocked, of that much he was thankful. Twisting the top off a Heineken, he took a large swig and walked back over to the bed. As he sat down and settled himself again his phone beeped, alerting him to a message. It was Todd Carson. He was at the airport and about to board a plane for Istanbul.

'TC, you bloody ripper. The cavalry is on its way!' He swigged again on the bottle.

Actually, this espionage shit is pretty cool, he thought.

16

ISTANBUL

'Good evening, Milko, this is Faisal Khan. A friend gave me your number.'

Matt jolted out of his light doze and nearly fell off the bed in his haste to get to the audio receiver. He turned up the volume and grabbed the pen and notepad from the bedside table, ready to transcribe Khan's side of the conversation. Matt hadn't expected the Afghan to make contact with the Russian arms dealer so soon; not this evening, anyway. A quick check of the small Bose clock radio confirmed that it was indeed late; nearly 10.30 pm. Matt rubbed his eyes; he had fallen asleep about an hour ago. He was still suffering from the effects of jet lag.

Khan continued talking and Matt scribbled down the important details: nine pm exchange tomorrow and something about payments received and cash still owing. It didn't make much sense. He heard Khan laugh and then the conversation ended. Matt held the receiver hard against his ear. Khan was still moving around. Drawers opened and closed and the Afghan cursed a few times, then there was a squeal of the door to the hotel room opening and closing. After this there was nothing, no audio at all. Even though it was early evening and freezing cold outside, Khan had obviously left his jacket behind.

'Shit!'

Matt checked the handheld GPS receiver to see if Khan was on the move with the sports bag, but there was no signal.

Matt put his shoes back on and grabbed his windbreaker. He looked at the safe and briefly considered taking the pistol with him, then decided against it. He wasn't anticipating any contact with his target; this was strictly recon. But without the benefit of tracking and listening devices Matt would have to do this old school.

• • •

Matt caught up with Faisal Khan a few hundred metres down the street from the Hotel New House. The Afghan moved with ease through the evening crowd. He had a black plastic bag over his right shoulder and he carried something else in his left hand.

Khan cut through the grounds of an old mosque and stopped for a moment. Watching him, Matt realised that in his left hand he was holding a map. Khan looked at it and adjusted his course. He walked off again down another side street and then stopped when he came to a laneway with a sign indicating that its name was Hoca Rüstem Mektebi. Here Khan stopped for a moment and looked around.

Matt put his head down and kept walking; he had already positioned himself amid a group of men who were walking alongside him and so remained undetected. Khan's eyes passed straight over them and back down the street. Seemingly confident that he was unobserved, he entered the laneway. Matt stepped out from the group of men and approached the lane cautiously, just in time to see Khan throw the black plastic bag over the fence of a compound that was opposite a pink hotel.

What on earth are you up to, Faisal? Matt wondered. *Was that cash? Surely it was being done electronically?* Had he seen Khan just set up a dead letter box? It occurred to him that he might have missed something; he hadn't heard both sides of the conversation, after all. *Perhaps they are doing it the old-fashioned way,* he reasoned. This was the exchange location for the weapon, of that Matt was certain. Faisal would tell them that the cash was on the other side of the wall; but that was the part that didn't make sense.

Khan kept walking straight down the lane and out the other side; Matt thought it better to not follow. Pulling out his phone he leaned against the wall of a small coffee and sweets shop of the type that were so ubiquitous on the corners of Istanbul streets. He brought up Google Maps, then zoomed in on his own location.

Lightning crashed across the sky, making Matt jump slightly at the noise. The rumble from the thunder went on for almost half a minute and in the distance the noise of more thunder echoed, reverberating across the water that separated European Turkey from Asian Turkey and over the minarets that were now sounding the night-time call to prayer. Matt shivered in response to the noise and the cold.

Satisfied that he knew where to go, he started back up the small street that he had just walked down and took a left, and then another left; he would approach the lane from the other end, he decided. There were two small walls at one end of a courtyard that separated a private residence from one of the hotels in the street. If Matt could get into location inside the first courtyard, he would be able to see the handover occur. He tried the small wooden gate and found it unlocked. A gap in the plaster rendering gave him a great view down the road.

Matt slowly made his way to the hotel. Things were happening faster than he'd anticipated. TC and JJ wouldn't be arriving till later tomorrow and the possibility of them getting to the hotel before he needed them in position was remote. It seemed he was going to have to monitor Khan by himself for the rest of the day and into the evening up until the handover.

17

SAMANDIRA ARMY AIR BASE, TURKEY

Rachel moved into the dimly lit hanger where Glyn's men had set up their vehicles and equipment. She juggled a roll of topographical and city view maps as well as various other intelligence overlays. The hangar, tucked down the very back of the Istanbul Samandira Army Air Base, was discreet enough to be hidden from prying eyes while close enough for the snatch team to get into Istanbul and recover the 'package'. The back gate was metres away and now manned by the Turkish military on a strict need-to-know basis when it came to arrivals and departures.

Earlier in the afternoon the SBS guys had changed into flight suits for the dirty job of breaking down the pallets and organising, cleaning and double-checking all the weapons and explosives that they might need. The Turkish military had been very helpful in the offloading of vehicles and pallets from the C-17, and a liaison officer, Major Evren Faruk, was standing with Glyn and Bluey next to the lead car. The Turkish major would be attached to the mission for the duration of the operation on the ground in Istanbul, ensuring that the team would have no problems with the overzealous Turkish police.

Glyn had already spotted her walking out of the small side office where they had set up the MI6 signals support team. He smiled at her as he saw her awkwardly juggling the paperwork.

'We have a drop-off location, Glyn,' she said. 'Milko has been in contact with an Afghan by the name of Faisal Khan – or, rather, Khan called him. They are set to meet tomorrow evening in a laneway outside some hotel.' She placed the maps on the bonnet of the black armoured cruiser and handed the location coordinates to Glyn. 'Here's a copy of the conversation as well.' She passed over a page of typed notes.

Glyn looked them over. His eyes narrowed when he read about the money transfer arrangements. He turned his attention back to Rachel.

'Rachel, you've met Major Faruk Evren, haven't you?'

'I have. Hello, Major.' Rachel smiled.

'Hello, Rachel. Please, anything you need, just let me know. I was saying earlier to Glyn that I can offer troops and aircraft, tanks – whatever we need to achieve this task.'

'Thank you, that's very kind, but I'm sure we can handle this.'

'Of course, of course, but as you are a guest in our country, my government is keen to make sure that you have all the necessary resources at hand. As you know, we are busy ourselves with our own internal issues and we don't want this to escalate into a major international incident.'

'I understand,' said Rachel. 'I know that government to government an agreement has been reached to let us deal with this in the first instance. Of course, if I need anything I will be sure to ask.'

'I have a question, Rachel,' interrupted Glyn.

'Yes, what is it?'

Glyn had turned his attention back to the telephone transcripts. 'Do we need to wait until the money transfer has taken place before the snatch or is that immaterial?' he asked.

'That's a good question; I think that we should wait. We can monitor it from the van – no doubt it will be an SMS, so that's hardly a challenge. If there's any delay, though, my priority is securing the weapon.'

'Okay, got it – we'll update our plan and get ready for the snatch.' He smiled and placed his hand on her shoulder, causing her to tense up. 'Why don't you go and get your head down for a bit? I'm going to tell my guys to get some rest now ahead of orders at six am.'

'Yes, that's a good idea.' Rachel was far from tired at this point, but she knew that the fatigue from the last few days' planning would slowly start to register and she wanted to be refreshed and alert for the next day. Rachel stepped back, away from Glyn's touch, and headed back to the office.

The three men watched her go.

'You should back of a bit, sir,' said Bluey. 'She has an important job to do, you know.'

'She'll be fine – something tells me she can handle herself,' Glyn replied with a wink. He opened the door of the armoured Land Cruiser and took an iPad from the front seat. He consulted the note Rachel had given him, then entered the coordinates into the military mapping tool, Falcon View, and zoomed in on the screen.

'I've seen you toying around with young ladies before,' Bluey persisted. 'Remember that waitress in Poole? You practically drove her insane in a matter of weeks.'

Glyn looked sideways at the warrant officer. 'Bluey, go tell the lads to get their heads down, then meet me in that room over there.' He indicated a room at the far end of the hangar, which, judging by the long tables and chairs had probably once been a briefing room for the maintenance crews. 'We'll use it as our operations room and I'll give orders there in the morning. Let's get this plan tightened up.'

'Will do, boss. Do you need anyone else or just me?' Bluey knew he had overstepped the mark; he also knew that Glyn would let it roll.

'Just you and Major Faruk here. Ten minutes, okay?'

Both men nodded.

Glyn headed towards the room and ten minutes later, on the dot, he looked up from the maps he had spread over the long tables to see Bluey and the Turkish officer enter.

'Here, I made you a wet.' Bluey handed Glyn a cup of milky tea.

'Thanks. Take a look at this, Bluey.' Glyn had placed a clear piece of plastic over the city map and tapped it down. Using a blue marker, he had circled three different areas; he had also circled a fourth area in red.

'This circle here is the Nowy Efendi Hotel.' Glyn pointed to the red circle with the point of a pocketknife. 'From the Falcon View flyover of this alley, the Hoca Rüstem Mektebi laneway seems small indeed – in fact, it's not even wide enough for more than one vehicle to pass, a car could park up on this curb, but it would be tight to get past in another vehicle, and it's only about two hundred metres long.' Glyn moved the tip of the knife to a large car park circled in blue. 'This is the Katli Otopark, down the hill around seventy metres from the entrance to the alley. It's a multi-level car park. It will make a great staging area prior to us moving in on foot. At nine pm there should only be a few people around, meaning we can move up this street and then into the alley fairly fast. The vehicles can follow after a one-minute gap. We should have it all wrapped up by then.'

'You don't want to hit each side simultaneously?' Bluey pointed to the other end of the alley.

'No, it's just too tight and the possibility of a blue on blue is far too great. If we do it this way, then we can have a team down either side and be on top of them before they can react. Judging by the street lighting on this Google Earth imagery, we won't even need NVGs. We can roll in there with discreet weapons and two snipers, one either side of the alley, for overhead cover.'

'Got it. What time do you want to roll then?'

'I think we need to get into the car park at around six pm. We need to hire some cars first thing tomorrow. We can't arrive in our armoured cruisers or the whole world will know what's going on. Let's take care of that after orders.'

'Sure, I'll get Ganley and Donoghue on it.' Bluey wrote down a reminder in his notebook. 'Do you think these Russians are going to bring any firepower? Anything we haven't thought of?'

'What's more powerful than a nuclear weapon?' Glyn looked up from the maps and smiled at his 2IC. 'Nothing we can't handle, mate,' he said. He sipped on the tea and tapped his iPad with his pen. 'I'm going to get these orders done then get my own head down.'

18

SAMANDIRA ARMY AIR BASE

'That's it then. The lads are loaded up and we're ready to move.' Glyn checked his own Heckler & Koch MP5K model machine pistol and adjusted the three-point sling. He closed the Aimpoint covers and turned off the switch of the red dot sight. The weapon bounced back by his side and he closed his bomber jacket over the top of it.

Bluey adjusted his own kit. 'The guys will be glad to get on with it, to be honest, all day in here rehearsing and listening to confirmatory orders starts to get a bit old hat after a while. No offence, ma'am, but even your briefs are a bit dry when you've had to sit through them every hour on the hour since six am. Anyway, how do I look?' Bluey straightened his shirt over his discreet body armour and holstered his pistol.

Rachel nodded her approval. It was four pm and they were running according to schedule. She looked across at the three hire cars, all different makes and models, all loaded with SBS operators – Britain's finest. A car containing an advance party had already left the hangar an hour ago. Their job was to scope out the car park and then make their way to the restaurant on the corner. From there they could provide commentary and alert Glyn to the Russian's arrival.

'Any news from the advance guys yet, Glyn?' asked Rachel.

'Oisín reported in five minutes ago.' Glyn looked at his watch then adjusted the microphone in his ear, making sure the cable from the mic to the radio receiver on his belt was hidden. 'It's quiet and the car park is near on empty. They've parked up on the third level on the northern side. There's a set of stairs we can use to make our way to the ground floor and out into the street. I suggest you keep the Transit van up there; it's out of the way and because of the open sides of the car park you'll still be able to provide a listening over-watch.'

'Got it.' Rachel kneeled on the concrete floor of the hangar and zipped up her small backpack. Standing up, she slung it over her right shoulder. 'I'm all set too.'

'Once we park up, the lads will move to the three different start points. When you're ready, let me know and I'll give the word to move in. I think it will take about thirty seconds for us to get to the start of the lane and then make our move down it. No more than thirty seconds, that's for sure.'

'Okay. As we discussed before, it sounds like there's going to be a money transfer of some sort. Most probably it will be electronic. Once we've detected it, I'll let you know.' Rachel hesitated. 'Actually, if I think it's going to wrap up without evidence of a money transfer, I'll still give the word. Either way, our main aim is to retrieve that weapon.'

'Understood. We've tested the body cams and they're all linked back to the monitor in the van, so you'll be able to see and record everything as it happens.' Glyn rotated the small bezel on the camera into the 'on' position and ensured it was fastened tight to his jacket.

'Shall we set off then?' Rachel turned towards the white Ford Transit; Glyn grabbed her hand before she could step away. Startled, she turned. He was gazing down at her, a sombre look on his face. 'What's the matter?' she said.

'I want to ask you something.'

Rachel frowned. 'What is it? Have we forgotten something?'

Glyn gave a sheepish grin. 'No, nothing like that. I thought I'd ask you out for a drink. Just in case this all goes pear-shaped, then at least I've asked, you know? Shown my intent.'

'Right, I see,' Rachel said crisply. She was annoyed that he had chosen such an important moment to turn personal. She was attracted to him, that was certain, but this was hardly the time or place to act on any attraction. Besides, there was something inside her warning her off him – not to mention the ever-present thought of Matt in the back of her mind.

'So, what do you say?' Glyn persisted. 'After all this is over, will you have a drink with me?'

'No. No, I don't think that's a good idea at all, Glyn.' Rachel pulled her hand away from his. 'Let's keep this professional, shall we? We need to go now; we have a job to do.'

Glyn laughed. 'Okay, Rachel – but you'll change your mind.' He opened the door of the lead car and turned to shout, 'Let's go, lads, three minutes apart. Move now!' He banged the roof of his own car and got in.

'She knocked you back, hey, sir?' said Johnny Brookes, the Alpha Team driver, as Glyn climbed into the seat next to him.

'Ha, you know me, Johnny – I love a challenge. C'mon, let's go meet some Russians.' Glyn smiled.

19

ISTANBUL

Faisal checked his watch; it was five minutes to nine. He scanned the restaurants and cafes along the main street. Everything seemed normal for this time of the evening and he couldn't see any sign of the Turkish military. Most of the cafes were full of tourists either smoking shisha or eating their main meal for the day. The brightness of the streetlights and noise and laughter emanating from the cafes and restaurants on the tourist strip disorientated Faisal slightly; even the busiest of the city streets of Kabul lacked the energy of Istanbul.

As he had done the night before, he turned down the side street nearest to his hotel, and then turned down a second street that took him into the more traditional area of the city. Nearing the start of the narrow laneway, he squinted, his eyes slow to adjust to the sudden darkness. One lamppost at either end of the lane splashed only a little light into the street. The faint glow from the windows of the boutique hotels pierced the many shadows, but not enough for Faisal to get a good look at his surroundings. Not far along was a small delivery van with a few men standing next to it. Faisal couldn't quite make them out; there were maybe three or four men, he decided. He approached slowly. One of the men turned and, seeing the Afghan, started towards him. As he came closer, Faisal could see that everything about him was short, from his stature to his arms to his blond hair.

'Faisal, hello, my friend, how are you?' The blond man's accent was unmistakably Russian. He extended his hand and Faisal shook it.

'Milko?' he asked.

'No, no, not me.' He moved in and started to pat down the tall Afghan, feeling his waist for a weapon and his body for a bomb. 'It is not possible to be too careful, don't you agree?'

Murmuring his assent, Faisal stood tall and still as the Russian completed the frisk. It was amateurish at best and Faisal grew in confidence. This guy wasn't military at all; he was more like a hired thug.

'What is this?' the Russian asked, pulling Faisal's phone from his trouser pocket.

'Just a telephone.'

Satisfied with the answer, the Russian returned the phone to Faisal. If he had asked Faisal to empty his pockets, he would have seen that there was something there besides the phone: a small garage remote with two buttons.

'Where's Milko?' asked Faisal.

'I'm right here, Faisal.' Milko emerged from the other side of the van. He was taller than the first Russian, but then that wouldn't be hard. In his white chinos, black polo and sports coat, he looked like he would have been just as at ease getting out of a Ferrari in Monte Carlo as a Ford in an Istanbul laneway. He removed his jacket and placed it on the bonnet of the van. Faisal could see the butt of a pistol poking out from the top of the waistband of his trousers. The other men were armed too, Faisal noticed, with AK-SBRs, a short-barrelled version of the AK-47 at the ready.

'Are you expecting trouble, brother?' said Faisal.

'Of course, I always expect trouble; you don't deliver a package like this without some insurance. But, having said that, I see no reason why this shouldn't go smoothly.' Milko waved his hand slowly in a half-circle to encompass all of his men. 'As you can see, we have *all* the firepower.' He laughed.

'Yes, that is clear,' said Faisal. 'God willing, it will go smoothly. So, do you have the case for me to see?'

Without turning his head, Milko gestured to someone behind him. 'Vasily! Show our Afghan friend the case!'

The sliding door to the small van flew open. Faisal and Milko walked slowly towards it. Faisal couldn't see inside the van in the dim light.

The Russian who climbed from the van was a bald-headed, big-nosed mountain of a man. In his hand, he held a silver suitcase. It was larger than Faisal had expected. Vasily opened the lid of the case and shone a torch on the contents.

Faisal could see it was the real deal. Clearly military made, it was exactly the same as the replica he had seen all those years ago in Quetta, except there was power to this one. A small receiver in the bottom left showed that it was connected to a transmitter somewhere. Small red numbers clicked over, disappeared and then reappeared – no doubt linked to the trigger initiator somewhere in Russia.

'Now you must fulfil your end of the bargain, Faisal,' said Milko. He walked over to his jacket, pulled a small bottle of vodka from an inside pocket and took a swig of it. 'Call who you need to call and let's finish this.'

• • •

Matt strained to see from his position in the small courtyard at the end of the lane. A large tree in the corner created a dark shadow for him to hide within and the large crack in the wall gave him a great view down the lane. He hadn't reckoned on it being this dark though. He could see shadows moving around a van located about seventy metres away. He couldn't make out how many men there were, but he could hear most of the conversation via the listening device on Faisal Khan's collar. The Russians were hard to understand through the audio, so he was relying on Khan's part of the conversation. As far as he could tell, the case was there, and now Khan was going to contact his handlers to get the final payment transferred.

Just then, a movement high up in a building to his right caught his attention. Freezing, Matt watched as a suppressor was slowly eased through the window of a drycleaner's shop. Matt's hand flashed to his own weapon as he pivoted towards the threat, feet shoulder-width apart, and dropped into a stable firing position; he gripped the handle ready to engage. He recognised the suppressor; it was most likely attached to an AK-101, a Russian assault rifle. While not particularly powerful, at this range it would be deadly and was more than a match for Matt's Heckler & Koch P30SK pistol. Clearly the weapon was covering the lane, though, and the guy on the other end of it wasn't a pro; a sniper would be seated well back in the room and would probably have cut the glass and laid mesh from the ceiling to floor to enhance the dead space and avoid detection. The suppressor pulled back slightly and then was laid to rest on the windowsill, further pointing to a lack of competence.

Confident that he hadn't been compromised, Matt settled back down to watch the show.

C'mon, Faisal, don't stuff this up, mate, Matt urged silently. *Just get the case and we can all get the hell out of here in one piece.*

• • •

Faisal tapped a message into his phone then sent it to the number Hassan al-Britani had given him. A few seconds later his phone vibrated with a return message requesting that Faisal send a picture of the inside of the case, and in particular the small plate at the top of the lid which contained the military equipment number.

'I need to take a photo of the case, Milko.'

'Of course, it's here, take the photo as you need, my friend.'

Milko scanned up and down the lane and then glanced up to where his sniper was set up. Satisfied there was no rush, he searched his pocket for his cigarettes and lit one. He offered the packet to Vasily, who accepted without thought. The other two Russians stayed at the front of the Ford Transit, covering the entrance to the lane.

Faisal snapped a photo and sent it back to the same number. The five minutes he spent waiting for a response felt like a lifetime. Faisal could sense that Milko was getting annoyed.

Milko lit another cigarette. Faisal's phone finally beeped. Embedded in the WhatsApp message was a screenshot of a bank receipt. It showed that fifty million US dollars had been deposited to a bank account in the name of a Turkish agricultural company. Faisal handed the phone to Milko, who smiled his approval. He slapped Vasily's back and then threw the phone back to the Afghan.

'Well done, Faisal. You are the proud new owner of a nuclear weapon.' Milko helped Vasily lower the suitcase onto its wheels. 'Well, the Taliban are, anyway.' Milko laughed. 'Just remind your friends, the final fifty million needs to be sent to me in order to activate the weapon. No cash, no bang.'

Faisal nodded; the Russian was irritating him now. He placed his phone back in his pocket and thought about pressing the garage remote just to make a point.

. . .

Glyn looked down at the message that had just flashed up on his phone. It was from Rachel.

All call signs this is GOLF ACTUAL, move now.

With that Glyn jumped out of his seat and his team followed him out the door of the small cafe closest to the lane. Three other groups of men poured out of the restaurants and cafes just up the street and seconds later they were all arranged and into their rolling start.

The Turkish and foreign civilians alike watched in awe at the speed of what was unfolding around them. Men seemed to be running everywhere, the cafes emptied in some sort of organised chaos.

Alpha Team filed out on the left and Bravo Team on the right, weapons up and staggered so they could all fire if required. The snipers at the rear of each team had discarded their long bags in the street and had their SR25 rifles up and at the ready. They all disappeared into the entrance of the dark alley. Glyn had thought there would be more light than this and cursed himself for not taking NVGs.

The SBS teams had run no more than a few metres down the lane when two shots rang out; while suppressed, they were still loud enough to register. John Higgins, leading Bravo Team, dropped to the ground as the rounds crashed into his small Kevlar chest plate.

'Fuck it, I'm hit.' He rolled to the left and into the gutter, out of the line of fire. 'The window at the end of the street!' he yelled. After quickly checking his vitals and establishing that he'd taken both shots to the body armour, he jumped up and attached himself to the back of his team.

Stuart Ganley responded faster than seemed humanly possible. The guy in front of him stopped dead in his tracks and took a knee, and Stuart placed his weapon on his shoulder and steadied himself. He locked on with the SR25 and let rip four rounds; the Russian sniper fell forward through the window and down into the street.

The Russians started to fire back down the alley in unison. The 7.62mm short-barrelled AKs made a deafening noise, but the untrained Russians, not used to firing in low light conditions, all fired high over the heads of the SBS teams, as was usually the case with men who had limited training in firing in the dark.

Glyn positioned himself against a wall and brought up his MP5. He punched the weapon forward on its sling and laid the red dot sight on the first muzzle flash, letting off fifteen rounds – full auto. Milko was dead before he could even get his second round off. Thirteen of the bullets pulverised his skull and the last two split his throat, making a hell of a mess all over the side of the small white delivery van. Glyn switched targets, putting ten more rounds into the flashes coming from the second AK. Vasily's body was punched repeatedly by the slow-velocity 9mm rounds, each one doing more damage than the last. He fell back into the van's open door, stone cold dead.

The rest of the two teams made short work of the other Russians. The SBS operators had years of training in fighting with these types of weapons in close quarters and every shot found its mark in that narrow alley.

Glyn and his two teams raced towards the Transit. They had got to within a few metres of it when a huge explosion blew the wall opposite the car to smithereens. Rubble showered down on them and dust and debris filled the lane. The men rocked back in shock, choking and gagging on the thick concrete dust that filled the once empty space.

'What the fuck was that?' said Glyn.

'Well, it wasn't nuclear or we wouldn't be talking about it, bro,' replied Semi Taufolo.

Glyn did a quick scan of his teams, making sure they were all still combat effective. Then he caught a glimpse of someone running towards the end of the alley, dragging what looked like a suitcase. 'Get after him, Semi!'

'On it.'

Semi took off at full speed, climbing over the broken bricks that had once been a wall.

• • •

The blast on the opposite side of the road had reverberated through Matt's hiding place and thrown him back off the wall. At the time, he had been weighing up his own options. Dazed, he got up and remembered that a moment before there had been a firefight in the alley. He had seen the sniper fall from the window and remembered that he had been impressed by the speed at which he had been engaged after firing. He had no idea who was on the other side of the shooting, but they were clearly well drilled. Small controlled bursts from 9mm auto weapons, double taps from suppressed 5.56 and a sniper who was more than handy with a 7.62. These guys were good.

Shit – Faisal! thought Matt. He looked down the alley through the crack in the wall and could see that half of the Nowy Efendi Hotel was now on the other side of the road and in the street.

'Should have known that's what was in the black plastic bag, Faisal – you've got form for it, after all,' Matt muttered to himself. He adjusted the volume on the listening device receiver and could hear that Khan was running somewhere. His breathing was laboured and Matt could hear the wheels of the case being dragged along the footpath. At that moment, in the distance, sirens began to wail.

Time to get out of here, thought Matt.

He jogged over to the gate and made his way out of the

courtyard, only to bounce off a giant who was turning the corner at that exact moment.

'You right there, bro?!'

Matt was about to go for his pistol, but thought better of it when he saw the short-barrelled 10-inch C8 CQB weapon.

The two faced off. Matt heard the giant say something and then realised that he was pressing a switch on the front of his shirt. He spotted the bone microphone in his right ear and recognised it as the type of communications device favoured by elite units.

'I'm all good, mate, what about you?' asked Matt. His mind was racing to interpret what was going on. Clearly this guy was a Pacific Islander, but was he a contractor or state-sponsored – and if the latter, what state? Australia? The UK? The UK was more likely given the weapon that he was carrying. SAS, SBS, SRR? Either way, Matt had to get out of there and fast. He thought about sweeping the Islander's legs out from under him and then making a getaway down the street, but all the distances were too great – he would be fired on in an instant and besides, regardless of their size, Islanders were always more athletic than they seemed, especially if they were in this job. Sweeping his legs might be an act of suicide.

The big guy stepped slowly to his left and walked around Matt, never taking his eyes off him. 'I'd suggest you get out of here, pal,' the Islander said. Then he jogged off down the hill, in the opposite direction to that which Matt knew Khan would have taken.

Matt didn't need to be told twice. *That was a lucky break*, he thought. He took off at speed up the street towards the hotel.

• • •

In the back of the van, Rachel sat staring in shock. As if the snatch going kinetic and Faisal Khan taking off with the weapon hadn't been bad enough to watch . . . She looked again at the image she had paused on Semi's body cam.

'Matt Rix,' she whispered. 'What on earth are you doing here?'

20

ISTANBUL

Faisal looked quickly back over his right shoulder. Behind him the evening crowds were still getting on with life, jumping on and off trams or milling around the numerous food shops lining the busy streets, completely oblivious to the carnage that had occurred barely a mile down the road. The sirens had all but stopped. Faisal assumed that the emergency services were crawling all over the blast site by now. No doubt they would at first think it was a Kurdistan Workers' Party attack and they would take their time to process the scene. Satisfied he hadn't been followed, he turned down Evkaf Street and made his way to the hotel.

'Evening, sir,' said the young receptionist behind the desk, glancing up from her computer screen.

Faisal hadn't seen her before.

'Looks like you've been doing some shopping.' She gave him a friendly smile.

'Yes, there are some bargains in the markets,' Faisal mumbled. He wheeled the suitcase through the foyer. He pressed the elevator button to go up, then pressed it again, and again, and again. He looked at his reflection in the shiny doors and studied his face. His black hair was a mess from the wind outside. He ran a hand through it to move it back across to one side. His eyes were sunken and his stubble was peppered with grey. The two years he'd spent in that Kandahar prison had taken their toll. His reflection looked vastly different from his heyday as a Taliban intelligence officer in Uruzghan in 2010. Back then he'd had a long black beard and his shoulder-length hair was as black as could be.

The elevator doors finally opened and Faisal stepped in. He let out a sigh as the doors closed behind him and he pressed the number three. The handover had not gone well, but God willing he would get rid of the case tomorrow and be on his way back to central Afghanistan.

• • •

Matt caught a glimpse of Faisal Khan at the bottom of the hill and followed him as far as the Starbucks. Then, having reassured himself that Khan had entered the hotel unmolested, he entered the cafe. There were half a dozen other people seated at individual tables, all engrossed in either smart phones or books. None of them paid any attention to the Australian as he ghosted in. Pausing beside a vacant table at the front of the narrow shop, he undid his windbreaker and placed it over the back of one of the pine chairs. He turned on the audio to the listening device, his mind still on what had just happened. Clearly those other guys were chasing Faisal Khan too. But who were they?

His phone vibrated in his cargo pocket.

'Hello?' There was silence on the other end and Matt took the phone from his ear and looked down at the screen. It was an international number.

'Hey, who's this?'

This time the phone connected.

'Hey, brother, it's TC. How you doing?'

Matt smiled. Pulling the earbud from the listening device from his other ear, he glanced around the cafe to make sure no one was in earshot. 'Mate, am I glad to hear from you. Where are you?'

'I'm at your hotel. JJ is here too; we met up at the airport. We just need you to come and swipe that magic Visa card of yours so we can check in.'

'Sure thing – I'm only about five minutes out. I'll brief you up when I get there.'

'Roger that, bud, look forward to it.' The phone disconnected.

Matt decided not to listen to Faisal Khan anymore. He was in his hotel now, safe and sound, and presumably going to stay there until morning. Picking up his jacket, he stepped back out into the cold winter's night, relieved that he had support from two of the most capable operators he knew. There were too many unanswered questions about this operation.

Who were the guys that had intercepted the handover? Were they state-sponsored, or was another terrorist organisation trying to get its hands on the device? Whoever they were, they were surely now after Khan. It was up to Matt to make sure the

Afghan handed that case over to the CIA operators, as per his initial brief. He thought about calling Steph to update her, then thought better of it. He didn't want to talk to her unless there was no other option.

• • •

Faisal picked up his prayer beads from the bedside table and squatted on the floor of his hotel room, opposite the silver case. He rolled the small beads between his fingers, deep in thought. He stared at the case for a few minutes and then sat cross-legged. Taking his phone out of his trousers, he sent a short message to Hassan al-Britani.

I have the case, but there was an issue. Some men attacked us during the handover. I think Milko and his men are all done. I want to get this to you as soon as possible.

He didn't have to wait too long for the reply.

No problem. Let's meet tomorrow. I will send you the location in the morning. Relax.

Faisal had an uneasy feeling about this. Relax? How could he relax?

He looked at the case again. What was it Milko had said? Another fifty million or no bang . . . Faisal thought about it. With Milko dead, the case was only good for parts, unless someone other than Milko was controlling the trigger – which of course was a very real possibility. Faisal couldn't work it out. Perhaps Hassan al-Britani had sent men to kill Milko and now he would come for Faisal. Maybe this was all his doing? Faisal jumped up and lifted the heavy suitcase onto the bed. He undid the latches and opened the lid. The insides were a complex mix of solenoids; wires and a long silver cylinder, which Faisal knew contained the plutonium. There was a small Uniden radio and, down the bottom, the initiator that had to match the same number as that on the remote trigger in order to work. The red numbers on the initiator slowly clicked over, changing every few seconds. It was held in place by a couple of small black cable ties.

Faisal went over to his Adidas sports bag and rummaged around inside, looking for his small pocketknife. He finally located it, and then he spotted a small round disc in the bottom of the bag. He tried to pull it out and found it was stuck fast. He opened the knife and cut the disc out; it had been fastened using a superstrong adhesive. He held the disc up to the light and rotated it in his thick fingers, reading the name inscribed on the quarter-inch-thick side: *Retrievo*. On closer inspection, he could see that it was solar powered as well as having a small watch battery in the back, presumably for when it was being used like this – hidden in the bottom of a bag. Faisal knew exactly what it was; someone was tracking him.

He placed the GPS tracker on the bedside table and then began to pull the room apart. Years spent working first with Pakistan's Inter-Services Intelligence and then as an intelligence officer for the Taliban had made him more than just suspicious; he was also as tech-savvy as his Western counterparts. He rechecked the bag, and then went through every drawer and cupboard. He checked the bed and found the listening device that Matt had screwed into the base. He carried it to the bathroom, planning to flush it down the toilet, but thought better of it. That would only alert whoever had put it there to the fact that he was on to them. He took it back into the bedroom and placed it gently on the desk, then he picked up the remote control, selected an Arab news station at random and turned the volume up. Returning to the case, Faisal cut through the cable ties, disconnected the cylinder and placed it on the bed. He looked around the room and finally went over to the bathroom. Looking up to the ceiling, he noticed that it was comprised of large foam tiles held in place by an aluminium frame. He could push these open and get access to the ceiling. He then dragged the chair from behind the desk to the bathroom, placing it in the shower. Getting up on the chair, he pushed up on one of the foam tiles and lifted it into the space above. He removed the next one and then another from the cross-sections of the frame. He twisted on the screws with his knife and undid a handful, removing the ribs of the ceiling itself. Faisal heaved the case up onto his shoulders and pushed it through the gap he had created and then followed it up into the ceiling cavity. He pushed it slowly across the framework and hid it down one side of the dark space. Satisfied it wouldn't be spotted with a casual look up into the cavity, he lowered himself back down and replaced the galvanised ribs and white tiles until the ceiling looked the same as before. If anyone came for the case, at least he would have his own bargaining chip.

Faisal took the chair back out into the room and jammed it up against the handle of the door and then secured the internal latch and the deadbolt. He checked the balcony for an alternative escape route should he need it. It looked like there was no other way out, unless he risked a jump of some considerable height to the balcony below. The fire escape stairs could be an option, but a locked grate secured them. He went back inside and picked up the metal chair and then went out and bashed the small lock until it snapped off.

Moving back inside, he withdrew the Browning from the safe where he had left it and placed it on the bedside table then picked up the GPS tracker again. He looked at it for a time then, jumping up, he went over to the wardrobe and took out the cloth laundry bag he had spotted there during his search. He stuck the tracker to the inside bottom of the bag and then stuffed it with a t-shirt and a pair of socks before tying it up at the top. He placed the bag back in the corner of the room then settled back on the bed. It would be a long night. Someone knew he was there and someone wanted to know what he was saying and where he was going ... perhaps the fact that he was aware of it would work in his favour.

• • •

'Sweet digs, Matt,' said Todd Carson. The big American stretched out on the two-seater couch. He looked every bit the sports star he could have been, dressed simply in blue jeans, a white polo shirt and a black truckers cap; he looked more like Captain America than a captain in the Green Berets.

JJ opened the minibar fridge and removed three Heinekens. He flipped off the lids with a butter knife against his thumb and passed green bottles to the other two. 'Here's to the CIA – best business-class flight ever,' said JJ.

'I'll drink to that,' said Todd. They all clinked bottles and took a swig.

'Okay, boss – fill us in. It's all well and good to have an all-expenses-paid holiday, but I know there's a catch.' JJ took another gulp of the beer. 'You said something about that nut job Faisal Khan?'

'Well, shit, where do I start?' Matt shook his head. 'So, Steph Baumer contacted me and asked me to track Khan to a rendezvous with the Russian mafia, who were going to hand over a nuclear suitcase weapon. He was to deliver this same weapon to guys from ISIS – only they're not really ISIS; they're an Afghan CIA cell masquerading as ISIS to take the weapon off the streets, except that the Russians think they're the Taliban. Anyway, this evening I followed Khan to the rendezvous and there was a firefight. Someone – maybe the British SAS – tried to intercept the handover and now all the Russians are dead and Khan is back in his hotel waiting for word on where to go to drop off the nuke.'

Todd and JJ both stared at Matt, eyes wide and mouths agape.

'Are you completely insane? What language are you speaking, because it sounds like bullshit,' JJ demanded. 'It's bad enough that Faisal Khan is involved, but Steph Baumer? You never said anything about that bitch! Have you lost your frigging mind?'

Turning to Todd, Matt could see the American was looking just as incredulous. Thinking back on what he had just said, Matt had to concede it did sound bizarre now he had said it aloud.

'Right, well, how the hell do we get out of this mess?' Todd started to laugh. 'Jesus, Matt, how did Steph even get hold of you?'

'Don't ask,' Matt said ruefully. 'I think the way forward from here is to shadow Faisal Khan, make sure he delivers the weapon to the CIA and then we bug out of here. This needs to be done discreetly; I assume the SAS will leave no stone unturned in their hunt for him.'

'What makes you think they're SAS?' asked JJ.

'I ran into one of them in the street – a Tongan, I think. He's big and fit and he was carrying a C8, so I assume he must be working in the British military; just stands to reason that they're SAS, especially carrying that weapon.'

'Maybe, but I'd have guessed Special Boat Service not SAS,' JJ countered. 'The SBS has a rapid response team that recovers nationals. Lots of Islanders join the Royal Marines and then do the selection. If they're carrying C8s they could be Canadian, they're made in Canada you know? But as he was an Islander I assume that they're British.'

'Doesn't really matter, does it?' Todd pointed out. 'Either way they're going to be an issue.'

'Well, maybe, maybe not. It would be good to know who we're dealing with for when the time comes . . .' Tipping his head back, JJ chugged back the rest of his beer.

'Jesus – no way, JJ. I don't want any confrontation with another country's military, especially the British. I want to avoid that at all costs, regardless of what flavour SF they are.'

'Got it; no messing with the colonial masters.' JJ smirked. He grabbed another beer from the mini bar.

'Go easy on that too, mate. We might have to mobilise; you're no good to me pissed.'

'Pissed? Well, you could have told me that before I had access to free alcohol all the way from Dubai to Istanbul. Man's not a camel. Besides, it actually makes me more effective – I can control my aggression better with the edge off. Anyway, you're fresh out of beer; that was the last one. I mean, why don't they make man-size mini bars – this looks like it should be in a kid's cubby house.'

Matt lifted himself up to sit on the desk and thought for a moment. 'I think the Turkish security forces are going to be swarming the streets tomorrow. I don't know how Khan is going to get that case to anyone. It would make sense that the Afghan CIA guys would go to him. I think we need to keep eyes on the hotel.'

'Why can't we just contact those guys, tell them we're working with them?' Todd asked. 'Job's done then.'

'Huh, you're right.' Matt looked down at the ground. 'Why wouldn't Steph link me up with them at this point?' he wondered aloud.

'None of this adds up, boss. None of it.' JJ stood up and went to the window and looked out into the dark street below. 'I think you're being set up and I think you took the bait hook, line and sinker. Think about it; you were an easy mark. Pissed off to be thrown into an office job, craving some real action.' JJ turned back to face the two other men. 'I think you're a bloody idiot actually, skipper, and you're probably going to get us all killed.'

'Yeah, I'm beginning to think you're right, JJ. Thanks for the feedback, mate.' Matt smiled and shrugged. 'Well, you're both here now – what's say we see how this rolls? After all, it will be a great way to see the New Year in.'

'We need to keep an eye on your man Faisal,' Todd agreed. 'But I find it hard to believe that the CIA and the British wouldn't have some sort of foreign forces agreement for this. As far as I'm concerned there are a few unknown unknowns at play here. It could be that this is anything but vanilla.' He stood up and placed his hand on JJ's shoulder and looked over at Matt. 'It doesn't matter though; I mean, how much trouble could the three of us possibly get into?' Todd slapped JJ's shoulder. 'Am I right?'

JJ laughed and clapped his hands. 'Yeah, it couldn't get much more complicated for you, could it, boss?' JJ and Todd both laughed in unison.

Matt cringed at the possibility. He looked at JJ, the most violent and gifted martial artist he had ever known, and then across at Captain America. 'We need to play this smart guys,' he said. He looked at his watch. 'It's nearly midnight – go get some rest. I'll keep the audio on in his room; if there's any more movement I'll let you know. Let's reconvene here at six am and work out what to do. At the end of the day, Khan is sitting on a nuclear weapon; I'm in two minds as to whether we should take this into our own hands and go and secure it – especially after this conversation.'

Todd and JJ grabbed their bags and took off to their own rooms, leaving Matt to think more about the situation. Now that he had their perspective on it all, he felt increasingly uncomfortable with what was happening.

What if I am being set up? he thought. It was looking more and more likely.

Matt adjusted the volume on the receiver that was currently set to monitor Khan's room. He could hear the TV; Khan was watching an Arab news station. He could hear the Afghan moving around too – the audio was crystal clear. Matt sat on the edge of the bed and kicked off his shoes. 'What the hell are you playing at, Steph?' he asked aloud.

• • •

Faisal closed the door slowly behind him and made his way down the stairs, out the back entrance and into the street. He'd had to leave the room; lying there on the bed, a feeling of foreboding had come over him that he couldn't shake. It was just after one am now and, although it was late, the laneways were still alive with young people moving around from late-night bars to cafes. Faisal had changed back into his white shalwar kameez and oilskin jacket, so he looked out of place among the mostly Western-dressed Turks and tourists, save for some of the other travellers from the Middle East.

Crossing Sultanahmet Park, Faisal noticed the increased security presence. He could see that at one end of the park there was an armoured security car. It was stopped beneath one of the many clusters of streetlights that gave the whole park an eerie yellow glow and created shadows within shadows. Hanging around the car were four young police officers. They were dressed in the uniform of the Turkish tactical police and they were watching a rowdy group of male tourists with interest.

Faisal approached the entrance to the Blue Mosque.

'*As-salamu alaykum*, brother,' he greeted the caretaker sitting on the bottom step.

'*Salam*, how are you, my friend?' the old man replied. He blew warm air into his cold hands as he looked up at Faisal.

'I'm fine, thanks be to God. Can I sit inside, out of the cold, until the first morning prayer? My accommodation is a long way from here and by the time I get there it would be time to turn around.'

'Ah – of course, brother.' The old man stood. 'There's a small room off the back of the mosque, you can stay there; you'll find some blankets on the floor.' The old man waved him through.

Faisal removed his leather sandals at the top of the steps and went into the bathroom to have a quick wash. In the back room he found the blankets and made himself a small bed in one corner.

He lay there looking at the ceiling, thinking about the events of the last few hours. Someone was tracking him, the case was in the ceiling of his hotel room and the initiator was in his pocket. The Russians were very likely dead and Hassan al-Britani was yet to give him details of how the transfer was to take place. In fact, Hassan al-Britani had seemed altogether too relaxed in his text message, which in itself seemed suspicious. Faisal would need to be more cautious now. Things had certainly not gone according to plan.

21

SAMANDIRA ARMY AIR BASE

The white Ford Transit entered the hangar and came to a stop in front of the other vehicles, which had arrived a few minutes earlier. Rachel got out of the passenger seat and made her way over to where the men were either unloading weapons or standing around their hire cars. She singled out the 2IC, Bluey Reid, who was pulling a stretcher out of the trunk of the lead hire car, a precaution the guys had taken in case they needed to tab out of the area carrying a wounded operator.

'Where's Glyn?' she asked.

'He's in the heads, ma'am. He won't be a moment; he's just cleaning himself up.' Bluey placed the folded-up stretcher on the ground. 'Well, that went downhill fast, didn't it? I have to say, the old Russkies put up a bit of a show. Mind you, they didn't last long.' Bluey laughed.

'I'm not sure it's a laughing matter, Blue,' Rachel said seriously. 'It's a mess. There's a nuclear weapon out there and we have to recover it. As far as I'm concerned, it's not mission success – not by a long shot.' She looked around at the SBS operators who stood there in silence.

'It's partial mission success,' said Glyn from behind her.

Rachel turned quickly, startled by his silent approach. She watched him as he sauntered around to join the group. He was naked from the waist up; he had changed back into a flight suit and had the arms tied around his waist. He wiped his hands on the towel draped around his muscular shoulders. 'A dangerous weapons dealer is dead and now we'll go and get the weapon.'

'Right, of course – and how exactly do we do that, Glyn?' Rachel put her hands on her hips. She realised that she was being defensive because of the sudden appearance of Matt. 'I mean, help me out here, Glyn.'

'I'm working it,' Glyn said. 'I think a good place to start is to have the intel lads triangulate all the messages and phone calls made in the alley from 2000 hours to just after the explosion occurred. Your MI6 staff and our squadron intelligence guys should pool resources. They should be able to give us a target list of a few locations within a couple of hours.'

'I see.' Rachel's pulse raced and her mind quickly cast back to seeing Matt. Would he have made any phone calls? Why was he even there in the first place? She thought about raising it now with Glyn, but then stopped herself. She had to make some phone calls, find out if there was an Australian special forces operation that she wasn't aware of. She looked around at the group of men. They were all watching her, waiting for her reaction. 'That's a really good idea,' she said finally. She could feel her grip on the mission being prised from her.

'Of course it is. That's why I'm here, love – to give you good ideas.'

Ignoring this, Rachel said, 'I'll go brief them now, get them working shifts on it. But then we need to sit down and sort this mess out, come up with a better plan than just wait and see.'

'Fine. Meanwhile, I think it would be a good idea for us to do an after-action review, get a feel for exactly what happened.' Glyn turned to his men, who were still busy dusting off their weapons around the cars. 'Lads, go grab yourselves a wet. There's some pies and other fatty duff in the kitchenette – you can thank Bluey for organising that.'

'No problem, sir,' said Bluey.

'Let's meet in the operations room in twenty minutes and we'll go through what the hell happened back there.' Glyn towel-dried his wet hair and draped the towel back around his shoulders. 'Well, get going then! Jesus, I shouldn't have to say it twice.'

• • •

Twenty minutes later the SBS lads had their chairs assembled in a semicircle in the small room off the main hangar. They were busy stuffing their faces with hot pies and drinking sweet cups of coffee and tea. Rachel sat to one side next to a couple of her MI6 intelligence staff.

Glyn walked through the door, followed by Bluey and Major Faruk, the Turkish liaison officer. Rachel watched as Glyn strode over to the portable whiteboard and positioned it so they could all see the planning diagrams of the alley and the buildings and streets on either side. 'Right, let's go through this step by step, lads.'

They spent the next thirty minutes detailing their actions and compiling the after-action review that would be used in the official report to Whitehall. Each soldier went through his particular recollections and thoughts on what had occurred.

Towards the end of the debrief, Semi gave his account. 'When I took off after that squirter out the back of the alley, I bumped into what I assumed at the time was some lost tourist or something – but the more I think about it, the more that doesn't make any sense to me,' said the corporal.

Rachel froze. She knew he meant Matt. She hadn't yet had the opportunity to contact the Australian High Commission, but deep down she already knew the answer that they were going to give her. Should she tell them now that she knew who he was? She had been struggling with this ever since she'd seen his face on Semi's body cam. What was he even doing there? She just couldn't work it out.

'What doesn't make sense?' Glyn asked. 'What's the issue?'

'Well, he came through a gate leading from a courtyard at the end of the street. When I bumped into him he said something to me, I can't recall exactly what it was, but I could tell he was Australian. The interesting thing, though, is that the guy shaped up to me for a moment. I thought that was weird at the time, and now I think of it, I'm pretty sure he must be military or police or something similar. I mean, my weapons didn't shock him at all and he actually sized me up. Not my usual experience with civilians, especially after a big blast like that.'

'No, you're right – that is peculiar,' Glyn remarked.

'I know who it is,' Rachel blurted out.

The men all turned to look at her.

'Go on,' said Glyn. He straightened, lifting his chin in the air and looking down on her.

'It's Matt Rix, an Australian commando officer.'

There was some murmuring and raised eyebrows at this.

'Second Commando Regiment?' asked Bluey finally.

'Yes, that's right,' Rachel confirmed.

'I worked with those guys in Afghanistan, Glyn. They're legitimate – and I mean *legit*,' said Bluey.

'Yep, I know about them,' said Glyn.

'I've worked with them too,' Oisín chimed in. 'Jesus, what the hell is 2nd Commando Regiment doing poking around here?'

'I would like to know that too,' interjected Major Faruk. 'I like Australians, don't get me wrong, but their presence here makes me a little nervous. We have a history . . .'

Rachel looked across at the Turkish major, trying to interpret his remark, and saw his lips twitch. He was joking, of course, but this reference to Gallipoli had clearly gone over the heads of the SBS guys. Rachel nodded to show she understood and he gave her a wry smile.

'Leave it with me, and I'll see what I can find out,' Rachel said. 'I'm sure it's just a matter of wrong place, wrong time.' But something in her gut told her the opposite was true. Matt was there for a reason . . . but she had no idea what it could be.

22

ISTANBUL

Hassan al-Britani and Abu Brutali stopped at the edge of the wall leading to the side entrance of Faisal Khan's hotel. Large drops of water pattered from the terracotta guttering overhead, the remnants of an early-morning shower that had since dissipated. Hassan listened for any movement around the corner of the wall. When he was confident it was clear, the two men crept through the archway and made their way down the side of the wall and around to the fire stairs.

The sound of the dawn call to prayer resonated softly across the sprawling city. The beautiful sound continued to increase in volume as it echoed from minaret to minaret and out into the suburbs and countryside.

The two Brits looked at each other in the shadows.

'I'll go first, you follow,' said Hassan.

'Right.'

Treading carefully, the pair climbed the stairs to the third floor. Before exiting the fire stairs, Hassan whispered, 'Faisal Khan is as cunning as a fox, Abu. I will open the door; if it's chained you need to smash it down and then finish him in quick time. If it's not chained, we go in quietly. Cover his face and kill him. Do you understand?'

'Yes,' said Abu as he took his silenced Glock from his jacket.

'Good – let's finish this then.'

Hassan made his way slowly to Faisal's door and took out the room card that he had been given the evening before. The concierge had asked no questions when offered a thousand US dollars for his troubles, especially since he had taken a similar bribe a few days prior from the Turkish secret police. It was his lucky year.

Hassan unlocked the door and gently pushed it open, relieved to find that there was no chain across it. Abu Brutali placed the silenced pistol back inside the suspender holster in his jacket and crept past. The giant British–Lebanese man moved with the stealth of someone a quarter of his size. Hassan moved in behind him and the two approached the double bed in the dark. Abu gently picked up a pillow to cover Faisal's face.

Suddenly Abu stopped and Hassan looked past him, squinting to try to make out what he had seen in the dark.

Abu looked around in panic and pulled the pistol back out of its holster. 'Shit, where is he?' he hissed.

Abu made for the lights and turned them on. They could both see that the bed had not been slept in. The bathroom door was closed; Abu flung it open. Nothing.

'He's not here, Hassan.'

'Yes, I can bloody well see that, Abu,' the smaller man fired back.

'Do you think he is at the mosque, perhaps?'

Hassan slapped his hand against his forehead. 'Yeah, of course he is. I should have thought of that. Okay, let's just grab the case and get the hell out of here. We can finish him another time.'

The two men looked around the room. Abu opened the wardrobe doors and Hassan looked behind the curtains. They searched everywhere, becoming more frantic as time dragged on.

'Where is it?' Hassan demanded.

'I don't know, but it has got to be here somewhere.'

Abu turned over the bed and then the couch in the corner. Behind the couch were two plastic bags. 'What have we here then?' said Abu, picking up one of the bags.

'Don't worry about it, Abu,' said Hassan impatiently. 'It's not the suitcase, is it?'

'No, it's not the suitcase – but it's explosives and plenty of it. Detonators and detonation cord, and this vest as well. It's military grade, too; that's some serious shit. There's a radio frequency device and a garage remote, too.'

'Cheeky fucker, isn't he? Right, put the couch back and the bed too. Are you sure we've searched everywhere? It's got to be here!'

'It's not here, Hassan – it's not here.'

'He must have taken it with him.'

'Or run off with it,' said Abu. 'Maybe he's double-crossed us.'

'Well, it's lucky we had the foresight to ensure we had a bargaining chip then, isn't it, Abu? Let's get out of here – I'll call him and see what the fuck he's playing at.'

• • •

Matt Rix placed the listening device receiver on the bedside table and quickly dialled JJ's number.

'Hey, mate, we've got a problem here – grab TC and come down to my room.'

'Be two minutes, boss.'

Matt hung up and looked again at the receiver, amazed by the conversation he had just heard take place in Faisal's room.

Shit . . . I'm not sure I like where this is going, he thought.

• • •

Hassan al-Britani and Abu Brutali left the Hotel New House the same way they had arrived. They walked in silence to the top of the street, where Hassan stopped and turned to face Abu. He waited for a couple of young men who had alighted from the tram to walk past. It was now just past six am and soon the streets of Sultanahmet would be alive again, crowded with people.

'We need to find Khan and get that case. If Steph smells a rat, we won't get out of this city alive, Abu, let alone this country.' Hassan pulled his phone out and punched in Faisal's number. It rang out. He tried again with the same result.

'Let's get down to the Sultan Ahmed Mosque. It's just down the road; perhaps the pious bastard is hanging around there after the early morning prayers.'

The two of them headed down the hill towards Sultanahmet Park.

• • •

From across the street, Faisal watched the two ISIS operatives walk away. He had been sitting at the small cafe since returning from prayers. He stretched his legs, grateful for the outdoor gas heater that stood above his table, then rubbed his hands together and shoved them in his shalwar kameez to protect them further against the cold. He had been on the verge of returning to his room when he'd thought better of the idea, and his caution had been rewarded on seeing the two Brits coming out unexpectedly. He drained his coffee then paid the bill and headed for the hotel.

23

The single knock at the door alerted Matt to their arrival. Todd and JJ were dressed and ready to go. In variations of blue jeans and black windbreakers, the two of them looked like they were special forces trying to disguise themselves as tourists, which of course they were. As they entered the room, JJ handed Matt a takeaway coffee from the cafe downstairs. The three men sat down on the couches arranged on either side of the low brown table next to the window.

'What's the situation then?' asked Todd.

'Well, about thirty minutes ago, the two Brit guys that Steph has working as part of her supposed "Afghan CIA cell" were in Faisal Khan's room looking for the case,' Matt said.

'Just a tad rude, arriving uninvited,' JJ remarked. 'I hope Khan killed them and them him?' He laughed.

'No such luck, mate; Khan wasn't even there – and neither was the case, by the sounds of it. They definitely had it in for him though, and it was obvious from what they were saying that they've turned against Steph. In any case, they didn't find the nuke, but they found some explosives – not that we should be surprised by that, given who we're dealing with.' Matt took a sip of coffee, he winced at how hot it was then looked up to the faces of the other two to gauge their reactions; they were both stony-faced and professional.

'So where's Khan gone?' asked Todd.

'I don't know where he went, but I do know where he is now: he's back in his room. I heard him come back and he's been pottering around, coughing and snorting and doing God knows what in there ever since.'

'Easy days then. Let's get in there and pick him up, you can contact Steph and we can deliver the nuke to the British military guys who took out the Russians.' JJ slapped his giant paw on his leg.

'Nope, that's not going to work. I think Khan has hidden the case. We need to keep monitoring him and be there during the handover. I have a feeling that Steph is being screwed by these guys.' Matt trailed off; he lifted the lid off the paper cup and blew softly into the coffee to cool it down. 'Why else would they turn up at Khan's room looking for the case from Khan when he was always going to give it to them in the first place? Other than them wanting this over quick, it just doesn't make any sense.'

'What have they got to gain by double-crossing Steph though?' JJ countered. 'That doesn't make any sense either.'

'Actually, it makes perfect sense.' Todd stood up. 'Think about it: they probably don't want the actual suitcase weapon at all. Steph might want to get it off the streets, or perhaps her job was to have the cell destroyed and recover the weapon, and that didn't happen.

Remember, those things are big and cumbersome and the chance of detection is pretty high. It would be very complex for them to actually deploy the weapon against any meaningful target. It's the plutonium that they're after. They couldn't conduct the exchange themselves, right? They're a couple of opportunistic lads from the UK; there's no way the Russians would trust them with it. But if these guys really do have access to ISIS, then they could use Khan as a front man to gain access to the nuke and then sell the stable plutonium for much more than they – or the CIA, I should say – paid for it. They must have thought all their Christmases had come at once when this fell into their laps. I wouldn't be surprised if they're part of a sleeper cell and Steph didn't do the due diligence on them in the first place. They know ISIS would have access to scientists who could then weaponise that plutonium. It's more than likely that they don't even want the weapon for use in the Middle East; it's probably destined for the States. It would be devastating.'

Matt looked at Todd, then JJ, then back to Todd. 'Jesus, TC – where did that come from?'

'Can you keep a secret, Matt?'

'Yeah, I guess I could start,' said Matt.

'What do you think the CIA and Green Berets were training to do during the Cold War? This exact same thing against the Russians. The CIA would infiltrate their ranks, steal their codes and weapons and then the Green Berets would deploy inside their territories to detonate their own weapons against them. It's a little more complicated than that, but you get the picture.'

'You need to ring Steph, Matt,' JJ said urgently. 'I mean, she needs to know what the hell is going on.'

'I agree,' said Todd. 'She might be able to get some real resources onto this before those arseholes get hold of the case. You have to hand it to your man Faisal though – he's not stupid.'

Matt took out his mobile and looked at the screen. 'I hate talking to this chick.'

'Just get it over with, boss,' JJ advised. 'Then we can wrap this mess up.'

Matt pressed the only number on the speed dial. The ring tone at the other end confirmed the international connection had been established, and a scrambled voice assured Matt the connection was secure.

'Matt, how's it all going?' Steph said. She sounded relaxed. He visualised her sitting in the high alpine town, looking smug over a cup of warm chocolate.

'Your guys are in the process of double-crossing Faisal Khan,' Matt declared without preamble. He waited for Steph to respond, but she didn't. 'Steph, did you hear me? They broke into his hotel room and would have killed him. Now they're after the case.'

'Yes, I heard you.' Her voice was faint. He heard her cough into her hand, away from the handset. 'What are you going on about, Matt? The last I heard from them was that the drop-off was going to be later on today. Job complete, everyone can go home.'

Trying to repress his irritation, Matt said, 'Listen, Steph, I'll spell it out slowly for you so you can keep up. Your boys had no intention of going through with the drop-off you'd arranged. They went to Khan's room early this morning and were planning to take the case by force – but he'd hidden it.'

'Wait – what? You're not joking, are you?'

'I heard them, Steph; I had a listening device in his room. I assume they're working for the Islamic State; it doesn't take a genius to work that out. Jesus, Steph – you've just bought ISIS a nuclear weapon.'

'No, that's impossible.' Steph muttered something inaudible and then lapsed into silence. Matt could hear her tapping something on her desk. After a few moments she said, 'Matt, are you still there?'

'Yes, of course I'm bloody here, I'm waiting for you to tell me the plan! And I'm here because you sent me here – and now there's a nuclear weapon floating around the streets of Istanbul! What are we going to do, Steph? Huh? Let me tell you a good place to start: we need some reinforcements over here asap and we need to seal the place shut. You need to inform your bosses to tell the White House that we've probably lost this thing and have them mobilise the Turkish military.'

Steph fell silent again. Matt looked at the enquiring faces of Todd and JJ and shrugged.

Finally, the CIA agent spoke. 'Matt, we haven't lost anything. You see, there was no mission.'

'What?! What the hell are you saying?' Matt snapped.

'I'm saying you're on your own, Matt. I don't know you, you don't know me. That's what I'm saying.'

'Don't you dare, Steph! We need to get this sorted. You can't run from this like you ran from Afghanistan.'

'Bye, Matt – until we meet again.'

'NO! I swear to God, I will kill you, you fucking bitch!' But he was talking to a dial tone. 'Jesus!' Matt threw the phone across the room and it hit the wall, hard.

'So, it sounds like that's all sorted then,' said JJ, getting slowly to his feet.

'She's dropped us in it; left us here with no support. Can you believe that?' Matt made a fist and thought about putting it through a wall. 'We can't run away from this; we need to get this bloody suitcase and secure it. We need to find those Brits who tried to intercept the handover, find out what their role is in this whole bloody mess.'

From the floor, Matt's phone started to ring.

'Change of heart, perhaps?' said JJ.

Todd picked up the phone and tossed it to Matt.

Matt looked at the number; he didn't recognise it, but he knew it was local. 'Hello?'

'Matt, it's Rachel.'

'What?' Matt took the phone from his ear and looked at the screen again, then put it back to his ear. 'What?' he repeated.

'We need to talk, Matt.'

'Now's not a good time, Rachel. I'll call you in a few days.'

'Wait – don't you want to know how I got your number?'

He blinked. It was a good question; what the hell was she doing calling on the phone that Steph had given him? 'I'm listening,' he said.

'We need to meet; there are some things we should discuss in person.'

Matt sighed and ran his hand through his hair. 'Rachel, like I said, this is going to have to wait. Seriously, I am under the pump here on an important job and just don't have the time to—'

'I know everything, Matt. You're trying to find a nuclear weapon – and so am I.'

Matt fell back onto the couch. He looked up at JJ, wide-eyed, shaking his head slowly from side to side in disbelief. 'Okay,' he said into the phone. 'I'm staying at the President Hotel. There's a cafe downstairs – we can meet in there.'

'Good, I'll be there in thirty minutes.'

She hung up and Matt dropped the phone into his lap. 'What the fuck is going on, JJ?' he said.

'Was that who I think it was?' JJ asked.

'Yeah. She's here in Istanbul, can you believe it? She said she's looking for the same thing I am; she actually said she's looking for a nuclear weapon, JJ. This is like a bloody nightmare.'

'Who was it?' asked Todd.

'That was Matt's ex-girlfriend from London, who apparently is a purveyor of fine nuclear devices now, or so it seems.'

'This is crazy. Why is she here?' Matt rubbed his eyes with the heels of his hands.

Todd clapped his hands together. 'Right, so how about this for a plan? While you're catching up with your ex, JJ and I will go and shadow your pal Faisal; we can keep an eye on him and intercept the others if they try to take him again.'

'Yes, good, do that.' Matt was staring at the wall, his mind ticking over as he tried to piece together the last half-hour in his mind. He pointed to the shelf next to the TV. 'Take the receiver with you, so you can listen to his hotel room.' Matt got up and grabbed the pen and notepad from the bedside table. He scribbled down Faisal Khan's hotel address and room number and passed it to Todd.

Todd studied it and stuffed it in his jacket pocket. 'Let's factor in some scheds,' he suggested. 'Every hour on the hour we'll send a WhatsApp message to each other with our location; I'll make the group now. Make sure you provide a brief SITREP. Lost communications, we meet back in the lobby here as primary, Starbucks is the secondary. Got it?'

'Yeah, okay. That's good, Todd,' said Matt.

Todd and JJ left. Matt went into the bathroom and washed his face with warm water. He looked at his reflection in the mirror; he was fitter, stronger and looked more relaxed than he had a few years earlier when he was chasing Faisal Khan and Objective Rapier across the bad lands of Afghanistan. He reminded himself that he was in control of this situation. Brushing his hair back with his hands he took a deep breath. This mission had turned into a right cock up and now he needed to take hold of it and own it.

He heard his phone ring again in the other room and he strode in to pick it up. It was the same number that Rachel had rung from previously.

'Hi.'

'Hey, I'm downstairs,' said Rachel. 'There was no traffic on the road. What room are you in? It might be better to discuss this in private – there are a few people down here in the lobby.'

Matt told her the room number.

'Okay, I'm coming up now.' She hung up and Matt flashed a look across at the safe. He was in two minds as to whether to get out the pistol or not. Who the hell was she? Could he even trust her? Would she be alone? Why was she even here?

Matt paced up and down the room, his mind racing. Even though he was expecting it, the knock at the door made him jump.

Looking through the peephole he could see Rachel standing there. A black jacket covered one of her hands – the right. Standing flat against the wall to keep his body out of the line of fire, he reached for the door handle opened the heavy door slowly. Matt tensed, ready to grab her arm as she entered.

But Rachel didn't waste a second; she pushed straight past him and strode purposefully in the room. 'So imagine my surprise when I see that you're in Turkey,' she said, tossing the jacket she'd been holding onto the couch.

'What? *You're* surprised? What are you doing here, Rachel?'

He looked her up and down as she spun to face him. Dressed in bone-coloured moleskins, a dark blouse and black high heels, she looked like the last person in the world to be blithely talking about nuclear weapons. Her hair was pulled back in a loose ponytail and her cheeks were rosy from the cold outside.

'I guess we both have some explaining to do. It's about time I came clean with you.' She put her hands on her hips. 'I work for the British government. That guy you bumped into in the alley, he's with me.'

Matt felt the colour drain out of his face. 'What do you mean you work for the government?'

'I'm MI6, Matt. I have been since before we met.' She turned away from him and walked over to the lounge.

'Jesus, you can't be serious,' Matt said, following her. 'I thought you were in import and exports. Why didn't you say something?'

'And what would I say, exactly? I was hardly going to blow my cover on a guy who can't even commit.' She turned back to face him front on. 'So why are *you* here, Matt?'

Matt moved past her and over to the window. He gazed down at the small market stalls in the street below. The traders were in full swing now, hawking their wares to the early-morning crowds on their way to work.

He shook his head. 'I'm not sure, to be honest. It's all such a mess. This CIA agent, Steph Baumer, she tasked me with following this Afghan who was facilitating the exchange of the weapon from the Russian to her people in Afghanistan. Now she's ditched me because the guys that she had working for her have gone rogue and are trying to secure the weapon for themselves. I suspect they're working for or on behalf of ISIS.'

'I wondered if that was the case,' said Rachel.

Matt felt his eyebrows shoot up.

'Don't look so surprised, Matt – I've been monitoring this for a while.'

Matt dropped his face into his hands. 'Seriously, what the hell have I done, Rachel? I must be in a bloody dream. In the last three weeks, I've lost my job, my platoon – fuck, I've lost my whole identity. And now I've lost a nuclear fucking bomb! Jesus, Rachel – I've lost everything.'

'No, you haven't lost everything – not yet, Matt. You haven't lost me.'

He looked at her standing there: open, honest, vulnerable. At that moment, Matt felt ashamed of the way he had treated her; always keeping her at arm's length, never making her his priority. It was no wonder she had broken up with him. Yet he could see now the effort it had cost her; the strength it had taken for her to let him go. Matt remembered again the last time they had made love. It was on their final trip to Italy together as a couple. He had thought about it many times since.

They had finished dinner and had a little too much to drink. She made some joke about paper-thin walls and he had laughed and said that she moaned in English and that no one would understand her anyway. He moved in towards her and held her head with his hands. He kissed her softly on the lips, at first gently and then they both became more urgent.

He had pushed her back onto the bed and held her down by her slim shoulders while he kissed her open mouth. Their tongues met in unison and then he trailed wet kisses down her soft cheeks and neck. Her breathing became hard against his ear. Matt grabbed a large handful of breast and squeezed her through her shirt. She moaned encouragingly to him, as he undid her trousers with his free hand. She was equally as accommodating and had his cargos off and down his legs, using her foot to take them the final way past his feet.

Both had become more urgent and clawed at each other. He gently pulled her lacy knickers to one side, surprised at how wet she already was, and as he did she reached down and guided him towards her. He pushed slowly at first and then sank himself completely inside her. Rachel gasped at the sensation, pushing her hips high in the air to meet him. Matt paused, savouring her tightness and then began to move in and out of her in slow rhythmic strokes. He ground himself tight against her pelvic bone and adjusted the angle so that he maintained the pressure, she writhed underneath him.

Their tempo increasing and their breathing becoming hard, Rachel slid her hands under the back of his blue t-shirt and clawed at his skin as he started to slam relentlessly inside her. She loved that and Matt knew it. He knew exactly how she liked it. The urgency of their actions and the realisation of their pent-up frustrations made Matt finally release inside her. His body became taught above her, as his head collapsed against her neck and then on feeling his release she arrived with him, swearing softly in his ear and shuddering to completion.

They had laid there for what felt like forever, holding each other.

'I love you, Matt,' she said. It brought him back to the present.

'I know you do.' He paused, thinking of how to reply. 'I love *us*, Rachel.'

She smiled. 'Well, now we've got that sorted, I've got to get back to work. Perhaps you should come with me, I can bring you up to speed on the situation. You can bring your friends as well.'

He frowned. 'What do you mean?'

She nodded towards the coffee table. The three takeaway cups he, Todd and JJ had been drinking from were still there.

'Right, of course,' Matt said. He had never given her enough credit, he realised. He didn't really know her at all, while she seemed to see right through him. 'I'll give them a call now.'

24

ISTANBUL

Faisal eyed the latest of the listening devices that he had found. This one he had discovered in his jacket. He tossed it into the laundry bag with the other two and the tracking device. This time he ripped the place apart looking for evidence of any others, then, satisfied there were no more, sat at the small desk on one side of the dark hotel room and stroked his short beard. He considered the laundry bag, then shifted his gaze to the Adidas sports bag, which now contained the cylinder of plutonium. He allowed himself to imagine the havoc that could be wreaked by this, the sheer scale of death and destruction, then he thought about his son – a boy he had never really known.

Jumping up, Faisal pulled the small couch back from the wall and reached for the plastic bag containing the chest rig and explosives. He contemplated his next move as he ran his prayer beads through the fingers of his left hand. Allah was guiding him, of that he was now sure.

His train of thought was interrupted by the ringing of his phone. Taking it out of his pocket, he checked the number. His eyes darted to the door and then the balcony. He grabbed the Browning 9mm from the table as he answered the call. 'Yes?'

'Faisal, it's Hassan al-Britani.'

'I know who it is.' Faisal looked through the peephole of the door.

There was silence for a moment. Faisal wondered if the beast, Abu Brutali, was with Hassan. He could hear voices in the background, some of them speaking in Arabic and some in Turkish. He suspected that Hassan was still down at the Blue Mosque, based on the direction they had headed earlier.

'Where are you, Faisal?'

'I'm down by the water,' Faisal lied, walking back to the middle of the room. 'I thought it would be best if I kept a low profile.'

'Where's the suitcase?'

'It's in my room.'

'Don't play games with me, Faisal. Now tell me where the hell it is, or so help me God I will—'

'Don't be so sure my God will help you,' Faisal spat back.

He moved to the sliding door and, holding the Browning at chest height to cover himself, gently eased back one of the curtains to check that no one had climbed onto the balcony while he was talking.

'Why don't you explain to me why you were in my room earlier, Hassan? We had an agreement and now that I have the weapon, I'm not so sure that you're going to uphold your end of the bargain.'

'I swear to God, Faisal, your son is dead if I don't get that case.'

'Like I said, the case is in my room – but I have the plutonium cylinder with me, Hassan. You release my son and I will give you the cylinder and then tell you where the case is hidden.'

Faisal looked again at the laundry bag containing the listening devices. It dawned on him suddenly that they mustn't have been planted by Hassan. If they had, the Brit would know that Faisal was in his room. This meant there was a third party involved – probably the men who had killed the Russians. It was only a matter of time before they, too, showed up looking for the suitcase.

'You think you're so smart, don't you, Faisal? Well, you had better listen to what I'm saying. We need you to give us that cylinder; it's Allah's will, Faisal. You were selected for this mission and, to be honest, I don't give a fuck if you live or die, or your son either, for that matter.'

Faisal put the phone on speaker and placed it on the desk in front of him. He loosened his white shirt and pulled it over his head. 'I am listening, Hassan, and I understand what I have to do,' he said.

'Good. I knew you would come to your senses.'

Faisal picked up the suicide vest, placed it over his head and secured the straps. 'Where shall we meet then?'

'The prophet Mohammed himself, peace be upon him, said that the first Muslim to pray in the Hagia Sophia would go directly to paradise. I think that would be an appropriate place for us to meet.'

'Very well.' Faisal pulled his long white shirt back over his head and started to do up the buttons.

'Be there at five pm – and bring the cylinder, Faisal. Once you hand it over we will release your son. I proclaim in front of the mighty Allah that he will be free. You have my word. Once you hand it over your business with me is done, do you understand?'

Faisal looked at the time on his phone, three pm, plenty of time. He caught his reflection in the mirror as he placed the dark waistcoat over his shirt. 'Yes, I understand what I must do.' Faisal took the battery out of the garage remote and then placed his hand inside the bottom of the shirt and screwed in the small radio frequency receiver. He would put the battery back in the remote later, when the time came.

'Good – I will see you then, Faisal. God willing, you will do what I ask of you.'

'I will do what Allah requires.'

Faisal ended the call. He grabbed the silver cylinder out of the bag and unscrewed the three screws on the top. Taking the lid off, he tipped the cylinder upside down and a smaller dark cylinder dropped out into his hands. The protective casing was now all that separated him and anyone else from a radioactive death. He stashed the plutonium in a pillow and then repeated the process he'd gone through earlier to get the pillow and plutonium up into the ceiling with the suitcase. Next, Faisal opened the minibar fridge and took out two cans of soft drink. He inserted one into the silver cylinder and then stuffed some toilet paper in before placing the second can inside. He weighed the cylinder in his hand then, satisfied, closed it back up and screwed the lid shut. He placed the cylinder in his sports bag and checked his watch.

For a moment, Faisal considered taking the Browning with him, but decided against it. As he moved over to the safe to stash the pistol, something on the bed caught his eye. He turned his head in time to see his iPhone backlight go out. He froze, watching it. Nothing happened, and he assumed his mind must have been playing tricks on him. But as Faisal took another step towards the safe the backlight came on again. His heart began to beat in panic, for Faisal knew exactly what this meant: his phone was being tracked.

25

GEBZE, TURKEY

Matt jumped out of the small Ford Transit, JJ and Todd close behind. He looked around the industrial warehouse; the set-up was not dissimilar to what he had seen when he was on tactical assault duties. Vehicles were lined up one each side of the door, military on one side and civilian vehicles on the other. They were all reversed in, as was the practice. The SBS guys had laid out a set of gear beside each vehicle, in their team order, ready for them to throw on and roll out the door at a moment's notice.

Rachel led the two Australians and the American over to where the SBS guys were busy checking their second set of gear, adjusting lightweight body armour and preparing weapon configurations. Matt could tell they were readying themselves for an airmobile operation.

'Matt Rix, this is Glyn Thomas, the SBS troop commander,' said Rachel by way of introduction.

Matt weighed up the English officer in front of him. An inch taller than Matt and probably a few years younger, Glyn's athleticism was clear; obviously, he had been training consistently for the duration of his adult life and he had the looks of a male model. Matt put his hand out to shake Glyn's and Glyn offered a fist. There was a moment of confusion before Matt cottoned on and the two did a small fist bump.

'Nice to meet you, old chap,' Glyn said in a snooty British accent.

'Right,' said Matt. He looked around at Glyn's men, who were all eyeing him suspiciously. 'This is Todd, and this big fella here is JJ.'

Glyn greeted the two men in turn. He didn't pay much attention to Todd, but he showed interest in JJ. 'You *are* a big lad, aren't you? What the hell are they feeding you Down Under?' Glyn glanced over at his men and smirked. He picked up his silenced Heckler & Koch and checked it was clear before placing a magazine on and cocking the action.

'British backpackers mostly,' JJ replied easily. 'They come Down Under looking for a decent root.'

The SBS guys sniggered and Glyn screwed up his face. 'How charming,' he said.

'C'mon, Bear,' said JJ. 'I thought you'd find that funny.'

'Bear?' Glyn frowned. 'Whatever are you talking about?'

'Bear Grylls, of course. He's SBS, right? You look just like the goofy bastard. I bet you're an asset in a survival situation where you have to drink your own piss too.'

Matt watched Glyn's reaction to JJ's ribbing and gave a bit of a chuckle. If there was one thing Matt could count on, it was that JJ would try to get a rise out of someone he thought was a pretender or who was acting above their station.

'He was territorial SAS, not regular SAS, and definitely not SBS; and I don't look anything like him, I'll have you know.'

'Oh well, if you say so – you seem to be the expert on such matters. A hero of yours, is he?'

'That's what I love about you Australians, everything is a joke.'

JJ grinned and looked across at Glyn's men. They were all smiling waiting for his comeback. 'Well, you know what they say, pal, laughter is the best medicine, and from what I can see your face is curing the world.'

Rachel interjected, 'Glyn, we know where the Afghan is who took the case – Matt has been tracking him. If we get set up now we might be able to trap him in that location.'

Glyn leaned back against the Land Cruiser and shook his head.

'The bird's already flown the coop, I'm afraid. He's on the move now and so are we.'

'I don't understand,' said Rachel. 'What do you mean he's on the move?'

'The intel guys came back to me while you were out. Just as we'd discussed, Rachel, we picked up all the handsets, matched their caller profiles over the past few days and identified the handset that fled the scene – as well as yours, Matt, of course.' Glyn smiled.

Matt narrowed his eyes at the sly dig, knowing full well that a state-sponsored force would have that capability. He had reasoned that watching Faisal Khan, and even being in vicinity of the Russians, would not require him to ditch technology to fly under the radar; however, he hadn't counted on the British being there.

Glyn zipped up his flight suit. 'About ten minutes ago, the Afghan left his hotel in Istanbul. He's in a vehicle now. We haven't got any eyes on yet, but based on the direction we think he's heading to

Sabiha Gökçen airport. It's slow going in the city traffic, but once he gets on the freeway it will clear up.'

'So you think Khan's fleeing the country by air?' Matt shook his head at the thought.

'Oh, is that his name? Yes, well either that or the airport is most probably the target.'

'What? Don't be daft, mate – there's no way Khan is going to detonate a nuclear bomb in Istanbul. Why on earth would he? What has he got to gain? That's not the type of guy he is.' Matt looked to Rachel for support.

Glyn turned to address Rachel. 'Major Faruk has gone to organise some helicopters for us – Bell 412s from the Gendarmerie. They should be here soon. We can get a fix on the vehicle this Khan character is in with the support of the Turkish intelligence service.' He turned back to Matt. 'I can't go into how they do that – it's top secret – but we can vector on to the exact vehicle.'

Matt glanced across at Todd, who simply rolled his eyes. 'Top secret, no worries, Glyn,' Matt said. 'Understood.'

'Right, so can we grab some kit, get suited up?' said JJ, moving towards the weapons table.

Glyn held his arm out. 'Not so fast. How about we let the big boys sort this mess out. I think you three have done enough already, don't you?'

JJ pushed Glyn's arm away. 'You know what, Glyn, I'm jealous of all the people who haven't met you yet.'

He looked at Matt, who turned to Rachel. 'Tell this guy to back off, will you, Rachel?' said Matt.

'I think he's right, Matt. The duly authorised sovereign forces need to take care of this. I have no authority to allow . . . what are you now, anyway? Vigilantes, I guess. Well, I can't allow you to take part, I'm sorry.'

Glyn winked at Matt and then smiled at Rachel. They held each other's gaze for a little longer than was necessary, Matt thought, surprised by a surge of jealousy.

'Oh, right, I get it,' Matt said. 'You fancy her, don't you?'

'What's not to fancy?' said Glyn, standing straighter and taking a step forward.

Matt stood taller too, flexing his shoulders. 'Why don't you ask her how she knows me, see if she fancies you nearly as much?'

'Matthew!' Rachel struck out at him with both palms hitting him in the chest.

Matt took a single step back to steady himself, pivoting towards Glyn slightly, hoping to provoke a reaction from the English dickhead, so that he would be justified in teaching him a lesson in front of his men.

'Seriously, how dare you say that?' Rachel demanded. 'Who do you think you are? Go, leave – just go and sit in the other room with your mates and keep out of our way.'

Glyn put his hand on her shoulder.

'If you don't go and sit down, Matt,' she continued, 'I will have no option but to have you arrested.'

'I see, so I guess loyalty is a one-way street then, is it?'

'Just go, Matt. You're hardly in a position to be talking about loyalty, are you?'

Matt looked around at Glyn's men, all standing now and all armed. 'Right, I'll leave you to it then.' He gestured to JJ and Todd. 'C'mon, lads, looks like we're sitting this one out.'

Matt walked away fuming, closely followed by Todd and JJ.

The warehouse remained deathly silent save for the footsteps of the three men.

Outside, a gentle humming slowly morphed into the screaming of whirring rotor blades as three Bell 412 helicopters came to rest in the field adjacent to the industrial complex.

Matt closed the door of the small lunchroom behind the three of them. He could hear the troops, who had just finished dressing in their combat equipment, shouting orders and running from their vehicles to the waiting aircraft. No matter what impression he had gained of Glyn, there was no doubting these were among the best special forces operators in the world and Faisal Khan was doomed; no prisoners would be taken in an operation as important as this. Matt felt strangely saddened; he had never truly understood Khan, and while he had been a hell of a thorn in Matt's side when he was hunting Objective Rapier in Afghanistan in 2010, he couldn't help but feel there was more to Faisal Khan than met the eye. After all, Steph had her claws in him as well.

The drone of the loitering aircraft increased as Glyn's men lifted off then faded into a gentle humming again as they disappeared.

The door opened a crack and Rachel peered in. Matt looked up from the small table where he and the other two had pulled up chairs.

'I'm sorry, Matt. You know I can't authorise you to be a part of this – you do understand, right?'

'It's got nothing to do with that. It's the way you look at him.' Matt stood up and moved over to the sink, where he switched on the kettle and started to search for tea bags. 'Jesus, you would think there would be tea bags in here, wouldn't you?'

'Try the door above the fridge,' Rachel suggested.

Matt did as she advised. 'Here they are – thanks.'

'God, you guys are like an old married couple,' JJ exclaimed. 'Explain to me again why you're not hooked up already?' He looked across at Todd and the two of them laughed.

'Shut up, JJ,' said Matt. He looked over at Rachel, who was smiling at him, and he felt himself grow calm again. 'Who wants a brew?'

'Go on then, skipper,' said JJ.

'Strong black coffee for me if it's on offer, Matt,' said Todd.

'Sure.' Matt smiled at the big American.

'I'm going upstairs to monitor the situation; this should be sorted fairly quickly now,' said Rachel. 'Once the debrief is over I'll have my staff organise your flights home – or maybe you want to come to London, Matt? If you still have a few days off, that is . . .' She trailed off, looking down at her feet.

Matt leaned back against the sink and smiled at her. 'Yeah, that would be nice. Didn't you promise something about big fires and even bigger glasses of red?'

Rachel closed the door and left the three men alone. Matt handed the hot drinks to the other two and plonked himself down again. They sat for a moment in silence.

'I just don't get it. All those listening devices went dead and the tracking device showed that he hadn't moved, but now they say they're tracking him going to the airport?' said JJ.

'I had to laugh when Glyn kept saying they were tracking him and not that they were tracking his handset,' said Todd, taking a slug of black coffee. 'There's a big difference.'

'You think it's a come-on?' said Matt.

'Of course it is; experience in Afghanistan tells me that. And in any case, he wouldn't get the nuke through the airport – that's just stupid.'

'We can't discount his hotel room, boss,' said JJ.

'I agree, mate.'

'Plenty of hire cars out there; no doubt the keys are in the ignition ready for a quick response. I don't think they'll miss one for a few hours. Actually, they'd probably prefer it if we were out of their hair when they get back.' JJ smiled.

Matt jumped up and slammed down the rest of his warm tea. 'It wouldn't be the first time we've operated off reservation – let's do this.'

26

ISTANBUL

The Bell 412s rose high above the Istanbul traffic. First heading to the south and then adjusting their direction around to the north-east, the three dark grey aircraft flew two up and one back with about twenty metres separating them. Their rotors thumped through the low-hanging clouds and the small wipers on the front windscreens swiped back and forth, seemingly useless against the ever-present drizzle.

Glyn's aircraft was in the rear. He looked across at his signaller, sitting in a seat on the back wall of the aircraft, busy punching frequencies into his radio in an effort to ensure that the teams could all communicate. Stuart Ganley, his team sniper, sat in front of Glyn in the open door, while Major Faruk and an intelligence analyst with the locating equipment sat in the aircraft's newly configured centre seating. The other two aircraft carried the remaining men separated into two teams.

Stu adjusted his position. The heavy SR-25 sniper rifle lay across his lap and was tethered to the ceiling by a long green retractable cord. When conducting these types of operations back in the UK, with aircraft devoted to the CT squadron, he would have a thick padded bar across the door cavity; then he could rest the weapon on the bar and take some of the weight from his shoulders.

The two front aircraft started to track to the north, leaving Glyn's aircraft continuing on, heading towards the freeway and then out over the sea. The aircraft gained another hundred metres of altitude. Glyn watched as his assault force moved away in the other two aircraft to follow the line of hills in the distance. From this point his aircraft would seek out the target vehicle and then they would call the assault force forward.

Glyn tapped Major Faruk on the shoulder and indicated for him to put on the headset that was hanging on a hook behind the seat in front of him. 'Can you hear me?' He cupped his hand around the microphone on his own headset to shield it from the wind.

'Yes. I can hear you.'

'That's the main freeway to the airport, right?' Glyn pointed to the busy road below and adjusted the folds in his city map. He spun the map around and orientated it so that the freeway was on the aircraft's left side.

'That's it, yes.' Major Faruk leaned forward and had a good look at the roads below. He moved his head back into the aircraft out of the wind. 'How will we find the vehicle in among all the others?'

Glyn smiled at his signaller, Simon Reid. Simon was listening to a handset while watching a small screen on the front of a militarised olive drab box. He looked across to Glyn and gave him a thumbs-up.

'It's all taken care of,' said Glyn turning to the Turkish liaison officer.

Major Faruk nodded noncommittally then looked back out the open doors of the aircraft.

Simon was busy talking back to the warehouse, checking and crosschecking the information being provided to him by Rachel's staff. Rachel's staff had access to the whole suite of tools available to MI6. Satellite images, triangulation of data packets being sent and received from Faisal Khan's handset, traffic flow and congestion information – all this was being fielded by them and sent on to Simon. It wouldn't be long before the vehicle was identified; then it would be up to the pilots to find the best place to interdict it. They would need an opening of about thirty metres in front of the vehicle and a smaller opening behind it to lock it in place. The manoeuvre would be made trickier by the overhead wires and billboards dotted along the freeway.

Simon placed the handset to his radio pack between his knees and gestured to Glyn, who removed one of the earphones and leaned down slightly so that he could hear the update.

'We have a lock on the target vehicle; it's a van of some type.' Simon looked back at the screen, adjusting the resolution as the aircraft went through a darker bank of clouds.

'Sir!' Glyn tapped Major Faruk on the shoulder and moved closer to the Turkish officer's ear to be heard over the engines. 'Ask the pilots what speed we're travelling.'

Faruk undid his seatbelt and moved forward to talk to the pilots. 'Ninety knots,' came the reply.

Glyn referred to his map again. At ninety knots, they were moving at around 2.8 kilometres a minute, meaning they would intercept the vehicle in fourteen minutes or thereabouts. He calculated the vehicle's speed and how far ahead it would be in fourteen minutes and then selected an area for the intercept. It was only estimation, but it would have to do.

'At that point it's a two-lane highway in each direction,' he observed. 'It looks like the traffic is spread out around there.' Glyn pointed to an area of the map just past an interchange. 'Finding an opening might be tough though.'

Major Faruk nodded and shrugged his shoulders. 'We will just have to make it work.'

Glyn thought about it for a moment. The trained pilots of the Naval Air Squadron, especially the dedicated 815 flight, would be able to jam their aircraft into the smallest of spaces and force the vehicle to a stop; it would be over in seconds. Glyn didn't have the same faith in the Turkish police pilots, though – especially given that he would need to communicate through Major Faruk.

Glyn grabbed the small bone microphone from inside his flight suit and placed it into his right ear, and then he readjusted the large inboard earphones over the top. Turning the volume down on the earphones, so that the pilots talking in Turkish didn't distract him, Glyn looked down at his body armour, located his patrol radio and switched the channels to the all-informed network. He immediately heard his team commanders in the other two aircraft talking to each other, discussing their tactics once on the ground. 'This is Alpha Actual, prepare for update and quick radio orders, over.'

Glyn studied his map further while his men acknowledged his communication. Removing a pen from his flight suit pocket, he circled an area about three kilometres short of the airport between two fuel stations. He put the pen between his teeth and lifted the map up close to his face to study it further. The wind battered the map around and he placed it on his thighs, locking it in place with his knees. He then drew a line about a further kilometre forward and the military symbol for a blocking position; this would be set as his limit of exploitation. If they hadn't interdicted the vehicle before this point he would have the pilots move here and they would stop all the traffic with two of the aircraft and have the third aircraft chase Khan if he tried to escape on foot in the resulting traffic jam.

Glyn passed the map to Major Faruk and tapped the two locations; Faruk nodded his understanding and moved forward to brief the pilots.

Glyn keyed the presser switch on his fist microphone. 'Fairly standard interdiction, lads. My aircraft will conduct a positive ID of the target and we'll be the initial roadblock. If Stuart can make a positive ID of the individual, he will engage as per the rules of engagement for Global Pursuit. Bluey, yours and the remainder of my team under the command of Simon will land as close as you can to the rear of the target vehicle. I want a solid cordon to the rear and sides. Approach with caution in pairs. Have the pilots try to synchronise with us if you can, Bluey.'

'Acknowledged, sir.'

'Good, and one more thing: we need to be careful if he wants to fight back. Head shots only and make them count; there are going to be people everywhere – not to mention the fact that he has a nuclear weapon in his possession.'

Glyn looked off to his left and could just make out the other two aircraft flying side by side above the hills. Glyn's own aircraft moved from over the sea and back inland to intercept the freeway. Glyn gave Stuart the thumbs-up. Stuart checked the restraining bungy and adjusted his sit harness, testing the resistance. He opened the sight covers and positioned the rifle on his shoulder, moving his head to get a good eye relief. The weapon and firer were ready to engage.

'That's it, that's the vehicle!' Simon yelled to Glyn. He looked down again at the softly illuminated screen and confirmed it with the tracking system, then pointed at the black van up ahead.

Major Faruk moved forward once again to talk to the pilots and they adjusted their speed to match the vehicle's speed, giving Glyn time to weigh up the situation and come up with the final interdiction plan.

Glyn looked up ahead and saw the open area between the fuel stations approaching in the distance. 'That's the spot – tell them to get in front and land at that spot there!' Glyn yelled.

Faruk relayed this to the pilots. The aircraft picked up speed and started to descend. Looking out the side of the Bell 412, Glyn saw that the other two aircraft were now approaching behind them, fast.

Stuart skidded on his side against the movement of the aircraft, the SR-25 trained on the vehicle as the helicopter raced up beside it. 'I can't see anything through the windows.'

'What? What did you say?!' Glyn couldn't hear Stuart over the thumping wind coming in the side of the aircraft.

Stuart turned his head to face Glyn, to ensure his message got through. 'The windows of the van are too dark, I can't see who's in the back,' he yelled.

'Tell the pilots to drop in on him, Faruk. Now!'

Major Faruk leaned into the cockpit and pointed out the clear area ahead. The Bell 412 lurched as the pilot followed the instructions, and for a moment the aircraft seemed weightless as the blades changed pitch. Then it was turning and flaring at the same time. Glyn gripped either side of his seat to hold himself in place, quietly impressed at the pilots' commitment to getting the aircraft down onto the ground.

Stuart grabbed the top of the harness and adjusted the buckle, releasing himself from its grip. He struggled against the g-force and switched sides, then tensioned the harness again, repositioning himself and his SR-25 should he need to get a shot away from the other side of the aircraft.

As the Bell 412 dropped into the speeding traffic Glyn saw the vehicles in front of and behind the grey aircraft coming to a stop. Most of the drivers' mouths were agape, passengers' faces pressed up against the windows as they struggled to make sense of the situation unfolding in front of them.

The aircraft came to a stop twenty metres ahead of the black minivan, throwing up dust and debris into the already grey sky. Tiny stones hit the rotors, making little sparks as the blades spun.

As the grey dust cloud cleared Glyn could see the van driver clearly through his front window, his hands on the steering wheel and the vehicle now stopped. Down the road the other two aircraft had also landed, forcing a gap in the flow of traffic. Glyn's men were now racing in pairs towards the minivan. The men ran around the now-stationary cars, paying them no attention as they moved towards their intended target with their weapons up in the shoulder, looking through their scopes. They surrounded the vehicle and, before anyone watching could even comprehend what was occurring, a sound and flash grenade went off in front of the car, thrown by one of the assaulters. Two men on either side of the vehicle smashed their reaming tools into the door windows in time to the explosions occurring in front. The SBS assaulter's arms were inside the vehicle, the doors thrown open. The driver was unceremoniously dragged from the front of the car and man-handled to the ground, the huge Tongan straddling his back and pinning him down. The call came to Glyn that there was no one else in the vehicle.

'What?' He turned to the intel analyst. 'We must have the wrong vehicle, Simon.'

'No, that's definitely it,' the signaller insisted.

Glyn climbed out of the helicopter. Stuart unclipped and followed his commander. Both men pulled their balaclavas down over their faces as they walked towards the minivan.

Simon followed behind, staring at the screen, the signal getting stronger the nearer they got to the vehicle. 'This is it, sir. One hundred percent lock on this vehicle confirmed.'

Bluey held up a laundry bag. 'Only thing in the car, sir – and I suspect this is his phone that we found in it.'

'Ah, for fuck's sake,' said Glyn. 'We've been played.'

'We sure have,' his 2IC agreed. 'We shouldn't have fallen for it, Glyn. That's no good at all. And if you don't mind me saying so, if you were a little less focused on that MI6 lass and more focused on the task, I think we would have played this a whole lot better.' Bluey was red in the face and Glyn sensed he wanted to say a lot more than he had.

'This hasn't been entirely straightforward, Bluey. The intelligence pointed to him making a run for it and—'

'That Australian commando seemed pretty sure that Faisal Khan wouldn't be making a run for the airport, but you were too busy having a pissing competition with him to recognise the fact that he might just know a thing or two about this guy.'

Glyn opened his mouth to reply, but was interrupted by the arrival of Major Faruk.

'The police are on their way; I suggest you go back to the warehouse and I will handle them at this end. Once we question the taxi driver, I will let you know what information he has.'

Glyn nodded curtly. 'Let's wrap this up, Bluey. We can continue this conversation later.'

'I've said my piece, sir,' Bluey told him. 'Let's get back to the warehouse and get the vehicles ready. I suspect we're going to be heading back to Sultanahmet.' Bluey motioned for the others to get back on the helicopters and the lads followed his lead.

Glyn lifted himself back into his seat on the Bell 412, followed by the rest of his team.

This mission is turning into a farce, he thought.

27

ISTANBUL

The Turkish security officer was in the middle of delivering his punch-line to his two bored colleagues as Hassan al-Britani approached the gate of the Hagia Sophia. Hassan moved over to the two long plastic benches and opened his backpack. The guard kept talking as he put a hand in Hassan's bag and moved the contents around.

'What's this?' The guard stopped mid joke and pulled out a small black box, no bigger than a cigarette packet. He held it up, studying the device.

'That's a Netcom hard drive,' said Hassan. 'University essays and readings, that sort of thing.' His blue jeans and New York Yankees baseball cap gave credence to his claim to be a student. This wasn't the first time he had been to the museum that week and he knew how complacent the staff could be at the end of the day. Indeed, this was the first time that his bag had been checked; he was glad he had left his weapon behind.

The guard lost interest. Dropping the black box back into the bag, he waved Hassan through and finished his joke, laughing along with the others. Nothing exciting ever happened here – mostly because of the two vans of tactical police that were permanently stationed between the Hagia Sophia and the Blue Mosque, but also because of the significance of the building itself. First built in 537 as a Greek Orthodox church, it had changed hands between Greeks and Catholic crusaders and then, in 1453, become an Ottoman Empire mosque. Now a museum, the mosque was rich in religious history and tradition and had been largely overlooked in recent years by those who had less than wholesome agendas. Relatively speaking, a meeting between ISIS thugs and a Taliban intelligence officer was an insignificant moment in that rich history.

Hassan closed his bag and showed the local security officer his museum all-access pass.

Abu Brutali followed close behind him, looking down at his smart phone the entire time, giving the security guard only the most cursory of glances and a nod. He wore Western clothes too: black Nike runners, sweatpants and a white jumper that hid the top of a six-inch dagger. He wore a Canon camera around his massive neck. The two of them looked like a couple of British Lebanese lads on holiday, which was exactly the point. Breezing past the security they walked around a small tour group of Europeans marvelling over the remains of the original church near the entrance and made their way towards the outdoor kiosk.

Hassan purchased a bottle of water and then the two of them entered the building through the giant wooden doors that once sealed the cathedral shut from intruders and opened only to welcome the most important of visitors.

'Let's go up here, to the top level in the back corner.' Hassan led the way up the stone staircase that would take them to the upper levels of the museum.

'So, we get the stuff from Khan and then what?' Brutali asked.

'We get the plutonium, yes.' Hassan frowned at the giant. 'And then you take care of him. We can't have someone like him out there on the loose with a vendetta against us, regardless of his faith. You can have your fun with him – just make it quiet and quick.'

Brutali smiled and adjusted the blade against his thigh. 'That's a given.'

Hassan put his bag on the ground and kneeled down to open it. He pulled out the small black box, screwed in three small antennas and switched the device on.

'What makes you think he's coming armed?' asked Brutali. 'That we would need something like that, I mean.' He nodded at the box.

'Why else would he have had that suicide vest hidden behind the couch? He's coming ready for anything.'

'You sure that thing is going to work, Hassan?'

'It will work as long as he sticks to his usual pattern. If it doesn't work, none of us will know about it until we are at the feet of Allah.' Hassan put the device back in the bag and stood up.

'I would just prefer to stay a while longer in this life, Hassan. So much killing of infidels yet to be done.' Brutali laughed and pulled out the blade, spinning it around in his fingers.

'Put that away,' Hassan hissed.

Hassan looked over the edge of the balcony and then up at the huge dome of the mosque. Most of the visitors were starting to leave now.

'There he is!'

• • •

Rounding a corner on the top floor of the museum, Faisal spotted his two British adversaries. He was confident it would be just them. He had sent whoever was tracking his phone on a wild goose chase. Back in the hotel room, he had grabbed the phone and stashed it inside a second laundry bag along with some clothes that had been scattered on the floor. Grabbing the Adidas sports bag, and the laundry bags, he'd hurried out of the room. He ditched the laundry bag containing the listening devices into a room-service trolley standing unattended in the corridor, then took the elevator to the lobby and strolled casually out of the hotel and into the street.

Just around the corner from the Hotel New House was a line of taxis and limousines with private drivers. He had approached the car at the front of the queue, but saw that the driver was older; he looked like someone's kind grandfather. Faisal walked past him to the minivan that was next in line.

The driver was younger, well built and cocky; most probably Iraqi, judging by his looks. Faisal disliked him on sight.

'Are you busy?' Faisal asked. 'I have an urgent job for you.'

'No, I'm not busy,' the driver replied. 'Where do you want to go?'

'I have this bag of clothes and other items that I need delivered to Sabiha Gökçen International Airport; I have a friend who is waiting for it. Can you deliver it?' Faisal pulled out five hundred US dollars and thrust it into the driver's hands.

The driver gave a huge smile when he saw the money.

'For this much money, I would do a lot more than just drive this bag to the airport,' he said.

'There will be a man standing near the taxi rank with a sign for Hussain Al Daeib – give him the bag. He will give you another five hundred.'

The driver directed Faisal to put the bag in the back of the van. 'I'll take it straight away,' he promised. Then, with a wave, he eased the minivan into the early-afternoon traffic.

Faisal had watched him as he disappeared up the road and then turned and headed down the hill towards the Hagia Sophia.

• • •

Faisal had slipped inside the museum with a large tour group an hour before. When the guided tour commenced, he had quietly peeled off from the group in the main hall before taking up a position in a corner from where he could watch everyone come and go. He saw the ISIS operatives arrive and make their way to the top floor and Brutali playing with his knife. He knew what he had to do – not just for his son, but for countless others – and the reasons that he must do it were known only to him and Allah. Faisal faced Mecca and prayed for what might well be the last time.

The Afghan stopped a few metres short of the two Brits.

'Well, I'm here,' he said. He was pleased there was no else around.

'Where is it, Faisal?' Hassan demanded.

'It is in the bag. Order the release of my son and I will give it to you.'

'You're in no position to bargain. Just hand it over. I have no need for your son if you give it to me.'

Faisal considered this for a moment, then he opened the bag and pulled out the silver canister.

Hassan's eyes widened. He took a step forward and accepted the container from Faisal's outstretched hand. 'See? That wasn't so hard now, was it?'

'Now let my boy go, Hassan. I have done as you asked.'

'We haven't had him for days, Faisal. Why do you think we came to your room in the first place?' Hassan placed the canister inside his backpack and took off his baseball cap. He rubbed a hand over his cropped hair before placing the cap back on. 'Apparently, the retards who were holding him let him escape.' Hassan looked across at Brutali. 'I mean, what is it with Afghans? You give them one simple job and they screw it up.'

Brutali neither smiled nor frowned; he just stared at Faisal.

Hassan continued, 'So you see, we no longer had anything over you. That doesn't matter, though, does it – because now we have this.'

Faisal laughed, softly at first and then harder and harder. He held his own sides before wiping the tears from his eyes. He was laughing from relief that his son had escaped, as well as the affirmation of the task at hand.

'In that case, you are the one who is in no position to bargain. I thought that something wasn't right; I have been in this game for a long time, my young friend. I've dealt with Westerners like you for years.' The Afghan narrowed his eyes at the two Brits. 'You don't have anything, Hassan. I took the weapon apart; it's in my room. There are others looking for it, the ones from the alley, and they will find it and then it will be gone. You have nothing.'

Hassan spat at Faisal's feet. 'You're a slimy fucking Arab, that's for sure.' Hassan's British accent became more pronounced as his anger escalated. He waved a hand at Faisal. 'Just end this prick, Brutali, and then we'll go to his hotel and get what is ours. I've had about all I can take from this piece of shit.'

Brutali smiled he took off the huge black-and-silver ring that was on his right hand and placed it in his pocket. 'I'm going to enjoy this, you slimy Afghan prick.' He pulled out the long blade.

'Not so fast.' Faisal ripped open his shirt, exposing the suicide vest. He stood taller. 'First, I'm an Afghan, not an Arab. I'm also a Muslim, not whatever it is that you two think you are, and today I rid the world of your hate. Don't look so shocked; I told you before, Hassan: I'm not fighting the infidel. It's always been about defending my home from invaders.'

'So killing yourself and us here is how you defend your home, is it?' Hassan said mockingly.

'No. When I was in the Blue Mosque Allah finally revealed my purpose to me – and it's greater than just defending my home.' Faisal took the switch from his pocket and held it in the air. He took a step towards the two ISIS terrorists.

'*Allahu Akbar!* God is great!' he shouted at the top of his voice as he pressed the button on the remote.

Nothing.

He pressed again.

Hassan folded his arms across his chest and sighed. 'It seems that it is I that knows you, Faisal; you're too modern for your own good, my *old* friend. If you had just used a circuit instead of a remote . . .' Hassan nodded at Brutali. 'Kill him.'

'My pleasure.'

Faisal sprinted towards the balcony, preparing to jump off in the hope of sliding some way down one of the giant marble pillars. Brutali moved too, much faster than Faisal. The athletic brute caught him mid stride and yanked hard back on his hair. Faisal's feet slid out from under him. Still holding Faisal by the head, Brutali smashed his knee into the Afghan's back, so that he was bent over backwards, exposing his throat. Brutali's knife flashed from his side. Faisal saw the blade from the corner of his eye and struggled for all he was worth to escape the monster's grip. He tried in vain to lower his head and protect his neck, knowing only too well what was coming. Brutali laughed. Faisal swallowed hard and mustered the last of his strength, struggling against the immense grip that held him in place. Brutali lifted the knife high into the air in front of Faisal's face and then, in one swift motion, he punched the knife into Faisal's throat, sliding the razor-sharp edge inside of him and then straight out, severing the jugular.

Faisal gurgled on his own blood, his mouth opening and closing as he gasped for breath. He tried to scream but blood just sprayed from the artery. His eyes were wide, taking in the last sights they would ever see in this lifetime.

• • •

Brutali threw the now-limp Afghan up against the balcony parapet. The Taliban's blood flowed across the marble banister and pooled over the ancient Viking runes, carved by Halvdan, a Nordic merce- nary, more than one thousand years before. Brutali stabbed Faisal in the kidneys for good measure.

'That will do,' said Hassan. 'Let's go — we need to get to that hotel room before anyone else does.'

Brutali cleaned his blade on Faisal's white shirt then put the knife back in the waistband of his sweatpants. He watched with satisfaction as the life flowed out of the Afghan and pooled on the floor at his feet.

'It amazes me that you never get any blood on you, Brutali,' said Hassan, turning to observe the giant's immaculate white jumper.

'It's a gift.'

28

SAMANDIA ARMY AIR BASE

Rachel watched as the three Bell 412s lifted off from the field opposite the industrial warehouse. Glyn and his men crouched low as the aircraft departed, shielding their eyes from the water and debris kicked up by the spinning blades. Glyn was the first to stand and make his way across the open field and through the wire fence leading to the warehouse on the other side. The rest of his men followed, heads down, walking in silence.

Glyn came alongside Rachel and the two of them walked towards the building.

'Alright?' Glyn said finally.

'Well, no, not really.'

'These things happen. Now we just have to fix it.' Glyn strode ahead into the warehouse. Walking past the hire cars, he headed towards the armoured Land Cruisers. 'Get the intelligence guys to search for him. If they locate him, we'll pick him up.'

'He's off the grid, Glyn!' Rachel exclaimed. 'He used the time we spent chasing his handset to escape. Jesus, Glyn, don't you get it? He's a ghost now – gone!'

Glyn removed the weapon sling from around his neck and placed the Heckler & Koch MP5K on the bonnet of his car. He ripped open the velcro on the body armour and lifted it up over his head and arranged it neatly on the ground, then put the weapon on top of it. He stood. She could see that he was struggling to maintain his calm; clearly the big Welsh officer wasn't accustomed to losing. He might have hit the odd dry hole or two in Afghanistan, but this was different: he had been played. 'I'll get the guys organised and when Major Faruk gets back we'll head into Sultanahmet and search his hotel. We can look for clues, maybe catch him somewhere around there.'

'You've got to be kidding! The major mightn't be back for hours. Why don't you just get out there now?'

'I can't go outside these gates, not without Major Faruk. Can you imagine what would happen if we end up having a standoff with the police – or, worse, the military? Use your brains, Rachel. We don't need to start a war with Turkey.'

'There's probably a bit more at stake here than our international reputation, Glyn. Do I need to remind you that we are trying to recover a nuclear weapon?'

'Don't be condescending, Rachel.' He took in a deep breath. 'It doesn't suit you. I know only too well what's at stake – and that's why I'm not going without Major Faruk.'

The two of them stood looking at each other in silence.

Rachel turned to watch the activity behind her; the SBS operators were busy changing over their equipment and readying themselves for a vehicle operation. Rachel realised that Glyn must have already issued orders in the helicopters on the way back to the warehouse. She gave herself a mental shake. Glyn was right: this was just a setback. These guys were Britain's finest and it would take a lot more than this to stop the SBS from completing their mission.

'Listen,' Glyn said, 'once Faruk gets here we *will* deploy. And this time we'll go in heavy. I'll request a Turkish military cordon a mile around the hotel. We'll go in using gasmasks, CS and stun grenades, the works. I will search every inch of that hotel and every building around it until we either have him or are satisfied that he's gone. We'll get the CCTV footage from every camera in the vicinity and all around; I'll leave no stone unturned and we'll do the intelligence work necessary to track him down. This isn't the end, Rachel. He won't get out of Istanbul on my watch, and he won't make a fool of me again.'

'Is this about the nuclear weapon, or is it personal now?' she asked, without turning to look at him.

'Damn right it's personal.' Glyn took his arms out of his flight suit and tied the sleeves around his waist. 'Speaking of personal, let's go talk to that Rix guy. It's time we had a no crap conversation, find out what he knows about Faisal Khan and see what other information he might have.'

Rachel led the way across the warehouse to the lunchroom on the other side. She wasn't looking forward to explaining to Matt how Khan had made fools of her team.

She opened the door and took a step in. 'That's strange,' she said, looking around. 'They're not here.'

Glyn moved past her to the table.

'Well, they can't be far away; this mug is still warm.'

'Sir, one of the hire cars is gone,' said Bluey from behind them.

Glyn looked at Rachel. 'Looks like our boy has gone out on his own.'

'I'm not surprised,' she said, trying to hide her smile.

Glyn took his phone from the leg pocket of his flight suit. 'I'll ring Major Faruk, see how long he's going to be. I'll try to speed him up if I can.' Glyn punched out a number on the phone and put it to his ear, walking back into the main warehouse as it began to ring.

'I'm sorry about all this, ma'am.'

'So am I, Bluey. We should have wrapped this up back in the alley.'

'This reminds me of a job we did back in Northern Ireland in the early nineties. There was this bomber; he'd set fire to stolen cars and then blow up our lads and the emergency services personnel who responded. We caught him by stealing a car ourselves and planting it in a location that gave us an advantage. Sure enough, word got around and his network told him there was a stolen car up on the estate. He arrived to set the bomb and one of our snipers shot him in the head. Job done, simple as that.'

'Jesus, that's a bit brutal.'

'That's war. But my point is not to always be on the back foot. Sometimes, rather than all this responding, you just need to initiate something on your own terms.'

'How does that help me here, Bluey?'

'Maybe it doesn't, ma'am. My job is just to point these things out. But, you know what, ma'am, I think that our Australian friend knows the moral of that story. He seems to be doing things on his terms now.' Bluey smiled at her and for the first time she understood the pressure he was under; providing counsel to Glyn and keeping him in line while also looking after the welfare of his men. He had a massive responsibility and she was grateful for the advice.

'Thanks, Bluey.'

'You're welcome, ma'am.'

Rachel left the small lunchroom and climbed the rusted steel stairs up to what was once the foreman's office. Inside, the small group of MI6 and SBS intelligence analysts were busy typing away on computers and leaning over printed documents laid out on the trestle tables, trying to find something, anything, that might lead them to Faisal Khan or the weapon.

She walked past them to the small room down the back where she had set up her own computer. Bringing up Skype she dialled the most recent number of the office back in London, checking that her security token was making the call secure as she waited for the connection.

'Rachel, hi – what's the news? Have you got it?'

'Hi, Sandra. No, not yet.' Rachel noted that Sandra was wearing her dark suit jacket, clothing that she usually would only wear to Whitehall or highly important meetings. 'The last lead was us being played by the Afghan. We've regrouped and the operators are going back into Sultanahmet shortly.'

'He's sneaky, isn't he? But we knew that from the IED in the alley. He can't get far on his own, though, not with the weapon configured like it is. The airports have all been warned and we have agents and 'friends' with detection capabilities watching all the trains and ports. It's amazing the people who offer to help when they think they might be implicated in the loss of a nuke.'

Rachel sighed. 'You're right. I'd feel a lot more comfortable if we actually had it in our possession though.'

'Of course, that goes without saying, I guess. So, in other news, I checked out the name you gave me.'

'What?' Rachel sat up straight, all attention.

'My contact at the CIA says that Steph Baumer no longer works for them. In fact, she hasn't worked for them since 2010. Apparently, she brought the agency into disrepute. There was an incident in Afghanistan and my source said that she endangered multiple human intelligence sources. There was a closed hearing and she was formally disciplined then released from service. No one even knows her whereabouts.'

'That is interesting. So, she isn't in Italy?'

'No. I asked about the base you mentioned, and they're adamant that there has been no base on Mount Cimone since the end of the Cold War. They actually laughed at me when I asked about it.'

'That can't be right. I mean, why would he lie to me?'

'Rachel, I think it's time you accepted that Rix isn't exactly what he seems. In fact, I think he's quite possibly delusional. He has a long history with Faisal Khan, right? Khan escaped from prison and Rix decided to go after him, it's as simple as that. He's been sacked from his job back in Australia, probably because of PTSD and his obsession with Khan. He probably made the whole CIA thing up on the spot when you confronted him. It's just a coincidence that Khan is mixed up in this and you chanced across Rix because of it. Nothing more – certainly not some American conspiracy masterminded by a CIA station chief in Italy.'

'Oh my God. He's nuts? Is that what you're saying?'

'It seems that way. You weren't to know. And let's face it, I shouldn't lecture you about bad choices when it comes to men.' Sandra looked at Rachel sympathetically. 'Anyway, we need to discuss succession planning when you get back. There's not enough of us modern female spies and I need you to make a choice soon; I'm not getting any younger, you know.'

Rachel stared at the grey wall behind the computer screen.

'Rachel?'

'Sorry, it's just – oh, I'm such a fool.'

'Rachel, what I am saying is that you need to get that weapon. Then, I think it's time you stepped up and went fully clandestine. You topped your induction and skills courses and you've done a great job here at Global Pursuit these past few years. This is your moment now. Forget about Rix. You need to do everything in your power to recover that nuke. If you're successful, the sky is the limit for you.'

'I understand, Sandra.' Rachel focused hard on the computer monitor.

'Get the job done, then go clandestine for a while, come back and take my job and then I can retire. Milton won't wait forever for you to step up, Rachel. He'll look elsewhere if you're not ready.'

Rachel leaned back in her chair and thought about what she had achieved in the past. Then she thought about Matt. Could Sandra be right? Was Matt delusional? 'I just don't know if I'm ready to be Jane Bond,' she said aloud. 'I'm not sure it's the right time.'

'There's never a right time. Look, I have to go now – we have an update on Syria in a few minutes and I have to get some things together. Turns out the Russians want to use the situation as an extension of their own foreign policy, and the Americans are readying the 3rd Ranger Regiment to roll into Raqqa. It's all a bit of a mess. Keep me updated on events there today as you go.' Sandra waved goodbye and the screen went blank.

Rachel crossed her legs and scanned the small room. Tapping her fingers on the desk for a moment, she looked back at the pattern of her relationship with Matt. She slammed her hand on the desk. *How on earth had she wasted so much time on him?* She jumped up. 'Let's finish this,' she said to herself.

29

ISTANBUL

'Just pull the car up anywhere down this street.' Matt pointed to the turn-off coming up on the right-hand side. 'We can park down here and do our final recon from a few streets back.'

'No worries, Matt.' Todd changed down the gears of the Fiat sedan and turned into the small laneway that ran down the hill away from the old town.

'Jesus, there are a lot of police cars around,' JJ observed from the back seat. 'What do you suppose that's about?'

'Yeah, there's certainly a lot more than usual,' Matt agreed. 'No sirens though, which is strange.' He turned in the passenger seat to face JJ. 'Another coup, perhaps?'

'Imagine that: trapped in Istanbul with a crazy Afghan running around with a nuclear weapon during a coup. Not an optimal holiday, thanks, boss.'

Todd pulled the vehicle in behind a small delivery van. The street was quiet, as it was mostly the back entrances for the hotels on the larger road, plus some restaurants and a bookshop. A handful of men sat out the front of their businesses on old crates, smoking cigarettes and drinking Turkish coffee. They paid the foreigners no notice.

'Okay, lads, here's the plan. I'll go around to the front of the hotel and make entry through the main door. Give me ten minutes, and then you guys head around the back. Scope out the fire escape around there and see if you can climb across onto his balcony. If it's unlocked, make entry at exactly fifteen minutes from when we set our watches – on the dot! That will be the same time as I go in the front. If it's locked, put the outdoor furniture through the window, go noisy. The distraction will help me to get in and close on him. Either way, one of us will distract him from the other.'

'Classic.' JJ smiled. 'I hope it's locked.'

'Of course you do. Alright, let's all set watches and get moving.' Matt counted down from ten seconds and the three men all set their stop watches at exactly the same time. 'Try not to use those weapons if you can help it; I'm not all that comfortable with the fact that you even took them.'

Todd and JJ both smiled.

'Ah, they had plenty,' said JJ carelessly. 'I don't think they'll notice a couple of handguns missing.'

Matt shook his head in mock admonishment. 'Okay, I'll see you up there then.'

He watched as the two other men started off down the hill, and then he turned to head back to the main road. The hotel was a couple of streets up and it wouldn't take that long for him to get there. He strolled slowly, keeping an eye out in case Faisal Khan was on the move.

Matt got to the corner and looked down the street; it was deserted and the streetlights had just started to come on. The lighting bathed the hotel in a soft orange glow. Matt had to decide whether to enter through the reception area and take the elevator, or use the fire stairs like he had on the first day. In the end, he opted for the elevator. He stepped in from the cold. The heavy glass door closed loudly behind him. There was no one at the reception desk. Matt continued on towards the two golden and purple velvet arm-chairs near the elevator and then sat down. Taking out his phone, he pretended to be engrossed in a message, but in reality he was killing time to allow Todd and JJ the chance to get into position. He watched the foyer discretely in the mirror hanging on the wall. Checking his watch, he slowly stood up and moved towards the elevator, pressing the button to call it down. He looked down at the ground, but kept his situational awareness, monitoring for anyone who might enter or be moving around in the foyer.

The elevator doors opened and he got in.

Leaving the lift at Khan's floor, he checked his watch again. Matt took the circuit board from his jacket pocket and located the small hole in the electronic lock. He checked the time; twenty seconds to go. A noise came from within the room – a crashing sound and then some inaudible shouting. Matt pulled his t-shirt up and over the Heckler & Koch pistol that sat in the paddle holster in the front of his pants. He checked his watch again and waited then made entry. The door lock clicked open and Matt dropped the electronic circuit board at his feet. He pushed hard on the unlocked door, drawing the H&K as he took three quick steps into the hall.

Someone fired twice. The first round slammed into the door-frame making Matt flinch and the second hit him under his extended right arm, in his armpit and through the back of his shoulder.

'Ah, fuck!' Matt dropped the pistol, then, realising his pre-dicament, dived through the open bathroom door to his right, slamming it shut and locking it. With his good arm, he pulled down the shower curtain rail and jammed it hard between the door and the sink.

His assailant fired twice through the closed door and then three more times.

Matt dived into the bathtub and curled up, making himself as small a target as possible. *That did not go to plan at all*, he thought. Looking around for an escape route, he noticed that one of the panels in the ceiling was slightly ajar. *That's my exit*, he thought.

His assailant was now trying to kick open the door. Fortu-nately, it held firm, just. Matt heard him yell out to someone else in the room.

It was time to move. Matt jumped up onto the toilet cistern and smashed the ceiling panel with the palms of both hands. It lifted and then fell back into place. He winced. The pain in his right shoulder was intense. He glanced across in the mirror and saw the large red patch on his back from where the bullet must have exited. There was a huge kick at the door behind him and it folded in and then out again. Matt smashed again on the roof. This time the panel flew up and into the cavity above it. Ignoring the searing pain as best he could, he grabbed the metal beams and did a muscle-up into the ceiling. He tried to kip himself up and heard the door exploding against the wall just below his feet from the force of a kick on the other side.

Matt hefted himself further up into the ceiling, kicking his legs frantically to get his body up over the last little bit. He could see up into the cavity and looked around for where he would go. Down the far end he could just make out a metal case.

'Well, well, Faisal you crafty bastard,' Matt said to himself.

Suddenly he felt huge hands grasp his ankles and he was pulled down to the floor like a child's toy, hitting his head on the way down and passing out cold.

. . .

'Got ya!' screamed Brutali.

'Move out the way and I'll put a bullet in him,' said Hassan from the doorway.

'No, I have a better idea,' said the brute.

Holding his captive down by his neck in the bath with one hand, Brutali put the plug in with the other and then turned the taps on full. The water rushing over his head and injured shoulder brought the injured man back to consciousness. Drawing a breath in he got a lungful of water and started to cough and choke.

Brutali laughed.

. . .

On the balcony, Todd and JJ were trying to work out how to get through the heavy glass sliding doors. Not only were they locked, but there was no outdoor furniture with which to smash the glass. Khan had clearly taken the precaution of moving it inside.

'What the hell do we do now?' Todd said.

'We go through the front too,' JJ replied.

The pair climbed down the fire stairs at the back. They made their way through the small courtyard and then sprinted up the access stairwell on the side of the building, getting off on the third floor.

They ran down the corridor, looking for room 313.

'That one!' JJ pointed to the door of Khan's room.

Todd took a run-up and smashed his shoulder into it – only to bounce off.

JJ laughed. 'Allow me.' The big sergeant took four huge steps and threw himself against the door. He reared back, holding his shoulder. 'That's metal – it looks like wood. Jesus, who does that?'

The two men tried smashing the door together, but even with their combined weight they didn't make a dent.

'What was that?' said Todd, in response to a sound coming from within the room.

'Sounded like Matt yelling something,' said JJ.

'JJ, we need to get in there – fast.' Todd pulled out the pistol he'd recently liberated from the SBS equipment pile.

'What exactly are you going to do with that then?'

'I don't know – shoot the lock off, I guess,' said Todd.

'Bad idea. It's metal and you're more than likely going to end up shooting one of us.' JJ looked around for a fire extinguisher or something else with which to batter the door. As his eyes scanned the carpet, something drew his attention.

'Well, I'll be a monkey's uncle.' He bent down and picked up the circuit board. 'I know what this is – I bet it's how Matt got in.'

JJ located the small hole at the bottom of the lock and inserted the plug attached to the wires from the circuit board. He switched on the device and the lock clicked open. He pushed the door open hard and Todd made entry in front of him, pistol drawn. Three steps inside the door he came face to face with a small man in a New York Yankees cap who had just darted out of the bathroom. Over his shoulder JJ could see a giant of a man was in the process of drowning Matt in the bath.

The smaller guy raised his weapon, but Todd was quicker. He fired his own pistol twice, the first round smashing the guy in the chest and the second in the top of the head, but not before his adversary got off an instinctive shot himself, the bullet hitting Todd in the side of the leg and dropping the big American in the doorway, his own pistol falling out of reach as he writhed in pain.

'Shit, you alright, mate?' JJ said, looking down at Todd as he calmly stepped over his injured friend.

'No, I'm not alright – I've just been shot, you son of a bitch.'

The monster who'd been drowning Matt charged out of the bathroom and faced JJ head on.

JJ levelled the pistol at him; glancing sideways he could see Matt face down in the bath, the water red with blood. He focused back on the monster. 'Jesus, you're a big unit, aren't ya, champ?'

'Hassan!' the monster yelled. He spat at JJ, and palmed the weapon to one side, striking out at the same time with his other hand and hitting JJ in the face.

JJ fired the pistol off into the wall as his grip inadvertently released on the weapon. It dropped next to him with a thump. 'Here, hold this, Todd.' JJ kicked the weapon behind him. 'I'm going to have to give this guy his final grading.' JJ moved in fast, the first punch catching his opponent on the cheek.

The brute seemed surprised to find himself under attack, but he managed to block the second and third punches and the two men moved away from the bathroom door and into the larger room.

'Get in the bathroom, Todd – Matt's in trouble in there,' JJ yelled without taking his eyes off his foe.

'Oh, no worries, JJ. I'll just jog in there, shall I?' Todd dragged his limp leg behind him as he crawled towards the bathroom door holding the pistol in one hand.

The brute came back at him. JJ put his hands up in defence and the brute punched him hard in the side of the stomach and then snuck in an uppercut under JJ's guard, the blow rocking the Australian, who had to grab the monster on the way down to steady himself.

Jesus, there's no point boxing with this guy, thought JJ on the way down.

The big man held JJ by the shirt and continued to elbow him on the top of the head on the way down. JJ grabbed the monster's left leg and lifted it high, pushing the brute off balance, then ran him hard at the wall. The monster hopped on one foot, trying to get his feet back down, but he couldn't quite get the platform he needed and JJ smashed him hard against the TV set, then used his own head to strike his adversary under the chin as he got to his feet.

The brute laughed it off and nodded his respect at JJ. He took a step back and the two men faced off again. The brute feigned a punch and then kicked at JJ hard. JJ moved out the way of the kick and came in from the side. He swept the brute's feet out from under him with a solid blow to the back of his legs and then followed him to the ground. The brute went into a half-guard as JJ used his shoulders to smother his face and neck. JJ splayed his legs and hooked them under the bed to further pin the brute down on the carpet. JJ was used to holding people like this, but never someone so powerful. The brute rolled then lifted his hips to try to create some space so that he could get out from under JJ. The Australian commando waited for him to do it again and this time he let him have the gap, then smashed his fist down into the brute's face. He closed the hold again. JJ expected that this time the brute would make a triangle with his hand and try to get it under JJ's arm, which was pressing down on his windpipe, but the move didn't come. Instead, he could feel the monster moving his hand around down by his legs. Then it dawned on JJ, a little too late, what the brute was doing. His suspicions were confirmed as the cold steel entered his belly.

'Shit!' JJ rolled off him, a small dagger still in his stomach.

The brute slowly got to his feet, smiling at JJ.

JJ grasped the dagger and slowly pulled it out. It hurt, a lot, but he knew it wasn't bad – however he made out it was terminal. He collapsed to one knee, wincing and gasping, and the brute walked over to him.

'You fight well. You surprised me at first . . . your technique is very interesting. You attack to defend. I like it, I must say.' The giant straightened himself up and loomed high over JJ. 'But, at the end of the day, the blade is always the best defence.' He placed his hand on JJ's head and then removed the large knife he had killed Faisal with from his waistband. 'When I'm finished with you, I'm going to kill your two little friends.'

JJ coughed. 'You're really not that bright, are you champ?'

'Fuck you.' The brute spat the words out and lifted the knife high in the air.

JJ thrust up with lightning speed and lodged the dagger under the brute's chin, driving it through his mouth and up into his brain. He grabbed the large knife from the brute's hand and spun it around, lodging it into his chest for good measure, then kicked the dying man across the room.

'Fucking lightweight,' he said.

JJ walked back into the bathroom to find Todd and Matt sitting on the bathroom floor, both holding towels on their wounds.

'Oh, yeah right, thanks for the fucking help back there, lads, no dramas.'

'What?' said Matt wincing. 'I haven't seen you lose a fight yet, mate. Why would this be any different?'

JJ frowned at him. 'Here, let me have a look at that.' He pulled back the towel to inspect Matt's wound. 'Ah, That's nothing, boss.' JJ took Matt's towel and placed it on his own stomach. 'Don't mind if I borrow this for a bit, do you?' He looked across at Todd's leg. 'Oooh, that, on the other hand, might take some recovery.'

'Nah, it's not actually too bad. I'm just not sure how I'm going to explain it to work is all.'

Suddenly the lights went out. They heard a series of small explosions and shouting coming from somewhere nearby. The sounds grew louder as the explosions from sound and flash grenades came nearer.

JJ slowly lowered himself to the ground.

'I suspect the British cavalry have arrived,' said Matt as he grabbed another towel off the floor and placed it under his arm. He started to choke on the CS gas that was coming in through the doors and windows.

Four guys dressed in flight suits with black gasmasks and silenced weapons made their way into the room, torch beams crossing each other as they scanned their arcs.

'Get down! Get down!' came the muffled shouts.

I'm already down, you fucking retards, thought JJ.

30

ISTANBUL

'And so that's how we came to be in Faisal Khan's hotel room.' Matt leaned back in the chair and took the proffered glass of water from Rachel, who had entered the hotel dining room just moments before. Matt wondered who had painted the pictures that adorned the walls. There was a series of five that depicted summer sailing in the Bosphorus. They looked so peaceful. He let his mind wander back to the sight of sails on Lake Burley Griffin, back before he had been caught up in all of this, before Steph Baumer had lured him from Canberra to Italy and persuaded him to work for her.

He looked across the dining table at Major Faruk, who was busy taking notes. Only a handful of hours earlier, this hotel had been all chaos and shouting; now the Turkish military had taken it over and were conducting a clean-up operation. The SBS guys had all been debriefed and spirited away back to the military airport.

Their work done, they were almost certainly on their way back to RAF Brize Norton and reconfiguring for future tasking.

Rachel pulled up a chair next to Major Faruk and opened her small notebook. Matt extended his neck, trying to see what she was writing.

'How's your shoulder?' she asked finally, looking up at Matt.

'It feels okay, no damage. The round went straight through the armpit.' Matt lifted his right arm over his head to demonstrate that he still had the use of it. He winced and then put his arm back down on the table.

'Todd has been released from hospital,' Rachel told him. 'He seems to be fine, just a hole in the leg. In fact, he'll be on a plane back to the States tomorrow morning.'

'Oh, okay, so you took care of that then?'

'Yes, Matt. Just cleaning up the mess.' Rachel looked at him intently for a moment. 'Matt, Steph Baumer isn't in the CIA and hasn't been since 2010 – you do know that, right?'

'Uh . . . what?' Matt looked at her, trying to figure out what she meant. 'Are you talking about the deniability thing?'

'No, I'm talking about the fact that she never contacted you – you made it all up. I don't think you're very well, Matt. Maybe you haven't been well since Afghanistan.' She glanced at Major Faruk, who rose out of his seat and quietly slipped out of the room. 'I think you need to go home and get some help.'

Matt focused on the bluest of the paintings. The artist had captured a clear sunny day; the sailing boat was the focus of the painting, and the water was clear and calm, but on the horizon there was a dark line of clouds. There was a storm brewing. The artist had flicked some little lines of white and grey on the water near the horizon to give an ominous tinge to the waves in the distance. Matt focused hard on the painting. He sensed that at any moment the sailing boat might be destroyed. He was that sailing boat.

He turned to look at Rachel. 'That's what you believe, is it? That I made it all up. You've given up on me before we even really began.'

'It's time we both moved on, Matt. And I think you need to go and work out what's going on in your head. I have things I need to do too, and I can see now that waiting for a future with you won't do me any good.'

The door to the dining room opened and one of Rachel's intelligence staff walked in. She handed Rachel a piece of paper and then left again. Rachel read the note, her forehead creasing into a frown. Matt sensed that the contents had come as a surprise to her.

'What is it?'

'I think it must be some sort of mistake.' She read it again and shook her head slowly. 'Apparently, the case is a fake. There's no plutonium in the canister; it's just an alloy of some sort.'

Matt nodded and smiled. He looked at the painting again and then laughed. 'Can I ask you a question, Rachel?' he said, as he rose from his chair. He put his hands in the pockets of his cargo pants and stood tall, shoulders back, looking every inch the commando officer that he had been.

Rachel looked up from the note.

'How did you come to learn about the case in the first place?' Matt asked.

'We were given the information through the European intelligence sharing portal; it's a facility we use to cross-check and collaborate with NATO.'

'Well, I'm not a spook, but I think I know the answer to this next question. Who in Europe sorts the information and loads it to the portal, oversees its validity and so on?'

'Well, that's the CIA . . .'

As Matt strode towards the door she asked, 'Where are you going?'

Matt turned. 'I'm going to go put a bullet in Steph Baumer's brain, Rachel – something I should have done a few years ago.'

31

MOUNT CIMONE, ITALY

'On belay, climb when ready,' Matt called down to JJ. He felt tension on the rope and knew the big commando sergeant was making his way up to the spot where Matt had set up the anchor. Although the ascent was relatively easy, even in the dark, Matt had still opted to be tethered together. The rock was slippery in some places and a few feet of sheer face was enough to be impassable, at least to JJ.

'Seriously, we couldn't have just driven up the bloody road?' said JJ as his head appeared next to Matt's feet. He was breathing hard as he removed the backpack from his shoulders.

'That would sort of spoil the surprise, don't you think?' Matt pulled in the last few feet of rope and locked it off. 'One more pitch to go and then we can stash this gear and walk up the rest of that track that runs around the side of the facility.'

'Sure, sounds like a plan.' JJ clipped himself into the anchor that

Matt had created with the large prusik cord loop and then placed his end of the rope in the figure-eight belay device before clipping it back to his harness. 'Ready when you are, chief.'

Matt chalked his hands and then started to climb slowly up the rock face. He smeared his toes across a small crack, the 5.11 shoes providing the grip required, and he extended his right arm up to the next ledge. He winced with pain as his injured arm took up the weight. Removing a small 'rock on wire' from his climbing harness, he placed the piece of metal protection into a crack in the rock and pulled hard on the wire to test its strength. With his left hand, he reached between his legs and pulled up the dynamic rope, placing it in his teeth, before getting a better grip and then clipping the rope into the carabiner attached to the curved wire. JJ released some slack and Matt moved above the protection that he had placed. He continued up the rock face for another twenty metres, placing in protection every couple of metres.

He reached the top of the climb and looked over the crest, scanning for guards, dogs or sensors that might give the game away. There was no movement, just a gentle cold breeze that came and went every few minutes. Light was starting to prick through the clouds on the horizon and Matt could now see a little further towards the facility. The barbed-wire mesh fence was around thirty metres away across open ground that was covered in long grass; this would offer them some concealment from view.

Matt moved back to the edge of the cliff and started to pull in the rope. He sat down and placed a piece of eleven-millimetre tape around a large rock and clipped into it. Then he placed a prusik cord around a small tree growing a few feet away. He tested the anchor. Satisfied that it would hold JJ should he fall, Matt gave three tugs on the rope. He received three tugs back and then could feel JJ starting to climb. He pulled in the slack.

Fifteen minutes later the two of them were sitting under the small tree going through the equipment required. Matt took the Browning Hi-Power from the backpack and handed it to JJ, before taking out a second pistol of the same make and checking it.

'I'm not sure these even work, mate – that bloke at the train station couldn't get out of there fast enough once I gave him the cash for them. He seemed a lot more legit than the guys I brought the last weapon from though.' Matt rolled his eyes as he recalled the guys who had set him up with the Walther PPK at the Bologna train station the last time he was in Italy. 'Let's stash this stuff here; we'll come back for it if we need it.'

'Let me grab the bolt cutters first,' said JJ. 'We're going to need those.'

Matt searched inside the backpack and located the bolt cutters. He passed them over and then stood up. 'Let's get moving, I want to be inside the wire before sun-up.'

The two men half crawled towards the fence. Matt used the low ground to conceal their approach and then they moved in through a little re-entrant that gave them access under the fence. Matt stopped and checked the gap where the ground dropped away. 'This should be monitored, wouldn't you think?' he said under his breath. He took a good look at it and then back at JJ, who just shrugged. They crept under it and continued in the low ground to the wall of the first white building.

A few metres separated the three small and one larger building. The large building was obviously where the action was, judging by the two huge aerials and deep radar dish.

Matt approached the single white door on the side of the building and tested the handle. Finding it unlocked he opened it and moved inside, JJ right behind him. They found themselves in a long corridor with doors on either side. The fluorescent lights were all on.

Matt crept down to the first door and eased it open. A pile of chairs and tables were stacked in one corner of the small office; there was no sign of recent occupancy. He closed the door again then froze, startled by a noise down the end of the corridor. He and JJ stood immobile for what felt like an eternity, but the noise didn't come again. They moved off and checked the next room; it was as unused as the first, as was the next and the next. Then they came across a large open plan office. There were maps on the wall and writing on the whiteboard, including the date for the day's tasks: 23 April 1969. The clock on the wall had long since stopped too.

Matt moved cautiously back out into the corridor, JJ covering him. They continued around a corner. At the end of this smaller stretch of corridor was another office. Matt pushed open the door and cleared the room. At the far end of the office was a huge panoramic window that looked out across the mountains and over the little township of Abetone below. Matt moved to the window and gazed out over the world.

'There's no one bloody up here, is there, JJ?'

'Nope,' came the reply from the big sergeant. 'Not a soul.'

Matt leaned against the window and closed his eyes. 'It's probably for the best. I would have shot the lot of them.'

'Hey, check this out, skipper.' JJ was standing in front of a desk against the right-hand wall. Matt had glanced at it on the way in, but having established there was no threat had quickly moved on.

Now he could see the TV that sat on the table. In front was a GoPro camera, plugged into the wall. A small light indicated that it was charged. 'What the fuck?' said Matt.

JJ turned on the TV and then hit play on the GoPro.

Steph Baumer's face appeared on the screen. She was sitting at a huge frosted-glass desk in a large leather chair. The desk was in the very room where the two commandos now stood.

'Hello, Matt. At first I didn't think you'd have it in you to come after me. But then I got word you were on your way. It's hard to move around Europe undetected, especially on your own passport.' She smiled. 'It was time we wrapped up operations here anyway, to be honest, so we've moved to another location, not too far away.' She winked at the camera and pulled her seat in closer. 'I want to congratulate you. I guess you know by now that the nuclear weapon was a fake, so it wouldn't have mattered too much if you had failed in your mission. The Russians were testing us, to see if we would stop them offloading some of their old weapons. It so happened that at the same time the British were talking about pulling their funding on our joint operation, and I felt they needed a little incentive to stay the course – a quick win, so to speak. The SBS made short work of the Russians, which was obviously our main concern. It's just a shame that my knuckleheads showed their true colours when they thought the weapon was real. Still, I should thank you for solving that little problem for me as well – and they, in turn, solved my Faisal Khan issue, so it was win-win.' She paused, regarding the camera thoughtfully. 'It can be a confusing game at times, espionage, nothing is as it seems, but you should know that my role here in the CIA's Special Activities Division is to bring clarity to confusion.' She smiled. 'Thanks for your help, Matt.

There's no hard feelings, I hope. I'll look forward to working with you again in the future. After all, you're a fucking lion, remember. Oh, hang on' – she nodded to a person standing just out of view – 'someone else here wants to say a few words. A friend of mine.'

As the camera panned around Matt looked at JJ. 'Can you believe this crap?!'

'Hello, Captain Rix,' said a familiar voice. Matt spun back to the screen to see Australia's Special Operations Commander.

'Well, bugger me,' said JJ.

'I do hope you realise that there will be no tea and medals for this particular mission, Rix? You see, Steph Baumer thought you were the right man for the job and when the government approached us on behalf of our American allies, well, your commanding officer and I agreed that to make this look plausible one of our own would need to work off reservation.'

Matt looked at JJ. 'Jesus, the TAG call out was a set-up.' Matt turned his attention back to the video.

'Come home, Matt.' The commander looked intently into the camera. 'Report back to 2nd Commando Regiment next week. You too, Sergeant Jones. And good work, both of you.' The screen went dead.

'He knows my name,' JJ said, turning to Matt. 'Can you believe it? He knows my bloody name.'

The two men stood frozen for a moment, shock rendering them speechless.

Finally, Matt broke the silence. 'I have no idea what the hell has just happened, JJ, but it appears that we've just completed a joint mission with the CIA Special Activity Division sanctioned by our command.'

'Yeah, and SOCAUST knows my bloody name,' beamed JJ.

'C'mon,' Matt said, walking to the door. 'Let's get going.' JJ followed him out and into the cool Italian morning air.

'So, what now, boss?' The two of them looked out over the Italian Alps. 'What about Steph?'

'She can go to hell. It's time to forget about her, and it's time to move on.'

'Right, so what's next then for Captain Rix?'

'Well, I guess I better start by packing up my apartment in Canberra and moving back to Sydney,' smiled Matt.